Acclaim for Merline Lovelace

Call of Duty

"Fascinating, behind-the-scenes details. . . .
Gripping. . . . If you're a sucker for *An Officer and a Gentleman* or *JAG*, you'll eat this up."
—*Publishers Weekly* (starred review)

"Lovelace has made a name for herself delivering
tightly drawn, exciting tales of military romantic
suspense." —*Romantic Times*

Duty and Dishonor

"Fans of Tom Clancy and Scott Turow will love
Merline Lovelace. . . . Exciting . . . gutsy . . .
powerful." —*Affaire de Coeur*

"Sizzles with excitement." —*Nora Roberts*

"A great yarn told by a masterful storyteller. It
could have happened!"
—Brigadier General Jerry Dalton, USAF, Ret.

Line of Duty

"Strong, action-packed stuff from Lovelace."
—*Publishers Weekly*

"The best writer of military romantic suspense
today. . . . Fabulous . . . fantastic . . . dazzling . . .
extraordinarily powerful . . . has bestseller written
all over it." —*I Love a Mystery*

ALSO BY MERLINE LOVELACE

Call of Duty
Duty and Dishonor
Line of Duty

RIVER RISING

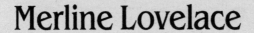

Merline Lovelace

AN ONYX BOOK

ONYX
Published by New American Library, a division of
Penguin Putnam Inc., 375 Hudson Street,
New York, New York 10014, U.S.A.
Penguin Books Ltd, 27 Wrights Lane,
London W8 5TZ, England
Penguin Books Australia Ltd, Ringwood,
Victoria, Australia
Penguin Books Canada Ltd, 10 Alcorn Avenue,
Toronto, Ontario, Canada M4V 3B2
Penguin Books (N.Z.) Ltd, 182–190 Wairau Road,
Auckland 10, New Zealand

Penguin Books Ltd, Registered Offices:
Harmondsworth, Middlesex, England

First published by Onyx, an imprint of New American Library,
a division of Penguin Putnam Inc.

First Printing, June, 1999
10 9 8 7 6 5 4 3 2 1

PUBLISHER'S NOTE
This is a work of fiction. Names, characters, places, and incidents either are the
product of the author's imagination or are used fictitiously, and any resemblance
to actual persons, living or dead, events, or locales is entirely coincidental.

This book is dedicated to the men and women of Air University who educate and polish the professionalism of our officers and senior enlisted personnel. Al and I spent some of the most challenging, stimulating, enjoyable years of our careers on the Air University campus.

WITH SPECIAL THANKS TO:

Colonel Scott McLauthlin, Air University Legal
Services, for setting me straight on the niceties of
murder and pretrial investigations.

Mr. Jim Whitaker, AF JAG School, for not batting
an eye when I walked into his office and told him
I was thinking of writing a sizzling potboiler set
at the school.

Major Doug Goodlin, Air Force Personnel Center,
for keeping my hand on the stick and my characters on the right track.

And especially to Colonel Robert Sander, USAF
Ret., chopper pilot extraordinaire. Thanks for flying those missions with me, Bob!

PROLOGUE

Rain pelted the earth hard and fast, almost obscuring the body sprawled amid a stand of pines.

Captain Joanna West nearly missed it as she jogged along River Road. To her right, the Alabama flowed gray and swollen from the storms that had made this the wettest spring on record. To her left, the manicured greens of Maxwell Air Force Base's east golf course shimmered under a haze of water.

With each stride, the captain cursed the light drizzle that had morfed into a torrential downpour and caught her miles from her quarters. She wasn't into exercise under the best of conditions. Racking up one hundred lung-squeezing miles in the seven weeks she'd spend at Maxwell as a student at Squadron Officers' School pegged out her fun meter at somewhere around minus ten.

She slogged along, thinking of all the things she'd rather be doing on what was left of this soggy Tuesday afternoon . . . like vegging out for an hour or two, or even logging in some research time at the Air University library. Her gray sweatshirt with BORN TO HOVER emblazoned in red stuck to her chest. Her shorts clung cold and clammy to her thighs.

Huffing, she calculated her remaining torture. Another half mile to the entrance of the minimum security prison situated at the bend in the river. Two and a half miles back to the students' quarters. She could do it, rain or no rain.

Maybe.

She'd just passed a bend in the road when a pale blur some yards off the road snagged her gaze. She blinked once, then again, in a vain attempt to clear her vision. Frowning, she swiped a hand across her eyes and squinted through the curtain of rain beyond the brim of her sodden ball cap.

"Oh, my God!"

She spun off the road and raced through the pines. As she drew closer, she cataloged the details with the instinctive precision of a helo pilot maintaining a hover in a howling crosswind, which Jo West had done more times than she cared to count.

That sprawled lump was a woman. A rider, in jodhpurs and a white blouse. Slender. Blonde. And very dead, if the small, dark hole in the center of her chest and the vacant eyes turned up to the rain were any indication.

Her heart thudding, Jo dropped to her knees beside the body. She'd flown enough missions since being assigned to a rescue unit to have gained a journeyman's familiarity with emergency medical procedures. CPR wasn't going to help here, though. The bullet had gone right through the woman's heart. The edges of the entry wound were singed black. Rain had washed away most of the blood, leaving only a stain of pale pink on her white blouse.

Jo sat back on her heels, aching to close those awful, staring eyes, to give the woman some semblance of dignity in death. She knew better than to touch her, though, or anything else in the vicinity. Swiftly, her eyes swept the wooded area around the body. She saw nothing. Heard nothing, except the rain weeping through the pines.

With a sudden spike of nerves, Jo shot to her feet. The skin on the back of her neck tingled at the possibility that the killer might be hidden among the pines. Watching. Waiting for another victim.

She cast a last, regretful glance at the woman. She hated to leave her so alone, so exposed to the elements, not to mention insects and animals.

Gulping, the captain spun around and sprinted through the pines. The federal prison facility was closer than the golf course clubhouse. She'd get help there. She ran for the road, throwing up a spray of water and pine needles with each step. She'd covered only a few yards when headlights stabbed through the curtain of rain.

Thank God!

She burst out of the trees and onto the road, arms waving, heart pounding.

"Hey! Hey, stop!"

The Bronco swerved to avoid her, fishtailing for some distance before hissing to a stop on the wet asphalt. The driver pushed out of the cab, his face tight beneath a crop of short, black hair.

"Do you have a problem, lady, or just some kind of a death wish?"

"There's a woman over there," Jo panted. "In the woods. She's dead. She's been shot."

The driver froze. His icy blue eyes sliced to the tree line.

"I need a ride to the prison," Jo gulped. "Unless you have a car phone? Hey! Mister!" She slapped a palm on the fender to get his attention. "Do you have a phone?"

He dragged his gaze from the trees. "Are you sure she's dead?"

"Yes, I'm sure."

She yanked open the passenger door. No phone, dammit.

"Let's go. I've got to notify the base police."

With callous disregard for the vehicle's interior, she threw herself into the passenger seat. Her drenched shorts squeaked on the seat. The driver joined her a moment later. His door thudded, shutting out the rain.

"Take the next left," Jo directed. "The prison's just ahead, around the bend of—"

"I know where it is."

The terse reply snapped her head up. Frowning, she caught the hard angle of his jaw, the nose that had been flattened at the bridge, the black hair, curling a little from the wet. The rugged profile triggered something in Jo's mind, a blurred memory, a fleeting image. Had she seen him somewhere on base? Maybe during her previous runs along River Road?

"Do you work there? At the prison?"

"No." A muscle jumped alongside his jaw. He shoved the car into gear. "But I spent some time there."

The scent of leather and drenched sweats seemed suddenly overpowering. The helo pilot pushed a single syllable through her throat with some difficulty.

"Why?"

Arctic blue eyes cut to her face.

"I killed a woman."

CHAPTER ONE

"I need to talk to you, Samuels. Get up here."
Major Carly Samuels hid a smile at the brusque order that snapped across the phone line. The commandant of the Air Force Judge Advocate General School was more noted for his killer legal mind than his personal or diplomatic skills.

"Yes, sir."

"Now."

"Yes, sir."

A few quick clicks of the keyboard saved the changes Carly had made to the latest draft of the *Air Force Law Review.* In a moment of sheer insanity, she'd agreed to edit the damned thing in addition to chairing the Military Justice Division and carrying a full load of instructing duties. Not exactly a smart thing to do with her mother's re-election campaign to the U.S. House of Representatives just heating up, but Carly hadn't been promoted to major ahead of her peers and been named to her position at the Air Force Judge Advocate General School by avoiding challenges to either her mind or her energy.

"I'm going up to see Colonel Carpenter," she informed her administrative assistant. "If my mother calls, tell her I'll stop by her place on my way home. I'm getting out of here early tonight."

"Right," the staff sergeant drawled. "That'll be about midnight."

"Seven," Carly said firmly, running a palm around the waistband of her uniform slacks to ease any hint of fullness from her blue blouse. A quick pat confirmed that her dark red hair was up, off her shoulders, and as smooth as she could keep it in this humid weather. "I'll be there by seven."

"Suuure you will, Major."

Ignoring his knowing grin, Carly left her office. As always, the dignity and somber elegance of the Dickinson Law Center gave her a little thrill of pride. One of the many institutions that, along with the Air War College, the Air Command and Staff College, and Squadron Officers' School, made up the campus of Air University, the Law Center had been Carly's home for six months now. Terrazzo tiles echoed her swift stride as she passed the law library and mock courtrooms paneled in the same rich cherry wood that graced the halls. Above the paneling, framed art decorated the hunter green walls. Congressman Dickinson, the now-deceased legislator whose district had included Alabama's capitol city of Montgomery and Maxwell Air Force Base, had seen to it that the facility named in his honor did him proud.

With the academic year in full swing, the center hummed with a subdued vitality that still gave Carly a high after six months. Almost four thousand officer and enlisted students from all branches of the service and a host of nations converged here each year to study everything from tort litigation and computer crimes to the legality of military actions during peace and war.

Born and bred to the law, Carly considered her assignment as chief of Military Justice something akin to putting a chocaholic to work in a Godiva shop.

Here she could keep her finger on the pulse of the air force's legal system, stay abreast of the latest cases, and directly influence future generations of air force lawyers . . . all without the hassles of her previous tour of duty as a staffer in the judge advocate general's office at the Pentagon. Still, teaching and editing the *Law Review* didn't provide quite the same degree of satisfaction as sending some scumbag child molester or gutless deserter to Leavenworth for an extended stay.

Which was why Carly didn't object when her boss waved her to a seat a few minutes later and proceeded to inform her that the base JAG had called to request an officer from the center to conduct an Article 32 investigation.

"Why don't they use one of their own?" she asked curiously.

"Because their chief of Military Justice is going to try the case if it comes to a court-martial and they need another field grade officer to do the pretrial investigation."

Her pulse took a little jump. "Are we talking the Smith murder?"

"We are."

Excitement shot through her veins. The murder had made all the local and most of the national headlines. Now, it appeared, she was going to get a chance to play in it.

"The Article 32 has to be done fast," Carpenter advised, "and it has to be done right. The folks over at the base are walking on egg shells with this one."

"No kidding! How often does a student at one of the air force's most prestigious schools stand accused of putting a bullet through his wife's chest? A wife who, by the way, just happens to be a lieutenant

colonel, a student at the same school, *and* the daughter of a four-star general!"

"That's just part of it." Carpenter leaned forward,
his bushy gray brows slashing into a straight line.
"The media hasn't gotten hold of this little bombshell
yet, but the only witness whose testimony puts Michael Smith at the scene of his wife's murder is Ryan
McMann."

She stared at her boss blankly. "Ryan McMann?"

"Obviously you're not a hockey fan."

"Hockey? You mean like in ice?"

"Is there any other kind?"

Carly turned on her best Alabama drawl. "Now
cuh-nol, suh, y'all know I was born and raised raht
here in Montgomery. To me, ice is what you poor,
ignorant Yankees pollute your bourbon with. Or,"
she added with a her quicksilver grin, "what a well-
intentioned gentleman slips on a girl's hand. Pref-
erably in great big chunks."

"If you had ever let the air force assign you north
of the Mason-Dixon line," her boss retorted, "you'd
know that Ryan McMann was once professional
hockey's answer to Magic Johnson."

Carly cocked her head, a speculative gleam in her
brown eyes. "Something tells me that 'was' carries
particular significance to this case."

"You're right. McMann spent the past two years
right here at Maxwell as a guest of the Federal Bureau of Prisons."

She sat up straight, her professional instincts fully
engaged. "Are you saying that the case against Smith
hinges on the testimony of a convicted felon?"

"You got it."

"What did this guy McMann do to land in prison?"

"He was convicted of possession of illegal substances and, ironically, a violation of the Mann act."

"The Feds went after him for transporting a minor across state lines for lewd and lascivious purposes? What is he, a pervert who preys on little boys?"

"The victim was a seventeen-year-old groupie who'd boasted to her friends that she intended to add McMann to her list of trophies. She also allegedly supplied the drugs the Feds found in his room at the time of the bust."

Carly didn't buy it. Sex and drugs were almost synonymous with professional sports these days. There had to be more behind McMann's conviction than the fact that he got high and made it with a seventeen year old.

"Why didn't he cop a plea and get off with a fine and a slap on the wrist, like all the other jocks?"

Carpenter picked up his silver pen and thumped the end on his blotter a time or two. "McMann's team was in the finals for the Stanley Cup at the time of his arrest. There was some talk that the big money guys arranged the bust and subsequent prosecution to get him off the ice, but that was only one of the wild rumors flying around at the time. Then the girl OD'd, McMann shocked everyone by changing his plea to guilty, and the rest is history."

"Now he's a key witness in a murder case." Carly blew a soundless whistle. "No wonder the folks over at the base are so nervous about this one."

"So, do you want it?"

"The Article 32 investigation? Are you kidding? Yes, sir, I want it!"

Carpenter allowed himself a small smile. "I told the base JAG you'd report to him in an hour. He'll have an office, the case file, and your letter of appointment waiting for you." The smile disappeared almost as quickly as it had come. "Clear your schedule for the next ten working days, Samuels. I don't need to tell you that this investigation takes priority over all other duties."

"No, sir."

Carly swept him a salute and executed a reasonably smart about-face. That particular maneuver sometimes proved tricky in the spike heels she wore to add a few inches to her scanty five-feet-three. She didn't consider her petite stature, dewy soft magnolia skin, and silky auburn hair a detriment to her profession. Nor did anyone else who'd spent more than two minutes in a courtroom with her. But she'd long ago learned to maximize her presence with hand-tailored uniforms, subtly dramatic makeup, and the extra leg-inches provided by high heels.

With a nod to the support staff outside the commandant's suite, Carly took the stairs that branched on either side of the impressive entrance to the center and headed back to her office. The thrill of the hunt she always experienced at the start of a case thrummed through her.

This was the law she'd cut her teeth on, first as an area defense counsel, providing everyone from dopers to degenerates with the defense that the Constitution and the Uniform Code of Military Justice entitled them to. Then as a prosecutor, sending those same dopers and degenerates to small, comfortless cells at Leavenworth. She didn't for a second doubt her ability to sort through the facts in this case and determine whether or not the evidence supported convening a court-martial to try Lieutenant Colonel Michael Smith for the murder of his wife.

As she strode through the paneled halls, she had no idea that her confidence in herself and her abilities would soon take a direct hit. Or that a former hockey player turned convicted felon would send her spinning into a foreign, frightening universe, one that existed on the far side of the law as she'd always practiced it. Her only thought as she cleared her desk and her schedule for the next few days was how much she'd missed the adrenaline rush a case like this always gave her.

Forty-six hours later, Carly flicked an impatient glance at the clock on the conference room wall.

Ten-fifteen. Lieutenant Colonel Michael Smith was supposed to have arrived at ten sharp.

Exasperation added an edge to her fine-boned features. She should have expected Smith and the high-priced, showboating criminal defense attorney he'd hired to keep her waiting. G. Putnam Jones had a reputation for theatrics that put O. J. Simpson's entire defense team to shame.

The attorney had already started playing his games with her. An Article 32 investigation didn't require the presence of the accused when taking testimony from witnesses, only that he be notified of the time and place of said testimony. Jones had assured Carly that he and his client would be there. Much as she'd like to, she couldn't just shrug off their tardiness. Not with the level of visibility that accompanied this case.

"We'll give them another five minutes," she told the stenographer seated at the far end of the conference table.

The paralegal nodded and went back to the racing magazine he'd brought with him. Restless and impatient, Carly strolled to the windows of the small conference room allocated for her use in the base headquarters building. Outside, another spring storm splattered the rain-soaked earth.

Sighing, she turned away from the depressing

scene and went back to the files stacked neatly on the conference table. She'd been through them numerous times . . . the initial reports from the military police who'd responded to the scene; the follow-up investigation by agents from the Air Force Office of Special Investigations; the medical examiner's and forensics reports; the field personnel records of Lieutenant Colonels Michael Smith and Elaine Dawson-Smith; a special file put together by the Air War College, where both the victim and her husband were students.

She drew that file forward, flipping it open again to the color photo taken of Elaine Dawson-Smith for the War College year book. It was a studio shot, in uniform, with the American flag as a backdrop. Colonel Dawson-Smith didn't need that dramatic splash of color to set her off, however. Her stunning violet eyes, classic features, and sleekly cropped white-gold hair would have caught anyone's attention even without that Mona Lisa smile.

The smile belonged to a woman on the way up and supremely confident that she'd make it ahead of everyone else. She almost had. She'd racked up all the right punches on her ticket: a distinguished graduate from the Air Force Academy; outstanding fitness reports as a maintenance and logistics officer; early promotions to major and to lieutenant colonel. She'd more than proved herself her father's daughter, and made no secret of the fact that she intended to wear all four of his stars someday.

Carly slid another photo out, this one from the crime scene investigation, and held it next to the studio shot. The stark, black-and-white print showed another Elaine Dawson-Smith, eyes staring vacantly at the sky, hands outflung. This was the woman who kept her horse at the base stables, who rode every afternoon, who got home late, when she came home at all, according to the husband accused of killing her.

Carly had spent hours reviewing the evidence that led to Smith's arrest and formal charging with the murder of his wife. Statements from a number of witnesses detailed Smith's vocal and increasingly violent arguments with his wife over the affair he suspected she was having. None of the faculty or fellow students at the Air War College could verify either the affair or Smith's claim that he'd been holed up in the library, working on his research paper, at the time of his wife's murder.

On the day of the shooting, Elaine Smith had driven from the couple's on-base residence to the stables. Her car was still parked there and her Thoroughbred was still in his stall when her body was discovered in the woods a half mile away. She'd been shot once through the heart. Ballistics tests confirmed the bullet was fired at close range from the .38 caliber Smith & Wesson "Ladies' Special" found under a layer of pine needles some yards from the body. Police records showed that the gun had been purchased by the victim's husband a year ago, reportedly for his wife's use. The weapon had been wiped clean of prints.

The evidence, although damning in its cumulative effect, was circumstantial to this point. Only one witness actually placed Michael Smith in the vicinity of the murder at the time it occurred. The same witness who now waited in the corridor outside.

Carly shot another glance at the clock. Ten-eighteen. She'd waited long enough. A quick adjustment straightened the alignment of the shiny silver-plated belt buckle at the waistband of her navy skirt. Her shoulders squared. Taking a deep breath, she walked to the conference room door.

"Mr. McMann?"

The individual leaning against the wall some yards away turned his head. Carly formed a swift impression of a ruggedly masculine face that wore the marks of his brutal sport under its deep tan. Of curly black hair tamed by a severe cut. Of a muscular body molded by tight jeans, and a white shirt that stretched taut across wide shoulders.

"I'm Major Samuels."

He didn't acknowledge the introduction by so much as a nod. Carly wasn't surprised. She'd had plenty of time to study the background file on Ryan McMann, too. There was no dearth of material. His arrest and sensational trial had grabbed the headlines for months. Sex, drugs, a tragic death, a superstar athlete who fell from grace with a crash. The media ate it up. The fact that McMann's wife had filed for divorce less than a week after his conviction had added another juicy postscript to his case.

Carly knew her key witness had gone through his own personal hell, and that he had little reason to cooperate in the investigation of another crime. Even with that insight into his background, however, she wasn't prepared for the stinging contempt in his ice-blue eyes . . . or for the sheer, animal magnetism of the man.

To her surprise, she realized that she'd forgotten to breathe. Injecting a quick pull of air into her lungs and a professional calm into her voice, she gestured to the open door.

"Would you come in, please?"

He didn't move, except to flick a glance at his watch. "Our appointment was for ten o'clock."

The deep, rough voice carried the unmistakable clip of his New England background.

"Yes, I know." She forced an apology. "I'm sorry for the delay. If you'll come in, we'll get started."

Still he didn't budge.

Carly kept her face impassive while she considered her next move. She couldn't order him to cooperate. He was a civilian, not subject to the military code that governed this pretrial investigation. When she'd called to request his presence here this afternoon, he'd flatly refused. He'd given a sworn statement to the police, he reminded her brusquely. If subpoenaed, he'd testify in court. Anything else the air force wanted from him, they could damn well put it in writing and mail it to him.

Ryan McMann hadn't liked her unsubtle hint that she'd be more than happy to work through his probation officer to gain his cooperation, if necessary. Any more than he obviously liked being here now.

Tough. The sleazoid was still paying the penalty for the crimes he'd committed. Carly wasn't particularly concerned about his likes or dislikes. She slid a touch of steel into her voice.

"The stenographer is waiting, Mr. McMann. As soon as I swear you in, we can proceed."

His blue gaze narrowed. Measured her. Then he squared his shoulders and strolled toward her. Absurdly, Carly had to fight the impulse to step back, to keep some distance between them.

He carried himself with the innate grace of a born athlete, but there was no mistaking the aura of controlled violence that came with him. He was a hockey player, she reminded herself. He made his living in what had become almost a blood sport. Or he had, until his conviction barred him from professional sports for life.

Carly had never watched a hockey game, either at

an ice rink or on TV. She'd barely made it to the football games that formed the heart and soul of the University of Alabama's athletic program. To be honest, she didn't have a lot of respect for the hulking bruisers who'd butted heads on the fields of play every Saturday afternoon.

She didn't make the mistake of categorizing Ryan McMann as a mere jock, however. The Mann, as his fans called him, had graduated with top honors from the University of Vermont before turning pro, where his skill on the ice and undeniable sex appeal had elevated him to the status of cult hero. His last contract had netted him a reputed seven figures. He'd pulled down millions more in lucrative endorsement deals and had been riding the crest of near adulation until one night with a seventeen-year-old girl destroyed his career and his marriage.

He'd risen too high and fallen too hard to have relied on physical prowess alone. Carly wouldn't let herself forget that fact.

With the width of the conference table between them, she picked up a printed form. She'd administered the oath often enough to know it by heart, but reading words made the process more official and impersonal.

"Please raise your right hand, Mr. McMann."

He complied, but the sardonic gleam in his blue eyes told Carly he knew exactly how much the sworn oath of a convicted felon was worth.

She got the swearing-in and the preliminary identification of the witness out of the way with cool efficiency. Waving him to a chair, she waited until he'd seated himself before taking the armchair opposite.

"Would you please describe in your own words—"

"I hadn't planned on using anyone else's."

"—your activities on the afternoon of Tuesday,

April twelfth," she finished calmly, ignoring his sarcasm.

He sprawled back in his chair. Those icy eyes drifted to the stenographer, to the framed pen and ink sketch of Air University's campus on the conference room wall, back to Carly.

"I left work at one-thirty and drove to the prison for a meeting with the education director. I left the prison at four-ten and drove home."

So he intended to make her dig for every detail. Fine. She'd handled more than one recalcitrant witness in her time.

"Did you see anyone or anything when you drove along River Road?"

"On the way in, I passed a dark green vehicle. On the way out, I almost ran over one of your officers."

"Captain West. I'm going to interview her after we finish."

His eyes mocked her, her investigation, and the judicial system that spawned them both. "We're finished, Major."

"Not quite, Mr. McMann. Describe the vehicle, please."

"I said it was green."

"Did you note the make and model?"

"You know I did. They're in the police report. So why are we going through this farce?"

"The air force doesn't consider the Article 32 investigation a farce, Mr. McMann. As I explained on the phone, this is similar to a civilian grand jury, which considers the evi—"

His mouth hardened. "I'm familiar with the grand jury process."

"Then you should understand that what I'm doing is separate and distinct from the police investigation that led to the arrest of Lieutenant Colonel

Smith. My task is to determine whether the evidence provides reasonable grounds to support the crime he's charged with. To do that, I want to hear a description of the vehicle you saw, in the words you would use if called to testify at a court-martial."

"And you think my testimony is going to carry any weight with a court-martial? Get real, lady."

"Describe the vehicle, Mr. McMann."

"Green."

"The make?"

"It's in the police report."

Carly knew any appeal to his sense of fairness would be totally useless, but she gave it a shot.

"From what I've read about your trial, Mr. McMann, it was a world-class media circus. Some people believe the networks convicted you before the facts in the case were fully investigated. Surely you can't want another man to go through the same—"

"Give it a rest. I don't care one way or another about your investigation or your accused."

"You should."

"Yeah? You want to tell me why?"

Shamelessly, she played the only trump card she had. "Because cooperating with authorities is a condition of your probation. I happen to know several members of the parole board personally, and I don't think they'd be happy to hear you've withheld information in a murder investigation."

The stinging contempt she'd glimpsed earlier returned with a vengeance. Blue eyes clashed with brown.

"Nothing like resorting to a little legal blackmail, is there, Major? And here I thought my lawyers had scraped the bottom of the barrel when it came to ethics."

"What was the make of the vehicle, Mr. McMann?"

He contemplated her for so long and with such open derision that Carly's temper sparked under her facade of professional detachment. Without changing her expression, she doused the brief flare. She'd never yet lost her cool when dealing with a witness and certainly didn't intend to start now.

She came close, though, when he rose, planted both palms flat on the table and looked her straight in the eye.

"It's in the police report, doll face."

Before Carly could respond, he turned and strode from the conference room.

CHAPTER TWO

"**B**astard," Carly muttered as the door swung shut behind McMann. Collecting herself, she turned to the paralegal. "That comment was off the record."

"Yes, ma'am."

"Why don't you take a break, Hendricks? It looks like we've got some time to kill until our next witness shows."

The sergeant clicked off his computer and stretched. Even in this age of minicams and videos, the court stenographer served a necessary purpose as a witness as well as a recorder.

"I'll go hunt down some coffee. Want a cup, Major?"

"No thanks."

When the legal tech strolled out, Carly straightened the stack of thick files and willed herself to calm. Despite her best efforts, McMann had gotten to her. Big time. It wasn't so much his attitude that irritated her as the contempt behind it. Where did he get off acting as though he owed his woes to the legal system, instead of to his own actions?

Well, he'd find out soon enough contempt and bullheadedness didn't deter Carly. She wasn't through with Ryan McMann yet. Her mouth tight, she pulled out a copy of the statement he'd given the police the afternoon of Elaine Dawson-Smith's murder. It elaborated on the bald facts he'd just related to Carly.

At one-thirty on Tuesday, April 12, he'd left the construction site where he was working while he served out his probationary period. He drove directly to Maxwell, entering through the Bell Street gate. The gate guard's log confirmed that he issued McMann a temporary visitor's pass at one-forty seven. McMann then drove across base, his route taking him past the Chennault Circle, home to Air University's major schoolhouses. Just after turning onto River Road, he passed a dark green Ford Taurus with its headlights on and a uniformed officer at the wheel.

He couldn't describe the officer's features. The drizzle had misted both McMann's windshield and the other driver's. Only after extensive questioning did he provide the final, damning bit of testimony that had resulted in Lieutenant Colonel Smith's arrest two days later. According to McMann, he'd caught a glimpse, a fleeting glimpse, of a silver oak leaf on a dark blue shoulder tab as the officer drove by.

After passing the Taurus, McMann continued to the prison, consulted briefly with the education director, then tutored inmates as part of the community service portion of his early release. At four-ten, he signed out of the prison. A few moments later, he'd swerved to avoid Captain West, then turned around and drove her back to report her gruesome discovery.

Was it just coincidence that put him on River Road at two such crucial points in time? Had he really passed a dark green Taurus or caught the flash of a silver oak leaf? And why in hell had Elaine Dawson-Smith walked from the stables to th .t deserted stretch of

woods in such a dreary drizzle? Had she gone to that
secluded spot to meet someone?

Her husband?

The unknown person she was allegedly having an
affair with?

McMann?

The timing would have been tight, Carly mused,
given the logs that tracked McMann onto the base
and into the prison, but he could have stopped long
enough to shoot Elaine Dawson-Smith. But why?
There was no evidence that he knew her, no record of
any previous meeting. Was it a chance encounter? An
explosion of rage and violence by a hardened criminal? No, that didn't fit. The crimes McMann committed and served time for weren't violent.

The questions dogged Carly, as they had the investigators who'd worked up the case file. A cynical Mc-
Mann had submitted to a lie detector test and passed.
Michael Smith, when confronted with the evidence
mounting against him, had submitted to the same
test and failed. The results of neither test were admissible in court, of course. Nor did they prove anything conclusively one way or another. Carly had
encountered too many false readings during her
years as both an ADC and a prosecutor to place any
confidence in them.

Blowing out a long breath, she thumped the file
shut. Maybe her next witness could answer some of
the questions piling up in her mind.

Spit-shined and spiffed-up, Captain Joanna West
knocked on the half-open conference room door fifteen minutes later.

"Major Samuels?"

"Yes. Come in."

"Captain West, reporting as ordered."

Carly returned the helo pilot's salute, then rose

and extended a hand. The younger woman took it in a firm, no-nonsense grip.

"Sorry I had to pull you out of class, Captain. This shouldn't take too long."

"Not a problem. We started a block on rescue and recovery yesterday." A grin split the young woman's lively face. "I do it a whole lot better than I listen to it in a lecture hall."

Carly didn't doubt her for a moment. The honey-haired pilot exuded a breezy confidence that could only have come from hands-on expertise at her profession. With less than five years on active duty, she already sported more rows of colorful ribbons on her uniform jacket than most officers with twice her time in service.

"Why don't I explain the Article 32 investigation process to you? Then I'll swear you in and take your statement for the record."

"Fine by me. Just between us, this is the first murder I've gotten involved in."

"Hopefully, you won't get involved in too many more during your career."

Her grin slipped into a grimace. "If I do, maybe next time I won't go all skittery and nervous. The colonel's eyes kind of got to me, so sightless and empty like that."

Her eyes had gotten to Carly, too, devoid as they were of all the promise, all the pulsing vitality that had carried Elaine Dawson-Smith so far, so fast.

Pushing aside the vivid image from the crime scene photos, she walked the captain through the air force pretrial process, from the initial on-scene investigation to convening a court-martial, should the Article 32 support it and the commanding general so order.

West proved a quick study. "Got it. The ground

crew got the case ready to fly. You're running the preflight checklist. If all systems are go, we power up for takeoff."

"That's close enough. Any questions before I swear you in?"

"Just one. If this case does go to trial, will I be called back to Maxwell as a witness?"

"That depends on what you have to tell me. Why? Do you have something coming up in the near future that may affect your availability?"

The captain glanced down at the diamond solitaire on her left hand, then lifted her shoulders in a careless shrug.

"Nothing that can't wait if it has to."

Uh-oh. Trouble in paradise. Carly didn't probe. She'd worn a similar ring herself a few years ago, until time and distance and separate careers had killed both the relationship and the passion it had sprung from. She'd gotten over the hurt and the regret, but didn't particularly enjoy talking about it.

Chances were the trial attorneys wouldn't call West back unless she came up with something startling during this interview. Something she hadn't included in her original statement.

She didn't. With a keen recall of detail, she recounted her actions exactly as she'd described them to the police that rainy afternoon.

"So you didn't see anyone in the vicinity of the deceased?" Carly asked when she finished.

"No one . . . except Ryan, of course."

"Ryan?"

"Ryan McMann." West shook her head. "I can't believe I didn't recognize him right away. He's sure changed."

Changed? Carly sat forward, her pulse skipping.

Another coincidence? This case already had a few too many of them.

"Do you know Mr. McMann personally?"

"Personally, no. Professionally . . ." The captain smiled. "I grew up in Wisconsin, Major. I also have five brothers, three of whom played hockey in high school and college. I slapped a few pucks myself before I was even old enough to tie my own skates. Ryan McMann is one of my all-time heroes."

Some hero. Carly kept the observation to herself as Jo West continued.

"I can tell you The Mann's total career goals, how many championships he skated in, what brand of wax he used on his stick, even the average number of minutes he spent in the penalty box per game."

"Quite a few, I'd imagine."

The drawled comment drew a smiling protest from the captain.

"Not compared to most of the pro players. McMann's a natural athlete, and one heck of a smart stick handler. He brought his own brand of respectability to the sport in addition to his mind-blowing skills on the ice. No one could believe it when . . ."

She broke off, obviously unsure of how much she should relate of the hockey star's background.

"When he pled guilty to transporting a minor across state lines, statutory rape, and possession of illegal substances," Carly finished for her.

"He didn't do it," the captain said flatly. "Whatever he said at his trial, he didn't do it."

The utter conviction in her voice made Carly blink. During their brief interview, she'd formed a solid impression of this woman's intelligence. She didn't seem the type to keep someone with proven clay feet on a pedestal.

On the other hand, McMann's potent brand of animal magnetism had affected even Carly for a few breathless seconds . . . little as she wanted to admit it.

"Mr. McMann's case isn't the one I'm concerned with," she said briskly.

"Sorry. Guess I got carried away."

"Is there anything else you can tell me about that afternoon, either before or after you found Colonel Dawson-Smith?"

"No, ma'am. I think we covered everything."

"Here's my card. You can reach me or my voice mail any time. Will you call if you remember anything, any small detail or impression we didn't discuss?"

"Roger that." She whipped up her right arm and executed a sharp salute, then spoiled the military effect with a cocky grin. "See you around campus, Major."

Smiling, Carly sent the stenographer off to lunch and flipped back through her notes. She'd go over what she got this morning. This afternoon she'd begin meeting with the long list of students and acquaintances of both Elaine Dawson-Smith and Michael Smith who provided evidence of their troubled marriage.

Wondering if Lt. Colonel Smith and his attorney would show for these sessions, she tried to reach G. Putnam Jones. His secretary apologized for his nonappearance this morning, explaining that he'd been detained in court and would call her personally the moment he finished.

Carly didn't kid herself that she'd hear from him any time today. He knew darn well she was expected to complete her report within the ten working days allowed in the Manual for Courts-Martial. He'd stall as long as possible, wait until her back was to the wall, then roll out the objections. Carly could hear them now. He hadn't had sufficient time to prepare. The pretrial investigation was flawed and prejudicial because his client hadn't been present at the interviews. The charges against Colonel Smith should be thrown out.

It was a dangerous game, one that might work in the civilian world but could seriously backfire in the military, where the accused could sit through the entire proceeding with counsel and learn about the government's case without playing any of their own cards. Carly would have given her client far different advice.

"Please remind Mr. Jones that his client is an officer in the United States Air Force and subject to the Uniformed Code of Military Justice. As such, Colonel Smith is required to provide me a statement, even if he chooses not to sit in on the other interviews." She glanced at her printed schedule of appointments. "Tell Mr. Jones that I want his client here at oh-eight-hundred on Thursday morning."

"I'll pass on the message."

That done, Carly waited for the rest of the long string of witnesses to appear.

Twilight had begun to darken the conference room's windows when she locked the files in her briefcase and left the base headquarters building. The mental image of the victim she carried away with her had become sharper, harder, more complex.

People had either loved Elaine Dawson-Smith, or they'd hated her. Interestingly, as many women fell into the first category as men. The colonel had burned with the intensity of a beacon, in class, at parties, even in her off-duty pursuits like riding and skydiving. With her stunning looks and razor-sharp mind, she was usually the focus of attention, which often amused and sometimes annoyed her.

She would have made a hell of a general, Carly thought as she headed for her car. The rain had finally stopped, thank goodness, and left her white MG glistening under the photosensor street lights triggered by the early gloom. A law school graduation gift from her grandfather, the MG had since racked up more than a hundred thousand miles. It still purred like a kitten.

On her return to Montgomery six months ago, the Judge had decided it was time Carly put the relic out to pasture. He'd even offered to buy her another, newer model, since her air force salary barely covered the cost of maintaining the Antebellum carriage house she'd insisted on purchasing instead of living at home with her kinfolk. Smiling, Carly had patted his whiskered cheek and reminded him that some relics only improved with age and hard use. His response to that bit of impertinence had made his nurse blush a fiery red and Carly grin.

The urge to see the crusty old barrister who'd fired both his daughter and granddaughter with a love of the law had Carly slinging her briefcase onto the back seat. She'd stop by the house, find out how her mother was doing in the polls, then spend a few hours with the Judge before heading home to transcribe her notes to her computer.

Wet pavement hissed under the MG's tires as she drove out the Bell Street gate. The cotton gin that spread its scent over the city or the base, depending on the direciton of the wind, loomed just outside the gate. Carly had grown up with its cloying, peanut-buttery stink. She never noticed it any more except on days like this, when low-hanging clouds caught the odor and trapped it. Wrinkling her nose, she whizzed past the gin and a few blocks of graffiti-scarred storefronts. The area outside the base was struggling to make a comeback. It had a ways yet to go.

Ten minutes later, she turned off the interstate that cut through Montgomery's heart and entered a world she knew and loved. The MG slowed, its low slung frame hugging the road as it took the curves along Woodley Lane. Moss-bearded cypresses leaned over the street, their branches forming a thick canopy. Banks of azaleas glowed pale and white amid darker, pinker hues. Gas lights flickered at the entrances to long, winding driveways.

Nearing her childhood home, Carly could almost taste the sour corn mash whiskey the Judge loved and would insist she sip to ward off the wet, almost feel herself relaxing as she dropped into the leather armchair beside his bed, kicked off her shoes, and plopped her feet on the hassock. She hummed in anticipation. The hum sank to a low groan when she turned off Woodley onto Melrose.

Parked cars lined the half-block long street, as well as the drive leading to the house at the end of the cul-de-sac. Lights blazed from every window in the gracious two-story Greek-revival. So much for relaxing, Carly thought with a wry smile. Her mother was hosting another of the lively cocktail parties that had won her almost as many votes and campaign contributions over the years as her shrewd politicking.

The daughter of a three-term member of Congress, Carly knew her duty. She'd have to make an appearance before she slipped away to see the Judge. Resigning herself to an hour of grinning and gripping, she wedged the MG into an open space along the curb. After swiping on some lipstick and checking her hair in the car mirror, she gave the legislative aide who did butler duty on these occasions a cheerful greeting.

"Hi, Jackson. Looks like you've got a crowd tonight. Anyone special I need to make nice with?"

"The lieutenant governor, the chairman of Alabama Electric, and a reporter from *Newsweek*," the aide replied succinctly. He and Carly had worked enough of these functions to know the drill.

"Point me in the reporter's direction."

"He's the one in the gray suit, talking to your brother and Parker."

The crowd shifted, giving Carly a glimpse of the tall, tanned blond standing next to her brother and the gray-suited reporter. As she started for the small group, she tried to understand her mixed emotions at the sight of Parker Stuart.

She'd enjoyed the time they'd spent together since they'd paired off at her mother's campaign kick-off party two months ago. Even more, Carly enjoyed his agile mind. A smoothly ambitious assistant DA, Parker had his eye on his boss's job. By all accounts, he had a good chance of nailing it when Steele retired next year, particularly with Congresswoman Samuels's political clout behind him.

Carly liked him. By his own admission, he more than liked her. But she wasn't ready for the commitment he already wanted from her. She'd gone down that road once. She wasn't going to race down it again. Making her way through the crowd, she looped an arm around her brother's waist.

"Hey, stud."

Dave returned her affectionate squeeze. "Hey, soldier girl. Did you finally convince the secretary of defense that you've got things under control enough to leave the base before midnight?"

"Did you finally convince my sister-in-law to trust

you enough to keep your cell phone turned on so she
can reach you when she goes into labor?" Carly returned sweetly.

"Oh, shit!"

Dave shoved his drink into his sister's hand and
fumbled for the phone tucked in his suit-coat pocket.
The comical look of relief on his face when he saw the
flashing indicator light had Carly laughing.

Pushing the phone back in his pocket, he reclaimed his drink. "I hate these damned things. I feel
as if I'm on an electronic leash."

"You *need* a leash," his loving sister retorted. "A
very short one."

Still grumbling, he waited while she greeted
Parker, then introduced her to the reporter. Within
moments, she was caught up in the twin passions
that had consumed the Samuels household for as
long as she could remember: politics and the law.
The law and politics.

After dissecting the platform put forth by her
mother's opponent, the status of the mandatory
school testing bill currently in committee, and the recent drug bust of the Auburn starting quarterback,
Carly excused herself.

"I need to find Mom, then go up to visit with the
Judge."

Parker stayed with her as she wove through the
crowd toward the vibrant redhead holding court on
the glassed-in veranda. An oasis of bright chintzes,
white wicker, and lush ferns, the veranda ran the
length of the west side of the house. Carly had spent
so many happy hours and dreamed so many girlish
dreams here. Tucked in a little island of privacy between two ferns, she and Parker waited to catch
Adele Samuels's eye.

"How about some dinner after you see your grandfather?" the assistant DA suggested.

"I'd love to, but I'm going to curl up with some leftover lasagna and a stack of case files when I leave here. I'm up to my ears in a pretrial investigation."

"And very pretty ears they are, too," he murmured, bending to nibble at one lobe.

She smiled, but hunched a shoulder and edged away an inch or two. The air force discouraged public displays of affection while in uniform. Nor did Carly consider a crowded cocktail party the appropriate time or place for such casual intimacy.

Parker took her withdrawal with good grace. "What's with the investigation?" he asked casually. "I thought you professorial types didn't work real live cases."

"I'm running this one for the base JAG."

"Colonel Dominguez?" His blond brows shot up. "Don't tell me you're working the Smith murder! How'd you snag that one?"

"I didn't. It snagged me."

"I'd give my eyeteeth to have someone hand me a juicy headline-grabbing case like that one."

"And very nice eyeteeth they are, too," Carly teased.

"Com'on, girl. Spill. Tell me the gory details."

"You read most of them in the papers."

"Most of them?" His friendly interest turned sharp and predatory. "What *didn't* I read?"

Carly hesitated. She was surprised that some enterprising, self-styled investigative reporter hadn't nosed out Ryan McMann's involvement in the Smith case before now. She could only imagine the media barrage that would erupt when one did.

"Look, I don't want this leaked to any of your reporter pals, but the key witness in the case is a former hockey player who served some time here in—"

"Ryan McMann!"

"You know him?"

Amazement blanked his handsome face. "You don't?"

"I didn't until I started on this case."

"Lordawmighty, Carly, The Mann led the NHL in scoring six, seven years. He's a legend."

She fought a sharp bite of irritation. For some reason, the idea of Parker and bright, breezy Captain West singing the praises of her uncooperative witness didn't sit well.

"Well, your legend is now a convicted felon. One who doesn't hold the legal system in high esteem, I might add."

"Give you a hard time, did he?"

"Let's just say that old she-mule the Judge used to ride the circuit on had more personality."

Parker tried unsuccessfully to hide a grin. The entire Samuels family loved to recount the tales of Carly's many childhood encounters with the yellow-toothed, cantankerous hinny put out to pasture on the family farm outside town.

"You shouldn't have any trouble getting McMann's cooperation," he commented. "He's on probation now, isn't he? Doing community service? Just yank his probation officer's chain a bit."

She hated to admit that she'd threatened to do just that . . . or that her recalcitrant witness had flung the threat back in her face.

"I read that he's doing his community service at the prison," Parker added. "Running some kind of counseling or education program for the inmates or something. I know the warden. I'll give him a call, get him to put some pressure on your witness."

"No, thanks," Carly said briskly. "This is my case. I'll handle it . . . and McMann. Look, Mother's waving to us. I'd better get in a quick a hug while she's between contributors."

The cheerful downstairs hubbub muted when Carly at last climbed the spiral staircase and walked down the carpeted hall to her grandfather's room. The plantation shutters at either end of the hall were closed to the night, but their pristine white paint brightened the gloom of the faded red and gray Aubusson runner and massive antique sideboard that dominated the center of the hall. Family treasures decorated the sideboard's many shelves, from the delicate Severes vase Carly's mother had purchased during her honeymoon in Europe to the stuffed and mounted bullfrog that had won Dave a ribbon at some science fair or another.

The Judge occupied the room at the end of the hall, as he had since the degenerative arthritis that was destroying him joint by joint had finally forced him off the farm. His nurse answered Carly's quiet knock, shaking her head when asked how he was doing.

"This rain's hard on him. Real hard. He didn't even want to go down to the party tonight. We've upped his prednisone to try control the inflammation, but at that level, the darned stuff eats into his liver and . . . "

"Now don't be going on about my problems," the Judge protested from the wheelchair drawn up beside a reading lamp. "I can't think of any subject less interesting to two pretty girls than an old man's liver."

That drew a snort from Betty, who'd passed fifty an indeterminate number of years ago. Carly crossed

the room, swallowing the pain that stabbed her at the
sight of her grandfather's bent frame and clawlike
hands. They were curled tight on the wheelchair
arms and knobbed with bony proliferations. Feathering a kiss on his whiskered cheek, she dropped
into the chair opposite his.

"Mom said she'd be up when she finishes working
the crowd."

"Sounds like a good one tonight. Betty, pour Carly
something to wash the tickle of all that talking down
her throat. Pour yourself a shot, too, while you're at
it. Maybe it'll loosen you up some."

As familiar with their routine as with her patient's
frequently improper suggestions, the nurse was already splashing bourbon into a single tumbler.

"Just a short one," Carly pleaded. "I've got some
case notes to go over tonight."

Her grandfather cocked a head wreathed in silver
gray. "Big case?"

"The pretrial on the Smith murder."

Like Parker, the Judge lit up at the mention of the
case that had grabbed the local headlines. Unlike
Parker, he didn't push her for details. He didn't have
to. One of Carly's greatest joys since her return to
Montgomery was the hours she spent here with the
Judge. She valued his wit and keen insight, and
trusted his discretion implicitly.

Accepting the tumbler from Betty with a smile of
thanks, she toasted her grandfather with the glass
and mentally braced herself. From years of experience, she knew better than to sip the cheap corn
mash the Judge bought by the ten-gallon keg from a
local distiller. The only way to survive its kick was to
down it in a few, heroic gulps.

As anticipated, the whiskey burned a hole at the
back of her throat before hitting her gullet with a fiery

fist. Her chest contracted. Beads of sweat popped out on her temples. When she could breathe easy again, Carly tucked a foot under her and gave herself up to the pleasure of her grandfather's companionship.

CHAPTER THREE

"Yo, McMann!"

"Yeah?"

"Warden wants to see you."

Even now, almost eight months after his release, that message prickled the skin on the back of Ryan's neck.

"We're almost done here," he replied evenly. "I'll..."

"Now, McMann."

Ryan's jaw locked. Technically he didn't answer to the warden any longer, only to his parole officer. But both he and the short, wiry guard who'd poked his head inside the classroom knew that particular legal nicety carried about as much weight inside the fence as a bucket of spit.

The inmate he'd been tutoring broke the charged silence with an anxious plea. "D...d...don't keep Mr. Bolt waiting, Ry. Please! Not 'c...c...c...cause of m...m...m...!"

Anger shot through Ryan at the kid's agonizing efforts to speak. Billy had made such progress this afternoon. Almost communicated a few coherent thoughts. Now near-panic clouded his pale blue eyes.

He shouldn't be here, dammit! They should've sent him to school, not prison. His nineteen years

and heavily muscled frame might qualify him as a
man, but his marginal IQ had made him the target
for every street tough in his Birmingham neighbor-
hood. Billy had no idea that the stolen Chevy his
buddy had told him to drive was being used as the
getaway car in a bank robbery. After his conviction as
an accessory, the only concession made to his lesser
involvement and impaired mental abilities was to
send him to a minimum security facility. Someone in
the legal system should have recognized his gulli-
bility as well as his complicity.

Yeah. Sure. As if anyone in the legal system gave a
shit about anything except scoring wins or making
headlines with their tough stance on crime, Ryan
thought with a familiar twist in his gut.

"I . . . I . . . I . . . "

"Calm down, kid. I'm going. Just look at these
pages, okay? We'll go over them together when I get
back."

Ryan left the education center with the guard.
Once outside, he hunched his shoulders against the
gray drizzle that misted the dormitories and white-
painted wooden administration building dominat-
ing the north end of the prison compound. The
seeping wet hadn't kept the inmates indoors. Their
work day officially began at six-forty-five and ended
at three. With a couple of hours to kill until dinner,
they attended classes, pursued hobbies, or crowded
the picnic tables set under the dripping pines to
smoke their precious cigarettes.

"Damned rain," the guard groused. "If it keeps
coming down and feedin' the rivers, we'll have to
put you men to work shoveling sand into bags pretty
soon."

Ryan didn't bother to point out that he wouldn't
be shoveling anything. He wasn't part of the prison's

labor pool any longer. He only returned twice a week to fulfill the community service portion of his parole.

Community service! Christ! If he'd known that his one act of careless kindness as an inmate would force his return week after week, he would have left Billy Hopewell to his narrow world of fear and illiteracy. Boredom as much as a nagging sense of pity for the boy locked in a man's body had prompted Ryan to try to teach him to read from picture books. Gradually, their private sessions had extended to informal evening classes that included other illiterates. Then the prison's educational director had pressed Ryan into service as an unpaid assistant.

She'd also testified on his behalf at his parole hearing, pushing for his early release in exchange for continued community service at the prison. Ryan hadn't asked for her support and sure as hell wouldn't have opted for this type of service if he'd had a choice. He hated coming back twice a week, hated the constant reminder of his own years as an inmate.

Well, he'd complete his probation soon. Two months, two weeks, four days, to be exact. Then he'd hit the road. To where, he didn't know and didn't care. The prospect of going where he wanted, when he wanted, without justifying his every move shimmered like a haze on the horizon as he and the guard cut behind the dining hall.

The stink from the Dumpsters and recycling bins lined up like tanks outside the kitchen door brought Ryan crashing back to reality. From the clatter of pots from inside the screen door, he knew the prisoners assigned kitchen detail that month were at the stainless steel counters and huge black range, helping prepare the evening meal.

Ryan and his escort were almost past the Dumpsters when the screen door banged back on its hinges. A beefy inmate in the prison green broadcloth work pants and a white T-shirt with the sleeves rolled up to his armpits shouldered his way out, dragging two hefty garbage sacks behind him. Sweat glistened on his shaved head. When he spotted the other two, a sneer dragged up his lip.

"Well, well, lookit here. Our big-time hockey star's come back for another visit."

Ryan ignored him, as he had for the better part of the past two years. Red streaked up the bull-like convict's neck.

"Hey, man, I'm talking to you!"

Ryan didn't break stride. The prison at Maxwell was designated a minimum security institution. With nothing except a chain-link fence separating it from the military base it had been built to support, the facility accepted only criminals with no prior record of escape, violence, or major medical or psychiatric problems. A few slipped through the screening process, however. Billy Hopewell was one. Gator Burns was another.

"I see you still got that hockey stick of yours up your ass," the street thug jeered. "Why don't you bend over and let me and the boys see if we can't—"

"Shut up, Burns," the guard rapped. "McMann doesn't have time to trade insults with you. The warden's waiting for him."

"The warden?"

Gator's eyes narrowed. Ryan felt them boring into his back until he rounded the corner. A few steps later, the guard peeled off.

"I gotta go see the doc. You know the way."

Ryan knew the way. He sure as hell knew the way.

*   *   *

"Hello, Mr. McMann."

The warden's secretary gave him the same polite smile she paraded out for all visitors, in or out of prison uniform.

"Hello, Mrs. Reeves."

"Mr. Bolt is waiting for you. Go right in."

Ed Bolt hadn't changed either his style or his tie in the years Ryan had known him. He still sat ramrod straight. Still wore his buzz cut so close that his scalp gleamed through the salt-and-pepper fuzz. Still didn't invite the man he'd summoned to his presence to sit.

This time, Ryan didn't wait for an invitation. He folded his long frame into a comfortable slouch in the chair in front of the desk and crossed one jean-clad leg over the other. To his immense satisfaction, tiny white lines of annoyance bracketed Bolt's mouth.

"I received a phone call a few minutes ago," the warden said without preamble. "I understand you're refusing to cooperate in the investigation of the Smith woman's murder."

Ryan's lip curled. The major hadn't wasted any time whining to her friends on the parole board. What had he expected? The lady might have the face of a Southern belle, all soft brown eyes, pink lips, and vanilla ice-cream skin, but she had the soul of a street lawyer.

"You've always been a hard-ass, McMann, but there's no reason for you to refuse to cooperate in this investigation." Bolt paused. "Unless, of course, you know something about the murder that you don't want to tell."

The ground shifted. Ryan felt it move and silently cursed the treacherous terrain beneath him. Jesus! Did Bolt know? Was he part of it?

No. He couldn't be. Ryan had heard no hint, no whisper of complicity by the warden. Willing himself not to sweat, he lifted a shoulder in a careless shrug.

"I have cooperated. I gave the military a statement the day of the murder, and talked to their special investigators a week later. That's all I'm required to do unless or until I'm subpoenaed to appear in court."

Bolt put his hands together, fingertip to fingertip. It was a familiar gesture, one Ryan had seen many times before. As it always did, the warden's carefully precise pose set his teeth on edge.

"The subpoena can be arranged, McMann. We can also arrange to have you serve out the rest of your sentence. Just to ensure your availability for the court hearing, you understand."

"I'm not going anywhere for two more months."

"You're not going anywhere for a lot longer than that if you don't cooperate."

Ryan knew what was coming even before Bolt's mouth curved in a small, tight smile.

"This isn't the NHL, McMann. We're not negotiating your next contract here."

They couldn't resist it. Any of them. The guards. The other prisoners. The warden. They loved to slide in that little dig, that sly reminder of how far the mighty could fall. Ryan had heard variations of the same theme so many times, the barb bounced off his hide.

Almost.

"I'm giving you a piece of advice, McMann. Report to Major Samuels before you leave the base today. Or plan on serving the rest of your sentence, with the possibility of a few more months tacked on for failure to cooperate in a federal investigation."

He dropped his hands and jerked his head dismissively. "That's all."

That wasn't all. Not by a long shot. They both knew it. Animosity hung in the air between them like an evil, many-headed chimera. It had sprung into life mere weeks after Ryan's arrival, when he flatly refused to help organize or participate in the prison Olympics. He'd been barred from professional sports for life, he reminded the warden. He wasn't going to be trotted out and made to jump through hoops like a pet dog in an amateur contest.

His stubborn refusal sparked an enmity that built between him and Bolt each week, each month, and made the years Ryan had spent under this man's jurisdiction a test of fortitude and endurance. He'd held his cool. Performed the extra duties meted out for every so-called infraction of the rules. Swallowed the guards' subtle insults and taunts. But never, *ever*, would he give another human being that kind of power over him again.

He was so close to freedom. He could taste it. See it hanging just above the horizon ahead of him. Almost hear the hum of his car's tires on the pavement as he headed to nowhere.

He left the warden's office without another word.

The sound of the door scraping open jerked Billy's head up. His muscular body was wedged too tightly in the one-armed writing desk to allow any other part of him to move. Futilely, he twisted around.

"Wh . . . what did the w . . . w . . . warden want, Ry?"

The door shoved back against the wall. Gator strolled into the classroom, followed by two other inmates in green and white.

"That's what we want to know. What did the warden want to see your buddy about?"

Gator ambled across the room and propped a boot on the chair seat next to Billy's.

"You talking to McMann, Billy-Boy? 'Bout things you shouldn't oughtta be talking about?"

The mists Billy had lived with all his life parted for a moment, only a moment. His momma had instilled a sense of right and wrong in him before she died. Sometimes he got confused and couldn't remember what was right and what wasn't, but he knew the things Gator and these men made him do were bad, real bad. Then fear hazed his mind once more. Only a gray curtain remained.

"I . . . I . . . I . . . "

Gator leaned closer, sweat and rain glistening on his bald head. The sour stink from his armpits stung the younger inmate's nostrils.

"Don't go all stupid on me, boy. You can talk when you want to. I heard you prattling on to McMann 'bout your momma often enough when we was in the same bay. You been prattling 'bout anything else during these little sessions with your buddy?"

Billy didn't answer. He couldn't. Gator's words fuzzed in his head, turned him all around. He wasn't s'posed to talk about what they did in the woods to nobody, no time, nowhere. Gator said so. Did . . . did he want to talk about it now?

"You want us to beat it out of you, boy? You're big, but not so big me and Jimbo and Pauly here can't hurt you."

"Why don't you try beating it out of *me*, Burns?"

Gator's boot hit the floor with a thud. He spun around, his teeth baring in a smile as he spied Ryan framed in the open doorway.

"Well, well, it's our big hockey star. Have a nice,

cozy chat with the warden? Why don't you tell me all about it?"

"Why don't you go to hell?"

"I will, McMann, I surely will. I 'spect I'll see you when I get there." The grimace that passed for a smile dropped from Gator's face. "What did you and the warden talk about?"

"That's my business."

"Yeah? Maybe me and the boys think it's our business, too." His black eyes glittered. "You talked to him about that bitch who got herself shot, didn't you?"

When Ryan didn't respond, Gator shifted on the balls of his feet. "What'd you tell him, McMann?"

The pride he'd been forced to eat a moment ago surged hot and raw into Ryan's throat.

"Go take a shower. You stink worse than the garbage you've been hauling."

"Oh, yeah? Maybe me and the boys should feed our big fucking hockey star some of that garbage."

The savage need to put his fist down someone's throat sliced through Ryan. His hands curled at his sides.

"You're welcome to try, Burns."

The last, feeble rays of the sun fought their way through the drizzle and slanted into the windows of the conference room appropriated for Carly's use. Great, she thought, her gaze on the trickle of sunlight. The first time the sun had shown its face in days and it waited until almost dusk to do it.

Sounds of desk drawers banging closed and the last conscientious employees finally departing for the day drifted down the hall. She barely registered either the time or the emptiness of the building. One elbow propped on the table, she played absently with the little pearl stud in her left earlobe and mulled over the statements she'd taken today from Smith's friends and classmates.

On the surface, they painted a damning picture. Several eyewitness accounts detailed the Smiths' last, violent argument at a party the night before Elaine Dawson-Smith's murder. Her husband had accused her of sleeping with someone. She'd laughed in his face and left. Another witness confirmed seeing the murder weapon in Elaine's possession. Her husband had bought the .38 for her, and knew she carried it in her purse. Even his friends described Mike Smith as a man hard enough and bitter enough to put a bullet through his wife's heart, wipe the murder weapon clean of prints, and drive away.

Carly was ready for her interview with Smith to-morrow. More than ready. She wanted to watch his face when he explained away the fact that he'd been seen driving along River Road at approximately the time of the murder.

Or had he?

Carly pushed out of her chair and moved to stand at the window. McMann's face hovered in her mind, tight with disgust, too damned handsome for his own good. Had he really seen a dark green Taurus? Had he lied to protect himself? Someone else?

McMann was smart, very smart, according to all reports. Smart enough to skew the results of the lie detector test he'd taken. Smart enough to concoct the story about seeing Michael Smith's car.

During his years as an inmate, he would have pulled work details all over Maxwell; around the stables, the on-base quarters. Did he know that the victim's husband drove a dark green Taurus and pull that salient and very damning fact out of his head

when the police questioned him? If not, why had he
refused to give Carly a statement?

That one wasn't hard to answer. He held her in the
same contempt he did all members of her profession.
He wouldn't throw her a tree branch, much less a
rope, if she were drowning in the muddy river that
surged closer and closer to its banks every day.

A phone shrilled in the distance. Once. Twice. A
third time. The unanswered ring grated on Carly's
nerves. She shagged a look at her watch. Five-fifty. It
hadn't take the building long to empty.

All except for the boss. The 42nd Air Base Wing
commander and his personal staff were still hard
at it. She could see the shine of fluorescent lights
through the windows across the courtyard.

She'd better get to work, too, if she was going to
meet the deadline for completing her report. Frowning, she sorted through the files on the conference table. She'd start putting her notes in order, weigh the
facts as presented so far on their face value. Then
she'd . . .

Afterward, Carly could never pinpoint the sound
that penetrated her consciousness at that particular instant. The whisper of footsteps in the carpeted
hall, perhaps, or the brush of an arm against the
doorframe. Whatever it was, she lifted her head and
turned toward it.

McMann stood framed in the doorway, his body
coiled under a blue denim work shirt, his expression
as tight and angry as the last time they'd squared off.
But this time his face held more than contempt. This
time, he sported a darkening bruise on one cheek, a
split lip, and a look in his eyes that set Carly's heart to
hammering with sudden, painful intensity. She got
to her feet, all too concious of the empty building behind him.

"What are you doing here?"

"Responding to your phone call."

"What phone call?"

He stopped two feet away. So close Carly could see the perfect crimson teardrop beading his cut lip. Too close for her to take more than short, shallow breaths.

"Don't give me that crap, lady. You know damn well what phone call. The warden relayed the message from your friends and strongly suggested I cooperate."

Shocked, Carly gaped at his battered features. "Are you saying prison officials used brute force to coerce you into coming here?"

"No."

"But your face . . . ?"

"My face isn't your problem. But the fact that I don't play your games by the same rules you do most definitely is."

Carly had learned a number of valuable lessons from her childhood encounters with the Judge's cantankerous old mule. One was to never show fear. Another was to dig her bare toes into the clover, plant both fists on her hips, and stare her nemesis down.

Both lessons stood her in good stead now. Her chin snapped up. Her shoulders braced.

"Before we carry this discussion any further, Mr. McMann, there are three things you should know about me. One, I didn't call either my friends on the parole commission or the warden . . . although I have an idea who did," she added in a low, furious aside.

Parker, damn him. As disgusted with herself for discussing an on-going case at a cocktail party as with Parker for interfering in it, Carly made a mental note to deal with the assistant district attorney later. Right now, Ryan McMann demanded her full attention.

"Two, I don't play games with a murder investigation."

He stared down at her, his blue eyes cold and dangerous. "And three?"

"Three, I don't respond to denigrating ephitets like 'lady' or 'doll face.' You can address me by my name, which is Samuels, Carly Samuels, or by my rank, which is major. Take your choice."

CHAPTER FOUR

Ryan couldn't remember the last time anyone had slapped a shot past the impenetrable shield he'd erected around himself since the day of his arrest.

For a moment, a crazy moment, he stood blade to blade with a woman who barely came up to his chin and felt the absurd urge to yield the ice to her. Hard on the heels of that impulse came the equally absurd and far more compelling urge to wrap an arm around her waist, haul her against his chest, and bury his face in the mass of wine-colored hair twisted up in a smooth coil.

The fight with Gator had started his blood pumping. The sight of the major with her chin at a touch-me-and-you're-dead angle stirred it even more. Heat shot through the lower half of his body, and disgust through the upper half.

Smart, McMann. Real smart. As if destroying three lives, his own included, with a single night of misplaced lust wasn't enough. One false step now, one ill-chosen word, and he'd wreak even more carnage.

That sobering reminder killed any wayward impulses, carnal or otherwise. The woman watching him with wary brown eyes seemed to take his silence as a signal that she'd scored a point. She lifted her chin another degree, then, to his surprise, offered a stiff apology.

"I didn't make the phone call that brought you here, Mr. McMann, but I'm afraid I may have said something to another attorney that caused him to do so. I'm sorry. I won't make that mistake again."

He stared at her for long moments, calling himself ten kinds of a fool for feeling even a fleeting impulse to believe her. He decided to ignore the apology.

"I'll take Carly."

"I beg your pardon?"

"You gave me a choice. I choose Carly. Titles like *major* . . . or *warden* . . . push the wrong buttons with me." He dragged out a chair. "Let's get this over with."

She didn't jump at the bone he seemed to be tossing her. Folding her arms across her light blue uniform shirt, she regarded him skeptically.

"Are you offering to give me a statement?"

"No, but you can run through that list of questions you wanted to throw at me yesterday."

"Will you answer them?"

"That depends on what they are."

"I see. Are these answers for the record?"

His smile had a bitter taste. "We both know nothing's ever off the record."

She cocked her head, studying him through thick lashes tipped at the ends with the same dark red as her hair.

"It sounds as though someone got hold of information you thought was given in confidence."

His answer was a careless shrug. He should have known she wouldn't give up. Not when there was still blood to draw.

"So who burned you, McMann? The prosecutor

who argued the case against you? One of the witnesses? The reporters who tried you on the nightly news?"

"You're not even warm, Counselor."

He watched her make the leap. Her eyebrows slashed downward. That incredible, sensual mouth firmed to a tight line.

"Are you saying someone on your own defense team violated attorney-client privilege?"

"I'm not saying anything. Let's just get on with this interview."

She wanted to, badly. He could see the impatience in her face as she studied him a moment longer. Then she rooted around in the black leather purse lying on the conference table and dug out a cell phone.

"I'll have to see if I can reach the stenographer and get him back to the base. In the meantime, you may want to go to the men's room and take care of that cut on your lip. It's bleeding."

Ryan smeared the back of his hand across his mouth. It came away rusted with red.

"Down the hall and to your left," she instructed as he pushed out of his chair. "Just past the . . . Sergeant Hendricks? This is Major Samuels. Sorry to do this to you, but I need you back on base. Yes, now. For a witness statement. No, you don't need to bring the printer. We won't need it transcribed tonight, only recorded."

Ryan left her issuing instructions to the court reporter and wandered through the empty halls. The custodial worker who'd let him in and directed him to the major's temporary office nodded as he passed.

Helluva security system. Locked doors and alarms to protect computers and files after hours, but one tap on a glass door, a few words to a night janitor and anyone could get in. Even an ex-con with a bloodied lip.

What the hell. The building's security wasn't his problem. Palming the men's room door, he fumbled for the wall switch. The overhead fixtures flickered, then poured down a flood of harsh white light. The image in the mirror took on several different shades of ugly.

Christ! No wonder the major had shot to her feet when he'd appeared in the doorway. He saw her face again, her creamy skin grayed with fear for a heartbeat or two. There was a time, he remembered bitterly, when he hadn't inspired fear in women. A time when someone like Major Carly Samuels wouldn't freeze up at his sudden appearance. They'd come after him in hordes. The groupies. The overeager fans. The talk show hostesses and senators' wives who loved to round out their scintillating dinner parties with a millionaire jock who also happened to hold a masters in electrical engineering from UVM.

For the most part, the women had amused Ryan. Some of them had humbled him with their sincere devotion. Until his marriage had fallen apart, though, none of them had ever tempted him.

A shudder started at the base of his neck and rippled down his back. In that black corner of his mind he saw again the face that would always haunt him. Laughing, sexy, and far too knowing for her years. Her brown hair feathering her cheeks. Her pink tongue teasing her lips.

Then came the stark black-and-white photo taken after her death. Ryan gripped the sides of the sink. He'd live with the guilt for the rest of his life. The regret. The disgust that spewed and churned like sulfuric acid in his gut. He'd killed that girl as surely as if he'd handed her the fatal dose of coke she'd mainlined after she'd been pilloried by the press, painted as a whore by Ryan's defense attorneys, jeered at by the fans who lined the courthouse steps. He'd killed her, and he'd accepted that responsibility by changing his plea to guilty midway through his trial.

Now another woman was dead. Her picture had leaped out at Ryan from the papers. Beautiful in a sulky, sultry sort of way. A general's daughter. An air force officer. Wife of another officer. A social, active woman with an extensive network of friends on base and in the local community, all of whom expressed shock and dismay at her murder.

Had Ryan killed her, too? Had he contributed to her death by keeping silent? Was she a member of the club?

Sweat pooled at the base of his spine. With a vicious oath, he jerked the faucet, boated his hands, and shoveled cold water onto his face.

The major—Carly—was waiting for him when he returned to the conference room a short time later.

"The court reporter's on the way. Would you like some coffee while we wait? There's a machine in the break room."

"No."

Ryan rolled out a chair. A small, prickly silence settled over the conference room. He let it stretch. So did Carly.

Her name suited her, Ryan thought, studying her through hooded eyes. It sounded soft on the ear, yet not sweet. She looked soft, too . . . on the surface. Subtle shadows deepened her eyes to chocolate brown. Her cinnamon hair showed glints of gold when she turned her head. Whispery little curls feathered the edge of her high cheekbones and teased at the pearl studs in her ear. Her tailored uniform shirt hugged a nicely rounded set of curves. He gauged her age at mid-thirties and wondered briefly at the absence of a wedding ring before dismissing the question. Her marital status didn't concern him, only her profession.

She was a lawyer. Like all of her kind, she feasted on the flesh of human tragedy. And she was so damned good at pulling on the mantle of detachment lawyers liked to assume. Behind that mask of feminine softness, she revealed nothing of herself. Her cool, self-contained composure irritated Ryan no end.

"Are you related to the Congresswoman Samuels whose face I see on billboards all over town?" he asked abruptly, wanting to strip away some of the mask.

"She's my mother. She's up for re-election this year."

"How long has she been in Congress?"

Something close to a smile touched her face for a moment. "Three terms, although it feels longer. One member or another of my family's been involved in politics for as long as I can remember."

"Pretty convenient that the air force would assign you to your hometown," Ryan observed cynically.

"Yes, it is," she replied before turning the tables. "What about you? Why didn't the court remand you to a federal facility closer to your home in Vermont instead of sending you down here?"

"I didn't ask."

And didn't care. By the time the sentencing phase of his trial had rolled around, Ryan couldn't claim Vermont as his home any longer. His ex-wife had rushed the divorce through and sold the house in

Burlington overlooking Lake Champlain. His parents were dead. Ryan had only shrugged when the judge sent him South, as far away as possible from the legions of angry, protesting fans who'd mobbed the courthouse steps each day.

As far as possible from the ice.

He hadn't expected to miss the cold and ice so much. Sometimes he dreamed about the frigid air that sliced into his lungs like razor blades when he tramped through the woods behind the house. The dreams were so real he could almost smell the turpentine of the spruces, feel the snow dragging at his boots.

From the first moment he'd stepped off the bus almost three years ago, Alabama's torpid heat had clogged his lungs. The mugginess, the creeping kudzu vines with their cloying scent, and the love bugs that swarmed, joined, and smashed against car windshields in black streaks had made him feel at first as if he'd arrived in a foreign land. Gradually he'd acclimated. He'd even come to appreciate the beauty of the moss-draped live oaks and the azaleas that flamed with color in the spring. But he missed the cold. God, he missed the cold!

He was still thinking about the way the winter sun sheened the frozen lake in shades of blue and white when the stenographer arrived a few moments later.

Carly waited until the sergeant had set up the small computer with its specially modified keys for rapid transcribing, then gave the time and the date. Indicating that she was continuing the interview with Mr. Ryan McMann, previously identified for the record and sworn in, she picked up exactly where they'd left off yesterday.

"Please describe the vehicle you passed on River Road."

"It was green, dark green."

"And the make?"

He'd tell her exactly what he told the police, Ryan vowed grimly. Nothing less. Nothing more.

"A late model Taurus with gold trim and wheel spokes."

An hour later, Carly used the building key she'd been given to lock the door behind herself and Sergeant Hendricks. An unspoken acknowledgment lay between them. They'd wasted their time. Mc-Mann hadn't added a single detail to the statement he'd given the police. Nor had he displayed any emotion, any expression that would indicate he knew more about the murder, the victim, or the accused than he'd stated for the record.

Yet Carly couldn't shake the sense that he was holding something back. She'd had to drag every word out of him. Even then, he'd kept his thoughts shuttered behind his bruised face. Guilt nipped at her, along with a twinge of empathy for the man. That split lip must have hurt like hell. Were his injuries her fault? Had they resulted from his initial refusal to cooperate . . . and the phone call she suspected Parker had made to the warden?

A fresh wave of anger gripped Carly. With a brief good night to the court reporter, she unlocked her car, slung her briefcase into the passenger seat, and dug into her purse for her phone. As she'd anticipated, Parker was still at his desk. He answered on the first ring.

"DA's office. This is Stuart."

"Did you talk to the warden about McMann?"

"Carly?"

"I want an answer, Parker. Did you call him?"

"Yes."

"Dammit, I told you not to."

"Hey, that's what friends are for. I help you out when you need it, you help me out when I need it."

"I didn't ask for and I don't need your help handling my investigation. Got that?"

"Yes, ma'am, I surely do."

His amused response rubbed her exactly the wrong way.

"I mean it, counselor. In legal parlance, butt the hell out."

"Okay, okay. Consider me butted." He paused. "Why don't you let me buy you dinner at Jubilee by way of apology?"

Her irritation rode too high even for dinner at Montgomery's best seafood restaurant. "Some other time. I've got work to do tonight."

He knew better than to push her. "All right. Some other time."

Still simmering, Carly hit the end button and dropped the phone back into her purse. She should head home, should review her notes and line up her questions before her interview with Colonel Smith tomorrow. Instead, she drove the short distance from the base headquarters to the JAG school. Before she could concentrate on Smith, she had to get a handle on the man whose testimony put the lieutenant colonel on River Road at the time of his wife's murder.

The B-52 mounted on a concrete pedestal at the juncture of Twining Street and Chennault Circle loomed huge against the dark cobalt sky. For once, no storm clouds blocked the moon hanging just above the bomber's wingtip.

It was a hunter's moon, full and round, the kind that used to get the hounds to howling out on the farm. Carly's lips curled at the memory. The Judge used to take her out to walk with him on nights like this. She'd breathe in the scent of honeysuckle closing up for the night with the same eagerness she breathed in her grandfather's tales of the cases he adjudicated during some forty years on the bench of the circuit court.

Leaving her MG in the well-lighted parking lot, she let herself in through the back door of the law center. A familiar mustiness greeted her when she walked into the library. Although today's legal professionals could access everything from state and federal statutes to supreme court opinions through computers, most law libraries still shelved bound copies of pertinent statutes for those diehards who got off on the real thing. Carly was one of them. She loved poring over the bound volumes, loved scanning the long, convoluted paragraphs that went on for pages. Somehow, the language of the law lost some of its elegance when transferred from the printed page to a flickering screen.

Despite her throwback tendencies, however, she could pound a keyboard as well or better than anyone at the center. With a smile of greeting to one or two of the students working assignments or researching case histories for presentation, she headed for one of the cubicles, dumped her briefcase on the floor and flicked on the terminal switch. The screen hummed to life a moment later. A quick sequence of commands brought up the main menu. Using her personal password, she went directly on-line to the National Legal Research Center's massive database and keyed in the subject of her search.

She sat back, tapping her nails against the desktop while the computer whirred. The results of her query flashed on the screen a moment later.

The U.S. versus McMann.

Fourth U.S. District Court, Northern District, State of New York.

Clicking on the case summary, Carly skimmed through the specific charges, a discussion of several motions to suppress made by the defense attorney during discovery, the preliminary hearings on admissibility, a summary of the trial itself. There was no appeal, which didn't surprise her considering that McMann had changed his plea to guilty halfway through his trial.

Propping her chin on the heel of her hand, Carly frowned at the screen. She'd prosecuted people for worse offenses than statutory rape with a willing seventeen-year-old and possession of an illegal substance. Far worse. McMann wouldn't have even come to trial in most states, given the overwhelming caseloads burdening the legal system these days. He could have copped a plea and received a suspended sentence, or ridden the trial out to the end and hoped the jury's sympathy would turn against the groupie who'd pursued him with such single-minded determination. Instead, the girl died and McMann changed his plea in midtrial.

Was the sensational trial just a ploy to pull him out of the Stanley Cup play-offs, as Carly's boss had hinted? If so, why had McMann suddenly come down with a bad case of conscience? Was there more to the situation than had made the press?

Deciding to request a copy of the verbatim transcript, Carly entered the governmental code that waived the standard processing fee for documents produced in the federal court system and zinged off the electronic form. A few moments later, the printer next to the monitor began spitting out page after page.

She left the law center twenty minutes later, her briefcase full. Given McMann's reversal of his plea in midtrial, the transcript didn't run to as many pages as some she'd seen, but it would give her a few hours of late night reading. Somehow, some way, she had to understand what made the key witness in her investigation tick.

She was just turning the MG onto Chennault Circle when she spotted a ponytailed figure jogging along the well-lighted sidewalk. With the Air War College, the Air Command Staff College, and Squadron Officers' School in full session, in addition to the JAG school and the half dozen other academic institutions that made up Air University, runners were a common sight along the Circle. She stopped for the jogger, who waved a thank you and crossed in front of the headlights.

Recognizing the sweatshirted figure, Carly hit the window switch. "Hey, Captain. Looks like you're racking up the aerobic points."

The young helo pilot she'd interviewed yesterday danced over to the driver's side of the MG.

"Not by choice, Major! Not by choice." Joanna West jogged in place, blowing out a puff of air that lifted her limp, honey-colored hair. "Trust me, I'd much rather fly into a storm to pull a crew dog out of the drink than waste perfectly good sweat like this. What about you? Working late?"

"Just finishing up." On impulse, she extended an offer to the young captain. "I was thinking about stopping at Tony's for a pizza. Care to join me after you complete your run?"

"Yes, ma'am! Give me ten minutes to clean up and I'll meet you there."

"You don't need a ride?"

"No, I brought my wheels to Maxwell."

"Good enough. I'll put the order in. What do you like on your pizza?"

"Everything the law allows," she answered with a grin.

The officers' dorms lined the circle just past the law center. Carly watched West disappear into the closest two-story building, then turned the MG onto the circle. A quick left took her along "Officers' Row."

The elegant senior officer dwellings reflected the French provincial style of architecture common to military housing constructed in the Southeast during the '20s and '30s. Symmetrical facades, pitched roofs tiled in red ceramic, dormer windows, and wrought iron columns all gave a sense of grace and dignity to the homes, similar in style to those at Barksdale Air Force Base in Louisiana and Langley in Virginia.

Carly had hers all picked out, a gracious three-bedroom on Inner Circle shaded by massive oaks. Much as she loved the converted carriage house she'd purchased, she'd rent it out and move on base in a heartbeat if given a chance at one of these beauties. She'd qualify for one soon enough. She was already on the list for lieutenant colonel. She should pin on within a year and, with luck, make full colonel while still at Maxwell. That promotion would depend on whether the commandant moved her into the deputy slot, as he'd hinted he would if she didn't step on it.

Which she could very well do, if she didn't get this investigation wrapped up soon, she reminded herself as she hung a sharp right turn outside the Bell Street gate. Her boss, his boss, and everyone up the chain of command were waiting for the results. The victim's father hadn't made any official requests for information on the case. He couldn't, without risking a charge of undue command influence. Yet the entire legal community felt the weight of his four stars. Carly's reading of the facts in the case and the sufficiency of the evidence had better come in right on target.

Much would depend on the crucial interview with Smith tomorrow . . . and on her assessment of McMann's reliability as a witness. She didn't kid herself that her impulsive invitation to Captain West had been motivated merely by friendliness. She wanted to pump her and, hopefully, get a clearer picture of The Mann as others saw him before his fall from grace.

Two beers, one Greek salad exploding with black olives and chunks of feta cheese, and a half a pizza later, Carly's mental image of the key witness in the Elaine Dawson-Smith murder case had blurred even more.

"You should have seen him on the ice, Major. He was something. Really something."

Carly toyed with her half-empty beer glass, content to let the helo pilot carry the conversation. Without conscious direction on her part, they'd drifted from talking about Maxwell in general and Squadron Officers' School in particular to the murder that had shocked the entire base to the key witness in the case. West wasn't at all shy about reinforcing her earlier testimonials on McMann's behalf.

She slouched against the worn leatherette booth and stretched her legs out comfortably under the Formica table top. A few skeletal crusts littered the tin pizza pan that covered most of the Formica.

"I remember the first time I saw The Mann in

action. My dad took me and my brothers to a Black-hawks game in Chicago. The Hawks got waxed that night, and Ryan was the reason. He scored two goals and assisted in two more. I'm telling you, Major, The Mann was fast as well as powerful. His slapshot was timed at one twenty point three."

"One twenty point three what?"

"Miles per hour."

She sounded slightly shocked that Carly had to ask.

"Ryan was named NHL player of the year right after we saw him play, and his team took the Cup."

"The Davis Cup?"

"No," Jo said, trying unsuccessfully to smother a smile. "The Stanley Cup. The Davis is awarded in tennis."

"Oh."

Taking pity on her obvious ignorance, the young pilot gave her a quick tutorial. "The Stanley Cup is the grandaddy of them all . . . the oldest continuous award in professional sports. Lord Stanley was the royal governor or something of Canada back in the 1890s and came up with the idea. Since then, the silver bowl's become the ultimate symbol of supremacy in the coolest game on the planet. The players would kill to see their names inscribed on the bowl's little silver plaques."

"Are we speaking literally here?"

West's grin flashed. "Well, they'd commit serious mayhem at least, which is more or less what hockey is all about."

"What about McMann? Did he commit mayhem on the ice as well as off?"

The laughter faded from the captain's face. "Ryan McMann played the cleanest game in the league. He won the Lady Byng trophy twice for sportsmanship and gave the fans someone they could look up to."

Yeah, right.

Carly kept the thought to herself, but after two sessions with McMann she couldn't place him anywhere near a pedestal, let alone atop it. Jo West remembered the man before his fall, so didn't have that problem.

"McMann also organized and chaired the Ice Buddies program, where the players sponsor a disabled child for a season. He even got the owners to contribute a percentage of the gate to various charities."

"Commendable."

"It's more than just commendable," the captain countered quietly. "I don't know how many kids the program has helped internationally, but I can tell you about one of them. My brother, Jack."

She played with a pizza crust, her lively face solemn for a moment. "Jack's school bus overturned when he was ten. The accident left him paralyzed from the waist down."

"Oh, no."

Shaking off the memory, Jo whipped out her infectious smile once more. "Jack's Ice Buddy designed and procured a specially equipped wheelchair for him so he could participate in our local hockey league. You ought to see him whiz across the rink. He'll mow down anyone who gets in his way."

Carly believed her. She suspected the captain came from a long line of intrepid Wests. Patiently, she waited while the younger woman washed down a crunchy bite of crust and picked up where she'd left off.

"McMann raised millions for charity during the course of his career. Whatever he did or didn't do in that hotel room the night before the play-offs, my brothers and I will always respect him."

"What about his personal life? I understand his wife divorced him."

"I think the marriage had been on the rocks for years. I remember reading an interview with his wife in *People* magazine. She described how tough it was being married to a superstar and talked about how much she hated hockey. She didn't exactly come across as a loving, supportive spouse."

As it had during her previous interview with Carly, the captain's gaze dropped to her left hand. Absently, she flexed her fingers. The diamond solitaire caught the overhead light and threw back tiny colored darts.

"Some people," she muttered, "can't seem to get it through their heads that a profession is more than just a job. It can get in your blood."

"Like flying?"

"Like flying," Jo admitted wryly. "And maybe lawyering?"

Carly acknowledged the hit with a rueful smile. "No maybe about it. Lawyering's been in my family's blood for three generations. And unfortunately, I've still got some to do tonight."

She reached for the check stuck under the edge of the pizza pan. "Put your money away, Captain. This is on me. I appreciated the company."

And the insights Jo West had given her into the ex-con who played such a key role in her investigation. The pieces still didn't quite add up to a coherent whole, but Carly found herself giving more weight than she had before to McMann's report of a dark green Taurus driving along River Road at approximately the time Elaine Dawson-Smith was killed.

She drove home thinking about that Taurus and the air force colonel allegedly at its wheel. As she turned into the narrow alleyway that led to her ivy-covered carriage house, she decided that she couldn't take the time to go through the transcript of McMann's trial tonight. For what was left of the evening, she'd review her notes and prepare for her meeting with the accused.

CHAPTER FIVE

"I didn't leave the library until after five on the afternoon of April twelfth, I didn't drive down River Road, and I didn't kill my wife."

Carly acknowledged the assertion with a neutral nod. "So you've told me, Colonel Smith. What you haven't told me is why no one can verify your presence at the Fairchild Library until you checked out at five-twelve p.m."

Michael Smith sat ramrod straight across the conference table from Carly. With his neat buzz cut, his Steve Canyon jaw, and his shiny brass accouterments perfectly aligned on his uniform jacket, he might have modeled for a recruiting poster. An engineer by training and a tanker pilot by profession, he sported several rows of ribbons on his chest. Only the small, still-angry scar cutting a jagged track through his left eyebrow marred his looks and gave mute testimony to a marriage that had spun completely out of control.

"My class at the War College includes more than three hundred colonels and lieutenant colonels," he replied. "The other schools on base, including your JAG school, bring in dozens more. I wouldn't expect the staff at the library to notice one among those hundreds."

He was as cold as his classmates and neighbors described him. Maybe he'd learned to wrap himself in that icy shield, Carly surmised, to keep from getting burned by his wife's scorching flames. Always remote and self-contained, he'd reportedly pulled more and more into himself as the academic year had progressed. At the same time, Elaine seared across the landscape of the school, brilliant, beautiful, driven, leaving her indelible mark on faculty and fellow students alike. Michael Smith barely rated a footnote when people spoke of the couple.

Standing accused of his wife's murder seemed to have driven Smith even further into himself. Carly struggled to find a weak spot in his impenetrable shield.

"What about the other patrons at the library? You didn't see or talk to any of your classmates?"

"No."

His attorney made a show of shuffling through a stack of papers and plucked one out with a flourish of a manicured hand.

"The Fairchild Library encompasses more than one hundred thousand square feet. I checked it out myself. It's easy to get lost in there or tuck yourself away in a study carrel out of sight of others."

"I'm familiar with the facility, Mr. Jones."

G. Putnam dipped his head. "I'm sure you are, Major Samuels."

Their civility barely ran surface deep. Privately, Carly neither liked nor respected Jones. He made no secret of the fact that he accepted only cases he felt confident of winning, or that his talents came with a hefty price tag attached. Briefly, Carly wondered how Lieutenant Colonel Smith could afford the man's fees. Making a mental note to check into Smith's finances, she picked up where they'd left off.

"The library's computers showed you didn't log on using your student ID until three-twenty."

"As I said in my previous statements, I brought my notebook computer with me. I used it to polish the final draft of my research paper, which I worked on from noon until about three. Then I logged onto the Library's computer to search for additional references. I checked them out a little after five and drove home."

"At which time you were notified of your wife's murder."

He didn't flinch, didn't blink, just drilled her with his gaze. "That's correct."

As a prosecutor, Carly had to admire his control. As a defense counsel, she would have advised him to show some emotion, any emotion. Granted, more than two weeks had passed since his wife's murder, two weeks in which Colonel Michael Smith had seen the thin curtain veiling his marriage ripped to shreds and his career, if not his life, put on the line. He'd been questioned, re-questioned, charged, arrested, and placed under a pretrial restraint that restricted his movements to the local area. Yet his face showed no signs of strain or sleeplessness. His gray eyes displayed not a flicker of panic or remorse.

"If you remained at the Fairchild Library from noon until five, Colonel Smith, can you explain why a witness spotted someone wearing silver oak leaves driving a vehicle identical to yours on River Road at approximately two o'clock?"

G. Putnam had been waiting for exactly that question. Leaning back in his chair, he steepled his fingers across his stomach. It was, Carly knew, his favorite pose, one that played well to juries. Calm, confident, almost paternal.

"The explanation is simple, Major. Ryan McMann is lying."

"Why should he lie?"

"For any number of reasons. Maybe he saw Elaine Dawson-Smith walking in the woods when he drove out to the prison. Maybe he followed her. Maybe he shot her."

"His prints weren't on the murder weapon, Mr. Jones. Nor do the polygraphs support that hypothesis."

With a wave of one hand, G. Putnam dismissed the fact that both McMann and his client had submitted to a polygraph, and only one had passed.

"The whole issue of whether or not Ryan McMann saw my client driving along River Road is a moot point. His testimony is impeachable under Subsection A, Rule 609, of your Military Rules of Evidence."

Dragging a copy of the Manual for Courts-Martial from his monogrammed pigskin briefcase, he flipped it open to a premarked page.

"As you know, Subsection A applies to witnesses convicted of a crime punishable by death, dishonorable discharge, or . . . and I quote here, Major . . . 'imprisonment in excess of one year under the laws which the witness was convicted.' "

It hadn't taken them long to reach the bottom line of the case. Carly didn't have to read from the manual. She knew it by heart.

"If you read further, sir, you'll see that Subsection C states that evidence of a conviction is not admissible if said conviction has been the subject of a pardon, annulment, or . . . and I quote here . . . 'certificate of rehabilitation of the person convicted.' "

"As of this date, Mr. McMann has not been rehabilitated," Jones countered. "There's no guarantee he'll satisfactorily complete his probation, much less receive a certificate of rehabilitation."

"But *if* he does and *if* he's called to testify," she shot back, "he'll state that he saw an air force officer wearing lieutenant colonel's rank drive a dark green Taurus along River Road at approximately two o'clock on the afternoon of April twelfth. At which point, the members of the court will have to weigh his testimony against Colonel Smith's assertion that he didn't leave the library until sometime after five."

It kept coming back to that. Smith's word against McMann's. A respected air force officer's versus a one-time hockey star and convicted felon. Even if the trial attorney successfully suppressed information regarding McMann's conviction, the odds were that one or more members of the court had heard of him and would know his background. Not everyone was as ignorant as Carly had been about hockey or its superstars.

G. Putnam had figured the odds, too. With a casual move, he smoothed the ends of his red silk tie inside his suit coat. The diamond-encrusted coin ring on his pinkie winked in the early morning light.

"Even with Mr. McMann's testimony, the case against my client rests solely on circumstantial evidence. No one saw Lieutenant Colonel Smith pull a gun on his wife. No one heard the shots or placed him at the actual scene. No jury will convict . . . if the case even comes to trial."

"That's up to the Air University commander to decide."

"I didn't kill my wife."

The stark assertion cut through the legal wrangling. Smith sat forward, a muscle twitching under his left eye. Sensing a crack in his impenetrable armor, Carly jumped to the attack.

"At this point, Colonel Smith, you've given me no reason to believe otherwise."

"I admit our marriage was coming apart at the seams . . ." he said stiffly.

"Why?"

"Time. Distance." He hesitated. "Other interests."

"On whose part?"

"Both of us, I suppose."

The terse reply carried a dismaying ring of familiarity. The officers selected to attend the War College in residence were top performers, driven by both ambition and demonstrated skill. They had reached that critical midpoint in their careers and, for many, their marriages. All too often at the War College, the fabled seven- or ten-year itch blossomed into a fatal rash.

Those officers who chose not to uproot their families and move them to Maxwell for the year found themselves at loose ends at nights and weekends. Those wives and husbands who accompanied their spouses spent months without the demands of their normal activities. For some, it was a time to socialize, to indulge in hobbies or hone their tennis and golf games. For others, the temporary idleness could lead to boredom, restlessness, and gnawing dissatisfaction.

The unique circumstances in the Smiths' situation added to those natural stresses. Two officers, each on their way up. One brilliant and, to all reports, close to the edge, the other quieter but no less ambitious, overshadowed by his wife's dominant personality. Both, it had been hinted, looking outside their marriage for whatever was lacking in it.

"Witnesses stated that they heard your wife needling you about your close liaison with a secretary at your last base," Carly said quietly.

"I didn't have an affair with that woman."

Evidently, Elaine Dawson-Smith had believed him. The tenor of her remarks that night had held more derision than anger. She'd confided to one of the other women present that her husband didn't have the balls to cheat on her.

No one could say the same about her.

"The same witnesses also heard you accuse your wife of having an affair here at Maxwell."

The muscle under his eye jumped. "I thought . . . I sensed she was seeing someone." He brought the words out stiffly, reluctantly, a private man forced to reveal his inner torments. "With all else that had started to go bad between us, the sex was always good. Until lately. Then Elaine didn't seem to want any. From me, anyway."

"You thought she was seeing someone else? Another student? Someone she met in town?"

"I don't know. She'd just laugh when I asked her what was going on and tell me there wasn't anyone I'd have to worry about. Lately, she'd stopped laughing, and we argued more."

"Like when she threw a glass at your head?"

"She was flying high that night, almost drunk. She'd sobered up by the time we got home, but it wasn't the first time she lost it in public. We talked about getting some professional help."

"Did you?"

"No."

"Why not?"

"Elaine woke up the next day convinced I was the one with the problem, not her. She was also concerned about the impact on her career . . . and on her father's appointment . . . if word got out that she needed help."

Carly had wondered how long it would take for

General Dawson to surface in the interview. Commander in Chief, Pacific Air Forces, General Ronald Dawson was responsible for U.S. Air Force operations from the west coasts of the Americas to the east coast of Africa—an area covering more than half the Earth's surface. A seasoned veteran and senior commander, Dawson had recently been nominated by the president as the next chairman of the joint chiefs of staff.

"Did General Dawson know about his daughter's problem with alcohol?"

"Not that I'm aware of. I didn't discuss it with him."

"Why not?"

Smith's eye ticked. "Have you ever met my father-in-law, Major?"

"No."

"If you had, you could answer that question yourself."

"I'd prefer that you answer it."

"Let's just say that neither my wife nor I wanted her father involved in our problems."

Carly wasn't going to get more out of Smith on that one. She saw the barriers going back up, the coldness descending.

She hadn't met General Dawson personally, but she certainly knew him by reputation. A decorated Vietnam War hero, he didn't suffer fools or malcontents willingly. He also believed in swift execution of justice. During Carly's stint at the Pentagon, he'd kept half the legal staff at the headquarters jumping through hoops with his demands for immediate, decisive action on sensitive cases.

The one weak spot in the general's armor, which he professed to fondly and publicly in several media interviews, was his daughter. He'd molded her, shaped her in his own image, took immense pride in the fact that she followed in his footsteps. Carly could understand why Elaine Dawson-Smith might hesitate to admit a failed marriage or a problem with alcohol to the father who wanted her to someday wear four stars, too.

"Tell me about your wife's daily trips to the base stables," she said, trying another tack. "Did she make a habit of exercising her mount even in the rain?"

"Rain, snow, or sleet." For the first time, a flicker of real emotion crossed Smith's face. Was it pain, or regret? "Elaine loved that animal. Sometimes I think it was the only thing she really cared about."

G. Putnam inserted a gentle rebuke. "Let's stay focused on April twelfth, Mike."

Smith took the hint. From then on, he kept his responses to the minimal required to answer Carly's questions. She terminated the interview an hour later, having gained nothing she didn't already know from the accused.

"When can we expect to receive a copy of your report?" Jones asked, snapping the gold clasps on his pigskin briefcase.

"When it's finished, Counselor."

Her lawyer's sixth sense put Smith at the scene of his wife's murder and the smoking gun in his hand. Her gut told her to dig a little more before she wrapped up her investigation.

"My report goes directly to the forty-second Air Base Wing commander for review," she explained. His staff will see that you receive a copy. You'll have five days from date of receipt to present objections if you have them."

"I expect we will," Jones answered. With a nod to the stenographer, he shepherded his client out.

* * *

With their departure, Carly suddenly needed away from the small conference room. She craved air, space to think, some quiet to anchor the thoughts swirling around in her head. Deciding to grab a few hours of privacy in her office at the law center, she left Sergeant Hendricks to finish printing out the transcript of the Smith interview.

As she crossed the parking lot to her MG, thunder rumbled in the distance. Oh, Lord! More rain. If these storms kept up, the Alabama would surely crest its banks. Local stations had already begun broadcasting warnings. To hammer the danger home, channel 6 had run a series of black-and-white stills from the great flood of 1929 on the news last night.

The Judge retained vivid memories of that devastating spring. Carly had grown up with stories about the incessant rains that brought the river over its banks and left almost a dozen Alabama cities totally submerged. Thousands of people had been stranded for days on rooftops and high hills. Raging currents made rescue by boat impossible.

As a result, the fledgling air group at Maxwell flew round-the-clock missions for weeks to drop food and supplies to stranded citizens. That heroic effort marked the first time U.S. aircrews dropped supplies during a major civilian disaster, cementing relations between the base and the community for the many decades that followed. Carly only hoped the Maxwell aircrews wouldn't have to provide such relief again.

The black thunderclouds piling up in the north changed her mind about her destination. With Michael Smith's statement still vivid in her mind, she wanted to time the short drive from the library to the stables, then walk the path Elaine Dawson-Smith had taken to her death. She'd better do it now, before the storm broke.

She followed Chennault Circle to the parking lot next to Air War College and clocked herself from there. After a short swing past the CADRE building, she took a right onto March Street. The golf course sat forlorn and deserted under the threatening gray sky.

March Street flowed into Mimosa, then into River Road. The turnoff to the stables appeared less than a mile later. Carly pulled into the lot behind the cluster of stalls. A quick check of her watch verified that the trip had taken less than seven minutes.

The medical examiner had fixed Elaine's time of death between one and three p.m. Her husband could easily have left the library, met her in the woods beyond the stable, shot her, and returned to the library. There were no witnesses other than McMann to prove or disprove his claim.

The only employee at the stables was a high schooler paid by the riding club and by individual members to feed and exercise their mounts in their absence. She came early in the morning, before school, then again after school. The agents from the Office of Special Investigations who worked the case hadn't located any riding club members who'd been in the vicinity on the afternoon of April twelfth.

Except Elaine Dawson-Smith. The investigators had carefully pieced together her movements on the last day of her life. She'd attended classes in the morning, had lunch at the Officers' Club with two classmates, taken advantage of a scheduled physical fitness block to drive out to the stables, ostensibly to indulge in her favorite form of exercise. She'd arrived just after one. Some time after that, she'd walked into the woods and taken a bullet through the heart.

Digging the crime-scene photos out of her briefcase, Carly exchanged her heels for the sneakers she kept with her racquetball gear in the MG's trunk and followed the horse path into the pines. It skirted the golf course for a short distance, then led to a broad, open field bordered by two fairways. Turning her back on the field and the manicured golf course, she crossed River Road and plunged into a stand of pines.

Moisture hung thick and heavy on the air. A spongy cushion of needles squished under her soles. Within moments, her short-sleeved uniform shirt lay limp against her breasts and her panty hose clung to her thighs like clammy Saran Wrap.

Aside from the distant thunder and the rushing roar of the Alabama less than a hundred yards away, the only sound that disturbed the stillness was the choking cough of an engine. A lawn mower, she surmised, one of those giant machines the inmates operated as part of the cooperative agreement between Maxwell and the Federal Bureau of Prisons. The base kept the prisoners busy. The prisoners kept the base trim and neat.

No doubt McMann had operated one of those machines during his confinement, or walked the perimeter, picking up trash. Carly tried to picture him in prison greens, one of the hundreds of men who blended into the background on the busy base. She couldn't imagine Ryan McMann blending in anywhere. Not with those slicing blue eyes and that lean, rugged face. That lean, rugged, *bruised* face. Anger shot through her again. She still hadn't quite forgiven Parker for his interference.

Preoccupied with thoughts of McMann, Carly

walked farther than she realized. Frowning, she turned and retraced her steps to where the path curved. Joanna West had spotted the body from the road, only a few yards off the path. The spot had to be near, maybe . . .

"Oh!"

She jerked back, narrowly avoiding a collision with the figure who lumbered out of the pines. Startled, she registered two instantaneous impressions. One, he wore prison greens. Two, he filled out the nondescript uniform in a way she'd never imagined it could be filled. The pants that bagged on most of the inmates clung to his thick, corded thighs. The white T-shirt stretched across a chest and shoulders roped with muscle.

Carly stumbled back another step or two, overwhelmed as much by his sheer size as by the grisly reminder of what had happened at or near this spot two weeks ago.

"What do you want?" she asked sharply.

"I . . . I . . . I . . ."

He didn't move toward her, didn't try to close the distance between them. He looked so startled, so frightened, that Carly's galloping pulse slowed to a fast trot.

"I . . . I . . ."

He swallowed convulsively. His Adam's apple bobbed under a chin lightly fuzzed with a blond shadow.

"It's okay. You scared me as much as I scared you. Are you working here?" She swept the area and caught a gleam of metal on the far side of the pine thicket. "Mowing grass?"

He nodded.

While he kept his distance and regarded her with a combination of nervous fear and wariness, Carly's mind raced. The military investigators had talked to prison officials and to those inmates on road and grounds duty the day of Elaine Dawson-Smith's murder. The closest crew had been detailed to the runway supervisor, who'd kept them at work clearing the field between the runways . . . less than a mile from the murder scene. None of the inmates had seen or heard anything, but Carly decided it was worth a shot to ask a few questions of her own.

"What's your name?"

"B . . . Billy. H . . . H . . . Hopewell."

In a gesture at once subservient and polite, he tugged off his hat. Carly's jaw sagged. Freed of the ball cap, his short, burnished curls framed a face that the Greeks might have immortalized in marble. Belatedly, she realized she was gaping.

"I'm Major Samuels, Mr. Hopewell. I work here on the base."

He nodded again, wringing the green ball cap with both hands.

"I'd like to talk to you."

Panic flared in his eyes. "Not s . . . s . . . sposed to t . . . talk."

"I'm aware that inmates aren't supposed to carry on casual conversations with base personnel, but this is official business."

"T . . . t . . . t . . ."

His face twisted in an effort of getting out the words. The struggle was painful to watch.

"T . . . t . . . trouble."

"No, you won't get in trouble."

He looked so close to tears that Carly found herself oozing gentle assurances.

"It's all right, I promise, it's all right."

"N . . . *not* all right. Ry says s . . . so."

"Ry? Ry who?" Her pulse jumped. "Do you mean Ryan? Ryan McMann? Do you know him?"

"My f . . . friend." His big fists mangled the ball cap. "Not right. Ry said so."

"What's not right?" She took a step closer, her attention riveted on his awesome face. "Did Ryan McMann tell you it wasn't right to talk to people? What aren't you supposed to talk about?"

"Can't . . . can't . . . talk. Ry said so. J . . . Joy said so."

"Who's Joy?"

The inmate backed away, his panic increasing with each question she threw at him. For an absurd moment, Carly felt like a predator stalking a prey at least a foot taller and a hundred pounds heavier than she was.

"Who's Joy, Mr. Hopewell?"

"I . . . I . . ."

With an inarticulate cry, he spun around and fled. Frustrated and a little ashamed of badgering him as she had, Carly watched him race through the trees. Moments after the trees swallowed him up, the mower's engine chugged to life.

She decided she now had two options. The first was to drive to the prison and make an official request to speak to Hopewell. The second option . . . The second was to have another chat with Billy's friend.

She set off for the stables. She'd check the OSI reports, find out who McMann worked for. With luck, she could catch him on the job this afternoon. Intent on her quick change of plans, Carly walked right past the tall pine that had partially obscured Elaine Dawson-Smith's body.

She didn't notice the limp cluster of pale pink woodroses laid at the base of the pine.

* * *

Flowers! The friggin' idiot dropped flowers where the Smith bitch got it!

Gator Burns snatched up the wild roses, cursing viciously. He'd figured something was up when he'd spotted Billy-boy stumbling outta the woods like a big, crazed bear. The fragile roses disintegrated in Gator's hamlike fist.

That fucking goonhead was gonna get them all fried! It was bad enough Billy had started crying like a baby at night, callin' for his dead momma, stuttering and stammering even in his sleep. Now he had to go drop flowers like he was decoratin' a goddamned grave.

Gator had worried that the kid might crack sooner or later. Looked like it was gonna be sooner.

Well, he wasn't letting no halfwit take him down. Hopewell had brought in some good bucks this past year, but Gator didn't need him. He had other inmates on the string, not as big, not as pretty, but eager enough to get their rocks off. It was time, he decided grimly, to put his prize stud horse out to pasture.

He backtracked to the mower he'd left parked just off the fairway and climbed into the seat. One foot worked the clutch. The other pushed the rusted pedal to the floor. The engine coughed and spit. The double circular blades rattled under their casings. Gator pulled the lever to raise the blades and let the clutch out. The mower humped and bumped down the fairway.

Good thing he'd worked it so's he got put on the same crew as the kid. Him and Jimbo both. Pauly was pullin' kitchen detail the rest of this week. Gator coulda got him off but he liked keeping someone in the kitchen. The guards came in for coffee, talked as if the inmates scrubbing the floors didn't have no faces, let alone ears. 'Specially Murphee. Ole Murph could shoot the shit with the best of them. He liked his coffee, Murph did, and sitting around on his fat ass. He also liked the money Gator slipped him to put him and Jimbo and Billy-boy on the golf course detail more or less regular. It was easy work riding up and down the grassy stretches. Convenient, too, for their little side business.

'Course, things got hairy on the East Course, where the greens hugged the river and deep ravines gouged right through the fairways. Cutting them slopes was tricky, 'specially on fairway number seven. A big, heavy machine like this wasn't angled right, it could tip right over.

A few moments later, Gator caught sight of Billy's mower up ahead. His boot stomped down on the rusted pedal.

CHAPTER SIX

Thunder rolled in from the north, sweeping toward the construction site like an oncoming tide. Scudding clouds sent shadows flitting across the partially shingled roof. The accompanying breeze cooled Ryan's bare, sweaty back.

He leaned heavily on his bent knee. With one hand, he slapped composite shingles onto thirty-pound underlay. With his other, he shot heavy-duty staples through shingle, felt, and wood.

Whap! Whap! Whap!

In a rhythm that matched the crack of the staple gun, he kneed his way along the plywood roof deck. The prickly composite shingles scraped like sandpaper on his palm and the reek of the tarred underpaper stung his nostrils, but Ryan barely noticed either. This was exactly the kind of work he wanted at this point in his life. Brutal. Mindless. Exhausting.

His parole officer had tried to convince him to take the job offered by the owner of a sporting goods chain, hawking football jerseys and baseball caps in a mall store on the east side of the city. Ryan hadn't wanted any part of it, any more than he'd wanted to organize the warden's prison Olympics. He'd put that part of his life behind him. Soon, he thought with a shaft of grim satisfaction, he'd put this part behind him as well.

Two and a half months and counting.

Two and a half more months of backbreaking labor. Two and a half more months of twice-a-week visits to the prison, followed by a final meeting with the parole board and a certificate of rehabilitation, which Ryan figured was about as useful as a wad of used toilet paper. Then he was out of here. His last sight of Alabama's red clay roads and gray, dripping skies would be the one framed in the rearview mirror.

He . . . *Whap!* . . . couldn't . . . *Whap!* . . . wait—

"Hey! McMann!"

The foreman's shout barely carried over the staple gun's ear-splitting crack. Ryan corkscrewed around, taking care not to let his knee slip off the deck.

"Yeah?"

"Lady wants to talk at you."

The foreman jerked a thumb toward the figure leaning against the fender of a low-slung white sports car. Even from two stories above the ground, Ryan couldn't mistake the woman's wine-red hair swept up under a blue air force flight cap or the slender, curving legs displayed below the hem of her uniform skirt.

He sat back on his heel, the gun dangling in his hand. What the hell was she doing here? How many times were they going to play out this farce? He knew as well as she did his testimony wouldn't count for squat with any jury, military or otherwise. Colonel Smith would walk, and his wife's death would remain a dark, tragic secret.

His jaw tight, Ryan shimmied butt first down the steep incline and grabbed for the ladder. When he hit the ground, his boots sank in the sucking clay churned up by the trucks that delivered supplies to the site. Weaving around stacks of lumber and bundles of shingles, he made his way to the waiting woman.

Jesus, she was something. Every man's wet dream come to life. Ryan's wet dream, anyway. As tight and angry as he'd been during their two short encounters, the woman had somehow managed to get under his skin. He'd punched his pillow more times than he wanted to count last night, trying not to think of her full, sensual mouth and red hair. Those high breasts and neatly flared hips hadn't exactly made the forgetting any easier.

She looked even better in the light of day than she had in the small hours of the night. So cool, even in this muggy spring warmth. So composed. As he'd once been. For a moment, Ryan let himself imagine how different things might have been if they'd met before . . .

His mouth settled into a grim line. He'd damned well better forget about before. Before was behind him. All he needed to do was get through today. And tomorrow. And the next two and a half months.

"What do you want?"

He did it deliberately, Carly decided. Tried to throw her off balance, to disconcert her by moving in close like this. She could see the sweat glistening on his broad shoulders, catch its raw, male scent. She refused to let his nearness get to her.

"I'd like to talk to you." She had to pitch her voice to be heard over the rifling crack of the staple guns.

"Without a stenographer? What do we have to talk about that isn't part of your investigation?"

"If we can go someplace where we can speak without having to shout, Mr. McMann, I'll . . ."

"Ry."

"I beg your pardon?"

"We dispensed with titles, remember. It's Ry, or Ryan." His mouth curved in the mocking smile she so disliked. "Take your choice."

"Fine. Can we get away from the noise, Ryan?"

He hooked his thumbs in the waistband of his jeans. Carly half expected him to refuse, and fully expected the added weight of his hands on his jeans to drag them down into x-rated territory. The damned things already rode well below his navel.

She'd never considered herself particularly susceptible to sweaty chests and washboard bellies. Grudgingly, Carly had to admit McMann could make a believer out of her.

"The crew's about to break for lunch," he said slowly. "I could take mine now."

"Fine. There's a pig stand a few miles back. If you're hungry, we could go there and eat while we talk."

"A pig stand?" His voice blended Yankee twang and overdone Alabama drawl. "I know I stink, sweetheart, but I don't usually eat with barnyard animals."

She lifted a brow. "One, you don't stink . . . much. Two, a pig stand is what we call a barbecue shack around these parts. And three . . ."

"I know, I know. You don't answer to denigrating epithets like 'sweetheart.' Sorry. It slipped out."

The apology surprised her. His hesitation about accepting her offer didn't. He stared down at her, his face unreadable, then abruptly agreed.

"Hang loose while I get my shirt and tell the boss I'm leaving."

Carly nodded, her gaze intent as she watched him cross the muddy site and shag a faded blue shirt

from a bundle of shingles. Shirt in hand, he headed
for a portable metal building that appeared to serve
as office, storage facility, and supply center. He
moved with an easy stride, his body as lean and
powerful from the rear view as from the front. Unbidden, the image of the boy ... man ... inmate
she'd encountered in the woods leaped into her
mind. He was bigger than Ryan. Far more muscled.
More ... more beautiful. She couldn't think of any
other way to describe him.

Yet for all the young inmate's stunning masculinity, he lacked McMann's lethal grace. Lacked, too,
the aura of danger that came with the broken nose,
the watchful eyes, the bitter intelligence.

What was the connection between the two men?
Why had this Billy Hopewell sobbed Ryan's name,
almost like a mantra? Why had he left his mower and
walked through the pines to where Colonel Dawson-
Smith had been killed?

The questions still buzzed through Carly's mind
when McMann returned, tucking a faded denim
work shirt into his jeans. He'd tried to clean up, she
saw. Water glistened in his neatly combed hair, and
the scent of industrial strength soap had replaced
that of healthy male sweat.

When she reached for her keys, he eyed the MG
skeptically. "Think it'll hold both of us? We could
take the crew truck."

She glanced at the pickup he indicated. She'd seen
rusted hulks in better condition used as planters in
backyards.

"It'll hold us. Just watch your head getting in."

He managed to fold himself in with little more than
a grunt or two. Carly slipped into the driver's seat
and keyed the ignition. With a smooth coordination

of hand and foot, she pushed in the clutch, shifted into reverse, and backed the MG down the dirt track.

The drive to the restaurant took only a few minutes. Screened on three sides and wreathed in the tantalizing scent of sizzling pork, the tiny, red-painted shack was crammed with locals. After snaking the MG through the dirt parking lot twice, Carly finally spotted a car pulling out.

"We might have to wait for a table," she warned.

"I get paid by the square, not by the hour. I'll make up the work if necessary."

She cut the engine, eyeing him through the screen of her lashes. There were better jobs out there, even for a parolee, but she didn't ask why McMann was slinging roof shingles. It wasn't any of her business and not pertinent to the case.

Contrary to her expectations, they lucked out and got a booth immediately. Or half a booth, anyway. They ended up wedged knee-to-knee on an L-shaped bench tucked in the far corner of the shack. A gum-snapping waitress hipped her way through the crowd to drop hand-lettered menus on the table and a wide smile on McMann.

"Interested in our specials today, handsome?"

"Maybe."

Still popping her gum, she rattled off a list that included five variations of barbecued pork and a solitary fried chicken platter, then left them to think over the choices while she got their drinks. Discreetly, Carly edged sideways to give McMann another inch or two.

"I can recommend the chopped pork sandwich."

"Eat here often, do you?"

"I used to. My grandfather's farm is just south of here, down Highway 331. Mom and my brother and I went to live with him after my dad died. We'd stop here whenever we kids could talk the Judge into hauling us to town."

"The Judge?"

"My grandfather."

"Another lawyer." The muttered observation didn't have the ring of a compliment.

"Actually, he never attended law school or passed the bar. He was appointed to the bench back in the days when formal schooling didn't count as much as common sense and a solid reputation in the community."

McMann's mouth took on the familiar, mocking curve. "Times have certainly changed, haven't they, Counselor?"

"Yes, they have."

Her calm reply took none of the sting from his smile. The waitress's arrival with two Mason jars brimming with iced tea did, however.

"Here you are, good lookin'." She plunked his jar down, then winked at Carly. "You got you a keeper here, Lieutenant."

"It's Major."

"Whatever. Y'all decided what you want?"

She took their orders for chopped barbecue sandwiches and a basket of onion rings, then left with another wink. Carly waited until McMann had added two heaping teaspoons of sugar to the already sweetened tea to pick up where they'd left off.

"Look, Mr. McM . . . Ryan. I can't answer for every member of the bar, but personally I'm very proud of what I do."

His spoon clinked against the glass jar. "What do you do?"

"When I'm not conducting Article 32 investigations, you mean? I'm chief of the Military Justice Division at the Dickinson Law Center."

"That's the two-story brick building on Chennault Circle?"

"Right. Have you been in it?"

"Only around it," he replied with a sardonic gleam. "Pulling weeds and picking up trash."

"If you'd been inside," Carly continued, "you'd see that it's one of the finest facilities in the country. We provide basic instruction in military legal practices to new judge advocates and paralegals, as well as advanced and specialized courses in such esoteric subjects as environmental law and forensic sciences."

He leaned against the wooden booth and stretched his legs out beneath the table. Or tried to. His feet tangled with Carly's. Politely, he drew them back and hunched forward again.

"You must be good if the air force picked you to instruct other JAGs."

"I am," she replied.

The smile came quicker this time, without the mocking edge. "So modest, too."

"It's the truth, the whole truth, and nothing but the truth."

His smile slipped into a crooked grin, and Carly felt her breath hitch somewhere down around the middle of her chest. Good Lord above! No wonder hoards of starstruck groupies had reportedly dogged McMann's every move. He could melt the ice with one of those genuine grins.

For a disconcerting moment, she forgot why she'd brought him to the noisy restaurant, forgot the investigation, forgot what he'd become. Then the laughter left his face and reality came crashing back.

"Too bad I didn't have you on my legal team," he said sardonically. "Maybe things might have turned out differently."

"You might have beaten the charges, you mean?"

"No. But I might not have killed a seventeen-year-old girl in the process."

"You didn't kill her." Carly had no idea why she was leaping to his defense. "The medical examiner's report said she died of a self-induced drug overdose midway through your trial."

"Yeah, right. After my team of scavengers devoured the few shreds of self-respect she had left once the media finished with her."

He threw back his head and took a long swallow of tea, as if to wash down the bitter memories.

"So that's why you changed your plea," Carly murmured. "You felt guilty about the girl's death."

The Mason jar hit the scarred table top. "I changed my plea because I *was* guilty."

"What?"

"I was guilty," he repeated. "Of everything the Feds charged me with. I transported a seventeen year old across state lines. I had sex with her. I was stupid enough to turn a blind eye when she pulled that coke pipe out of her purse and took it into the bathroom. That's why I changed my plea, Counselor. That, and the fact that I was sick to death of providing more flesh for your kind to feast on."

Carly wasn't expecting that slap in the face. She controlled her instinctive flinch and decided not to dignify his vicious attack with a response.

"I thought we had dispensed with titles," she said

instead, her voice several degrees chillier than it had been a moment before.

"Jesus!" He shoved his drink aside and leaned forward, disgust in every line of his taut body. "Don't you ever get riled? What the hell does it take to light your fuse?"

"More than you can dish out."

She knew instantly she'd said the wrong thing. A blue flame ignited in the eyes only inches from her own. The hand that had held the Mason jar whipped up to wrap around her nape.

"Maybe I haven't tried hard enough."

His palm was cold and wet on her skin, his breath warm and sugar sweet on her face. She didn't blink.

"And maybe I don't like being pawed in a public restaurant."

She refused to move, refused to let him see that his touch got to her.

His gaze dropped to her mouth, so close to his own. All he had to do was lean forward an inch, maybe two.

"Don't do it," she warned softly.

He hesitated, then nodded. Before he could pull back, gum popped right beside Carly's ear.

"Y'all want this lunch or you just gonna sit here and make cow eyes at each other?"

McMann's hand slowly dropped. Carly sat back, her nerves snapping. The skin where he'd touched her burned.

"I thought you two was never coming up for air," the waitress smirked.

Thumping down two heaping platters, she dug in the back pocket of her jeans for a bottle of the house's special sauce and the check.

"Have at it, folks. Yell if you want anything else."

The words exploded in Carly's mind. She wanted. She definitely wanted. Just a touch. Just a taste of the dark, dangerous man across from her. The realization shocked her all the way to her core.

A sick little suspicion that she wasn't any better than the groupies who'd mobbed him in his heyday lodged at the back of her consciousness. She'd wanted his kiss. She'd wanted his touch. She still wanted to satisfy a purient tug of curiosity and see if he lived up to his reputation as a world-class superstud.

Shaken, Carly slammed the door on that compartment of her brain. She'd drag her inexplicable, unexpected craving out later. Examine it rationally, coolly. Right now, she'd better concentrate on why she'd tracked him down to the southside construction site.

He, evidently, had the same thought.

"What I want," he said conversationally, as if he hadn't just set her skin afire with his touch, "is to know why we're here."

"I told you," she replied in an even tone that, thankfully, revealed none of her inner turmoil. "I want to talk to you."

He reached for the barbecue sauce. "About what?"

"Billy Hopewell."

She thought his eyes narrowed a fraction, but that might have been caused by the steam rising from the pork heaped on his plate.

"How do you know Billy?" he asked casually, thumping the bottle to get the sauce running.

"I met him earlier this morning . . . in the stand of pines where Elaine Smith was killed."

She hoped that would shock him, or at least get his attention away from that damned bottle. It did neither.

"He must have been on weeds and seeds patrol."

"Billy said you're his friend."

He shrugged. "I slept in the bunk below his for six months or so. I tutor him and a couple of the other prisoners twice a week. That doesn't make us friends."

Setting the sauce aside, he wrapped both hands around the dripping bun.

"He also said you told him not to talk to anyone."

"So?" He tore a chunk out of the sandwich.

"So I'd like to know what don't you want him to talk about?"

She waited with an impatience she refused to show while he chewed slowly, savoring the spicy pork with every evidence of enjoyment. He swallowed, then washed the sandwich down with a swig of iced tea.

"In case you didn't notice, Billy has a speech impediment. It gets worse when someone surprises or frightens him."

Both of which she'd done, she admitted silently.

"I've told him he doesn't have to talk to anyone, about anything, when he's scared or can't get the words out."

The mocking smile was back, raking across Carly's nerve endings like fingernails on a chalkboard.

"Any more questions?"

"Just one. Billy mentioned someone named Joy. Who is she?"

McMann couldn't have faked the blank look that crossed his face. He was good, but not that good.

"Beats the hell out of me."

CHAPTER SEVEN

The storm that had threatened all day broke just as Carly pulled into the parking lot behind the base headquarters. Lightning cracked across the black sky to the accompaniment of thunder that boomed like continuous rounds of field artillery. Sheets of rain poured down and produced an instant layer of silver on the asphalt.

Carly cut the engine, grimacing as winds buffeted the MG. This kind of storm spawned tornadoes. With a silent hope that McMann and his crew had climbed down off that roof, she debated whether or not to ride the storm out in the car. The prospect of an extended wait in the muggy enclosure of the little MG held even less appeal than a mad dash across the parking lot. Shouldering open the door, she abandoned her military dignity and raced through the rain with her briefcase held over her head.

The rain blew at almost a ninety-degree angle, wetting her from the neck down. She left a trail of squishy footprints as she made her way to the conference room, where she found the stenographer gone and the transcript of this morning's interview with Colonel Smith neatly printed and waiting for her. Shivering in the air-conditioned chill, Carly dropped her briefcase on the table.

Two thumbs and forefingers lifted her sodden

blouse away from her chest. She walked the length of the conference room shaking the upper portion of her blouse and had just turned back when a yellow stickie stuck to the wall at eye level snagged her attention.

Call Baptist Memorial immediately.

Her first reaction was fear—instant, sharp, and metallic. The Judge! On the crest of that wave came the more rational reminder that her sister-in-law had chosen the birthing center at Baptist Memorial to deliver her second child. Blowing out a quick breath, she grabbed for the phone. Two transfers and five minutes later, her brother picked up on the other end.

"Alison's water broke almost an hour ago," Dave got out in a near panic. "The pains are fifteen minutes apart."

"You're not in the birthing room, are you?"

"She won't let me in!"

Since her big, hulking brother had keeled over in a dead faint and broken three ribs the last time he'd tried to share the miracle of birth with his wife, Carly could only be thankful for Alison's insistence that her mother-in-law act as her labor coach this time.

"Is Mom there?"

"She's on her way in from the office. Listen, I dropped Suzy off at the house on the way to the hospital. Can you stay there tonight? I hate to leave the Judge and Betty to the mercies of a three-year-old."

"No sweat. I can handle Suzy-Q."

Dave didn't even bother to respond to that gross misstatement of fact. Suzanne Patricia Samuels had wrapped her aunt around her little finger the first time she'd scrunched up her wrinkled pink face and grinned a toothless grin.

"Betty said the Judge is pretty bad today," Dave warned.

The familiar pain clutched at Carly's heart. "He's bad every night now."

She replaced the phone just as another blast of air-conditioned air shot out of the vents. A shiver started at the base of her neck and worked its way down to her knees. Hunching her shoulders, she glanced at her watch. Almost three-thirty. The late lunch and long drive back to the base had eaten up most of the afternoon. She'd take her work with her and get what she could done at her mother's house . . . after she dried off.

She reached for the Smith transcript and had just wedged it into her briefcase along with the other case files when a young legal tech stuck her head inside the conference room.

"Major Samuels?"

"Yes?"

"Lieutenant Colonel Dominguez would like to see you, ma'am."

"Now?"

"Yes, ma'am."

With a rueful glance at her still soaked uniform, Carly slicked back her wet bangs.

"Okay, thanks."

Luckily, the offices of the 42nd Air Base Wing's Staff Judge Advocate were only a corridor away. Carly's wet heels made a little squeaking noise as she followed the legal tech through the halls of the sprawling headquarters. When she reached the offices of the base JAG, his secretary indicated that he was on the phone.

Carly's impatience mounted as the wait lengthened from five minutes to ten, from ten to fifteen. Finally, the little red light on the telephone console blinked off. After buzzing her boss, the secretary invited the major to go inside.

"Ah, Carly. Come in. Come in."

Short and pudgy, Dominguez sported a luxuriant black mustache that nudged the limits of air force allowances. He came around his desk and waved her to the leather chairs grouped around a low, mahogany table.

"Looks like you got caught in the storm."

"Yes, sir."

"And we've got more coming," the JAG commented with a grimace. "Would you like some coffee? Or a diet Pepsi? My wife got me started drinking the stuff and now I'm hooked."

"No, thank you. I was just heading over to my mother's house to dry off and stay with the Judge while she's at the hospital with Dave and Alison."

"The baby's on the way?"

Smiling, Carly nodded. As the governor's legislative assistant for environmental matters, Alison Samuels was well known to the Maxwell legal community.

"Well, I won't keep you long. I just wanted to hear how the Article 32 is going."

"It's going. I've interviewed the key witnesses and several of Smith's friends and neighbors."

"And?"

"And I still have a few questions that need answering."

"What's your gut feel? Do the preliminary findings support the charges and specifications?"

An odd reticence nipped at her. She wasn't ready to state her conclusions yet, particularly since Dominguez had a vested interest in their outcome. His office supported the Air War College commander, who'd preferred the charges against Smith. The Base

JAG and his staff wouldn't look good if Carly came back with a report that criticized their reading of the evidence.

"So far," she said slowly, cautiously.

"Good. When can I expect your report?"

"Right now, I'd say the end of next week."

The colonel's brow creased. "Why so long?"

"As I said, I still have some questions that need answering."

"Like what, Carly?"

She wasn't ready to voice her suspicions that McMann was holding something back. Nor did it occur to her to tell Dominguez about her surprising encounter with the odd young inmate in the woods this morning. She wanted to play with the pieces of the puzzle a little longer, see how they fit. When she didn't answer right away, a frown sliced down between the colonel's dark brows.

"Is there a problem?"

The edge to his voice surprised her. She tapped her fingertips on the leather-covered chair arm, eyeing him thoughtfully.

"You tell me, sir."

A flush rose above the collar of his uniform shirt. "You guessed it. I got a call from General Dawson's chief JAG. He wants to know what's happening."

"Just tell him that the investigation into the murder of Lieutenant Colonel Smith is still in progress. I plan to review the transcripts this weekend and start formulating my report early next week."

"That's all you can give me?"

"At this point . . . yes, sir."

"All right." He pushed himself out of his chair. The interview was clearly over. "I'll be expecting your report next week."

Diplomatically, Carly didn't reply that he could

expect it all he wanted, but he'd get it when she was satisfied that she'd fully executed her responsibilities as investigating officer.

Still, she felt the pressure as she lugged her overflowing briefcase along with her to her mother's house. If the Judge broke down and resorted to the pain pills that always knocked him out, she'd have some long, quiet hours to work tonight.

Long after midnight, silence had wrapped its arms around Carly like an old friend. Suzy, thankfully, had depleted her seemingly inexhaustible store of energy after two long games of hide and seek, one Barney movie, and another reading of her favorite bedtime tale featuring Taffy the golden retriever. Betty had gone to bed hours ago, almost as soon as the Judge had drifted into a fitful sleep. The nurse needed rest as much as her pain-racked patient.

Now Carly's back rested comfortably against the arm of the sofa in her grandfather's bed/sitting room. Her bottom angled into the cushions. Files spilled from her briefcase and formed an island of paper on the sofa and thick mauve carpet. Absorbed in McMann's trial transcript propped on her updrawn knees, she registered only peripherally the tick of the mantel clock and the raspy snores coming from the bed across the room.

They crucified the girl! The media, McMann's team of defense attorneys, even the prosecutor. The judge should have suppressed her juvenile convictions for possession and distribution. The prosecution should have objected more strenuously to the parade of "friends" who testified to her promiscuity and growing obsession with McMann. The victim's past record and reputation didn't obviate the facts in the case, yet the defense presented them as evidence of complicity in her own seduction . . . and the judge allowed it!

Carly's lips curled in disgust. If her grandfather had presided over this circus, he would've yanked both the prosecution and the defense up by the short hairs. The Honorable Harry Walters must have been senile.

No wonder the ABA regularly debated the independence guaranteed to federal judges by the Constitution. They were appointed, not elected, and held their seat for life unless impeached for and convicted of "Treason, Bribery, or other high Crimes and Misdemeanors." Thus insulated from outside influence, they were free to render impartial decisions based solely on their interpretation of the law. The same provision that guaranteed them their independence, however, also raised the ugly specter of incompetency upon occasion. This, Carly decided as she turned page after page, was one of those occasions.

The phone's shrill broke the quiet at just past two a.m. She dived for the receiver, trying to catch it before the second ring.

"Samuels residence."

"David Lee Samuels the Third finally made his appearance," her brother announced exuberantly. "The kid's got a set of lungs on him that won't quit. Can you hear him?"

He must have stuck the phone right in the baby's face. Carly winced at the screech that jumped over the line.

"I hear him, I hear him." With one hand over her mouth to keep from disturbing her grandfather, she demanded details. "Does he look like you or his mother?"

"He's got my hair and her nose."

"Thank God for small blessings. How's Allie?"

"Recovering, and profoundly grateful to Mom for standing in for me. Now she only has to nurse one baby instead of two."

"Is she up to talking?"

"Hang on a sec."

Alison came on a moment later, sounding tired and elated. "Hey, Carly."

"Hey, girl. Congratulations. David Lee the Third sounds like he's already staking a claim to his piece of the world."

The new mother laughed. "He's something, all right. Did Suzy wear you out?"

"She tried."

"Well, give her a kiss and *no* water if she wakes up in the middle of the night."

"Uh-oh. Too late."

Adele took the phone at that point and assured her daughter that Suzy's bedding already included a rubber mat under the mattress pad. Smiling, Carly hung up a few moments later and wrapped her arms around her knees, trying to visualize her new nephew, wondering when . . . if she'd give birth to a child of her own. She wanted kids. Lots of them. And a husband, if the right one happened along.

She'd come close to marriage once, just once. Sweet heaven, the plans they'd made, the dreams they'd shared. Then Steve had pulled a short tour in Korea and the magic hadn't rekindled when he shipped home fifteen months later.

Now Parker kept trying to edge her into different plans, different dreams. Children didn't excite him as much as the idea of taking over his boss's job . . . or running for her mother's seat when the congress-woman decided to stand down. He often said what a great team he and Carly would make.

Politics and the law. The law and politics. They were all she'd ever known. All she would know if she slipped into the relationship Parker wanted.

"What's puttin' that wrinkle between your eyes, missy?"

The raspy croak brought her head around. The Judge peered at her from his bed, the bones in his face almost skeletal in the gloom. Carly pasted on a smile and pushed off the sofa.

"I was just trying to get a mental picture of your great-grandson."

Her grandfather struggled to sit up. "He's here, is he?"

"Mmmm. Dave says he looks like Allie."

"Thank the Good Lord for small blessings!"

Grinning, Carly plumped the pillows behind him. "Exactly what I said."

"Allie okay?"

"I talked to her a bit. She sounded tired, relieved, and happy."

He nodded, leaning back against the pillows with a sigh. Blue-veined lids hooded his eyes as he took in the sofa lamp angled to beam its light away from the bed and the papers scattered across the floor.

"You don't have to sit up and watch over me all night, missy."

"I didn't plan to. I was just waiting on the news from the hospital and catching up on some work."

"That Smith murder?" he murmured.

"Mmmm."

She perched on the side of his bed, aching to curl

her hand in his, as she had so many times before. She
knew better than to touch him, however. The slight-
est pressure on his swollen joints caused an agony
that whitened his lips. The mantel clock ticked a few
moments of companionable silence.

"What would you think of a judge who allowed
four men who'd previously slept with a girl to take
the stand as witnesses for the man accused of raping
her?"

"I'd say McMann lucked out in the draw, or his defense team called in some mighty big chits to get the
case assigned to that particular judge."

"I had the same thoughts myself."

"I'm surprised the prosecutors won a conviction
with that kind of bias coming down from the bench."

"They didn't. McMann changed his plea to guilty
midway through the trial. He convicted himself."

"His attorneys didn't appeal the sentence?"

"He wouldn't let them, or so he told me today at
lunch."

The pillow rustled as the Judge angled his head
back. "You havin' lunch with your witnesses these
days, missy?"

"I thought I might get a better sense of his credibility if I talked to him on neutral turf."

"Did you?"

"No."

And yes.

In a very disturbing way, she'd gotten far more
than she'd anticipated. The back of her neck tingled, as though the wind whispering through the
towering magnolia outside the window had
touched it.

"Sounds to me like you've boiled the corn down to
the starch," the Judge observed. "The key witness in

one heinous crime admits his moral turpitude and
guilt in another. You have to decide whether you believe McMann, my girl, or Smith."

"I know," Carly sighed. "I know."

The decision didn't come easy. By Sunday night,
Carly finished reviewing her notes and the transcripts. On Monday morning, she decided on one
last interview. It was a long shot, but maybe Billy
Hopewell could give her some insights into his
friend Ryan McMann.

She drove the short distance to the prison just after
ten. For once, a hazy sun beat down. The muggy
spring felt more like high summer, heavy with a humidity that curled Carly's hair at the temples.

The sunshine held a false promise, however. The
radio announced that a low pressure system was
sweeping up from the gulf. Residents of Florida's
coastal resort towns had already started bracing for
high tides and the violent tornadoes these storms all
too often spawned.

The forecast for Alabama didn't look any brighter.
Weathermen were predicting the storms would track
north within the next forty-eight to seventy-two
hours. The governor had called a news conference
for later today to announce his decision to acti-
vate selected units of the State Guard to coordinate
sand-bagging efforts. Montgomery's mayor hadn't
waited for the governor. Bagging crews were already
hard at work along River Front Park.

It looked as though the base had pressed inmates
into duty, as well. When Carly pulled into the prison
parking lot, she saw air force dump trucks mounded
with sand spitting black clouds of exhaust into the
air while crews in prison greens piled into passenger
buses.

Carly angled around the trucks to find a parking space and walked the few short yards to the entry gate. Whistles and catcalls from the buses' occupants followed her until one of the guards rapped out an order to shut up. A few minutes la-ter, she was shown into the office of the assistant warden.

A tall, striking brunette in a summer suit of dark gray, Fayrene Preston greeted Carly with a smile and a no-nonsense handshake.

"What can I do for you, Major Samuels?"

"I'm conducting the pretrial investigation into the murder of Lieutenant Colonel Elaine Dawson-Smith. I'd like to speak to one of the inmates about it. I understand I need your authorization to conduct an official inquiry."

The prison official frowned. "Agents from your Office of Special Investigations interviewed all the crews working that part of the base on the day of the murder. Do you have reason to believe one of our inmates knows more than he told the air force investigators?"

"No. I'm simply following up on a conversation I had with a prisoner on Friday morning, near the site of the murder."

"Which prisoner?"

"Mr. Hopewell."

The brunette looked up sharply. "Billy Hopewell?"

"Yes. Is there a problem?"

"I'm afraid so."

When she hesitated, Carly leaned forward. "I understand he has a speech impediment, which worsens when he's forced to talk to strangers. I'll try to keep my questions—"

"That's not the problem, Major. Billy Hopewell is dead."

"Dead!"

"He was killed Friday afternoon. His mower overturned on a steep slope and crushed him. We found his body an hour after he failed to return from his work detail."

CHAPTER EIGHT

Billy Hopewell was buried in a southside cemetery on a gray, weepy Wednesday afternoon. A wrought-iron fence separated the tree-shaded burying ground from the suburb that had grown up around it. Cars whizzed by on the busy street beyond the fence, their passing shielded by a screen of ancient crepe myrtles.

With no known relatives to claim the body or personal effects, the Federal Bureau of Prisons would have quietly and efficiently arranged to have Billy's remains cremated and his ashes properly disposed of. No one in the vast prison bureaucracy cared if a former inmate wanted to shell out the necessary bucks for alternate arrangements.

With Ryan McMann's check in hand, the funeral director he'd contacted took care of every detail, from choosing the casket and outfitting the remains to ordering a dignified funeral flower arrangement and inserting the two-line notice of interment in the *Birmingham News* and the *Montgomery Advertiser*. Not that he really expected anyone to show for the simple graveside ceremony, the funeral director informed Ryan solicitously. But the deceased had been born in Birmingham and perhaps some friends might choose to make the trip.

None did. Ryan stood alone beside the fresh, gaping wound in the earth while the hearse driver who doubled as a deacon read the twenty-third psalm.

"The Lord is my shepherd, I will not be in want. He leads me to quiet waters and bids me lie down in green pastures."

The phrasing was just modern enough to jar the solitary mourner. Ryan didn't consider himself a particularly religious man, certainly not a righteous one, but he'd grown up grounded in hard-headed Yankee principles and High Episcopalian faith. At the darkest moments he still reached back to that core. Shutting out the hearse driver, he recited silently the phrases of his youth.

The Lord is my shepherd; I shall not want.

Regret, sharp and stinging, seared him. Billy hadn't wanted much. Hadn't asked for anything except the few careless crumbs of kindness thrown his way. Ryan should have spent more time with the kid, tried harder to instill some confidence in him, listened more closely when he tried to force out words that wouldn't come.

Yea though I walk through the shadow of the valley of death, I will fear no evil.

The kid didn't have to fear his evil demons any more. He wouldn't shrink into himself when the other inmates jeered him, or look out at the world through frightened eyes, or cry at night for his momma.

Surely goodness and mercy shall follow me all the days of my life; and I shall dwell in the house of the Lord forever.

The hearse driver closed his prayer book with a snap. "Amen."

"Amen."

The soft echo snapped Ryan's head around. When

he saw the woman standing just inside the gate, his insides went tight with fury.

She couldn't leave him alone. Couldn't give Billy even these few moments of peace. He swept his gaze over the formal dress uniform, the spit-shined back heels, the small bunch of waxy red gladiolas in her hand. Deliberately, he turned his back to her.

"We'll take care of everything from here, Mr. McMann."

"Fine."

"The headstone should be in place within ninety days. We like to give the ground time to settle, you understand." The driver tucked his prayer book in his pocket and stretched his chin in a vain attempt to ease the discomfort of his tie. "You can view it come the end of July."

Ryan didn't plan to hang around Montgomery long enough to view anything come July, much less the headstone he'd ordered. With a curt nod, he turned away. His departure from the small cemetery took him right past the silent, watching woman.

Carly didn't speak to McMann as he strode by. His closed face didn't invite comments or condolences any more than the rigid set of his shoulders under his dark suit coat.

The charcoal gray suit surprised her. Not that he'd worn it, but that he wore it so well. Up to now she'd seen him only in jeans and work shirts, or jeans and no shirt at all. The McMann she'd dealt with on previous occasions carried himself with a potent mix of strength, controlled violence, and raw masculinity. This one added power and a surface patina of sophistication to that combustible combination.

His pinstriped worsted hung in executive, tailored lines that only emphasized his athletic build. His pale yellow shirt with its white collar and cuffs had somehow stayed crisp in the humid spring warmth. He'd had his hair trimmed, Carly noted. Jet black and too short to make any pretenses to styling, the severe cut suited his lean features.

His shoes crunched on the gravel path leading away from the cemetery. Carly waited until the footsteps faded before following the path to the freshly dug grave. She wasn't exactly sure why she'd left her still-unfinished report to drive down here. Partly - because of a lingering regret that she hadn't gone straight to the prison after meeting Billy in the woods and talked to him before he died. Partly because of a nagging, irrational guilt. She couldn't shake the thought that her unexpected appearance and rapid-fire questions had upset Hopewell so much that he'd lost his concentration, taken his mower down that slope at too steep an angle, and died under its crushing weight.

And partly, she acknowledged with brutal honesty, she'd driven down to this little cemetery because she'd expected to find McMann here. From the moment she'd spotted the brief notice of interment among the death notices her grandfather always wanted read to him, Carly had anticipated another confrontation with McMann, another opportunity to get beyond his brittle outer shell to the complex individual beneath.

One look at his face had shattered that plan. The Mann wasn't in any mood to talk. Not to her anyway.

Slowly, she made her way along the gravel path to the tall, lanky attendant waiting beside the grave for the cemetery workers to arrive.

"Afternoon, ma'am," he said politely, swiping a handkerchief across the back of his neck. "This humidity is almost worse than the rain."

"Almost."

"Are those for the newly deceased?" He nodded to the blood red gladiolas.

"Yes."

"If you care to place them with the other remembrances, I'll tell the diggers to put them on the grave when they finish."

The other remembrances. Aside from the modest spray resting atop the casket, the only other tribute to Billy Hopewell was a small arrangement of white carnations. Pity washed through Carly. How sad that so few people cared for the young man in life or mourned his death.

Stooping, she placed the gladiolas beside the carnations. Her gaze caught on the card almost hidden among the white blossoms.

Sleep with the angels.
J.

Carly felt her pulse quicken. In her brief, one-sided conversation with Billy Hopewell, he'd mentioned two names. Only two. Ry and Joy. Could this "J" be Joy?

What had the inmate said? Something about Ry insisting it wasn't right. As did Joy.

What wasn't right?

Who was Joy?

Without a qualm, Carly plucked the card from the arrangement and made a mental note of the name and address of the flower shop stamped in blue ink on the back; the Flower Basket, out on Eastdale Drive.

She'd give them a call when she got back to the office. Or maybe she'd just drive out and talk to the shop owner. If she flashed her ID and her letter of appointment, she shouldn't have any difficulty getting the name of the customer who'd sent the flowers. For curiosity's sake if nothing else, Carly wanted to close the last loop before finalizing her report.

The carnations occupied her thoughts as she let the creaking wrought iron gate swing shut. She followed the path to the weed-grown parking lot, only to stop short at the sight of McMann leaning against the MG's fender.

Elbows bent, suit coat shoved back, he jingled the coins in his pockets. His loosened tie hung in a lopsided loop around his neck. The top two buttons of the pale yellow shirt yawned open to show a curl of dark hair at the base of his throat. Suspicion, distrust, and something Carly couldn't quite define clouded his eyes.

"What are you doing here?"

"Paying my respects."

"Yeah? Do you pay your respects to every inmate who ends up under a mower?"

"Only those I've spoken to."

The jingling coins went silent. He regarded her intently. "You told me you only spoke to Billy once, for a few seconds."

The guilt Carly wanted to deny stung her again. "I did only speak to him for a few seconds, but . . ."

"But what?"

"Well, I . . ." This was ridiculous. She had no reason to feel as though she contributed to the young man's tragic accident. But she did. Dammit, she did.

When she didn't reply, McMann's expression went tight and hard. Pulling his hands out of his pockets, he pushed off the fender.

"What the hell did you say or do to Billy?"

Carly's jaw set. She didn't particularly appreciate being grilled like this.

"I spooked him," she admitted curtly. "I threw questions at him so fast he couldn't get out an answer."

"Yeah, he had that problem. Or didn't you notice?"

"I noticed. All right? I noticed."

"But your kept after him anyway."

The disgust in his face singed her already prickling conscience. "Yes, I kept after him."

The confession cost Carly. Big time. She didn't often mishandle people the way she had the young inmate. Pulling off the flight cap, she scraped her palm across her damp forehead.

"I shouldn't have peppered him with questions like that. Not after I realized he had ... a problem. I should've handled him more calmly, more carefully."

"If you had, he might not have run away, jumped on that mower, and sent it tumbling down a ravine? Is that what you're thinking?"

"Maybe."

"Well, well," he said with caustic incredulity. "A lawyer with a conscience. Who would have believed it?"

The jeer pushed exactly the wrong buttons. She'd taken all she intended to take from Ryan McMann. Her hand swung upward.

His arm whipped up to meet hers. A brutal grip manacled her wrist. She gaped at his white-knuckled hold for several seconds before jiggling the flight cap that dangled from her fingertips.

"One," she said icily, "I raised my hand to put on my cover, not to slap your face, although I admit the idea holds considerable appeal at the moment. Two, I've told you before I don't like being pawed. And three . . ." Her voice dropped another dozen degrees. "You're hurting me."

His glance bulleted from her face to the arm he'd

captured. Disgust rolled across his features once again, but this time it was directed inward. His grip loosened.

If his gaze hadn't shifted back to hers at that moment, Carly would have snatched her arm away. The unremitting emptiness in his eyes held her frozen.

"I'm sorry."

He dragged the words from a place so dark and private that her own anger fizzled.

"I don't . . . I've never . . ." He drew in a harsh breath, began again. "Despite my record and all evidence to the contrary, I've never intentionally hurt a woman."

She believed him. For an insane moment, she believed him. Her heart thudding, she kept silent as he unwrapped his fingers and dropped a light kiss on the inside of her wrist.

"I'm sorry," he said again.

She nodded, letting him make what he wanted of the small movement. Her heart was still hammering when he climbed into the late model Bronco parked next to her MG and drove off.

She felt the imprint of McMann's mouth on her skin all during the drive around the south loop.

The late afternoon rush hour had already started. Every stoplight seemed to be working against her. Traffic jerked along at a stop-and-go crawl until well past Montgomery Mall, and moved sluggishly on the eastern bypass.

Carly barely noticed the delays. Hands locked on the steering wheel, she played and replayed those moments with McMann in her mind. Why had she deluded herself into thinking she could get past his impentrable barriers? Why had she let him get to her like that? And why in God's name did her flesh still burn where he'd kissed it?

A sick feeling curled in her stomach. This was the second time he'd touched her. The second time she'd allowed him to. She could have jerked her arm free. Withered him on the spot with a few well-chosen words. Walked away.

Instead, she'd stood rooted to the ground like one of his adoring, adolescent fans while he bent his head and pressed his lips against her wrist.

She couldn't understand her reactions. She'd never experienced this absurd combination of dislike and fascination for any man, let alone a key witness in an investigation. She had to shake this preoccupation with McMann, had to put this damned Article 32 behind her.

Grimly determined, she turned off the eastern bypass onto the old Atlanta highway. A three minute drive and one wrong turn brought her to the small strip mall that housed the Flower Basket Boutique and Gift Shop.

The shop owner was a small, cheerful woman with berry bright eyes and fluttery hands. She bobbed her head several times when Carly asked about the delivery to the southside cemetery.

"The white carnations? Oh, yes, such an odd little offering, don't you think? I recommended lilies or white roses . . . for the same price . . . but she wanted only the carnations."

"She? You mean Joy?"

"I think that was her name." The proprietress riffled through a cardbox filled with handwritten orders. "Yes, yes, that's it. Joy Matusi . . . Matusin . . ."

She stumbled, providing the perfect opportunity for Carly to lean across the counter and help her with the unusual name.

"Ma-tu-sin-ak," she enunciated. "Joy Matusinak."

She got the address and two digits of the phone number before the shopkeeper refiled the card.

"Is Mrs. Matusinak a friend of yours, dear?"

"No, in fact we've never met. Billy ... the deceased ... mentioned her."

"I see." She folded her plump hands. "Well, what can I do for you?"

A very satisfied customer left the Flower Basket a few moments later carrying a tissue-wrapped cluster of fresh-cut irises.

Fifteen minutes after that, a not-quite-as-satisfied Carly climbed back into her MG after striking out at the two-story brick and stucco Matusinak residence. More curious than ever about the connection between Billy Hopewell and the woman who lived in a subdivision that shouted wealth and privilege, Carly decided to try to reach Joy Matusinak by phone later that evening.

Dusk had fallen by the time she drove down the narrow alley to the converted carriage house she'd purchased in a moment of sheer insanity. Set at the rear of what was once one of Montgomery's most magnificent estates, the two-story, wisteria draped cottage echoed the French revival style of the main house. With its pumpkin-colored stucco, charcoal gray plank shutters, and arched dormer, it more than made up in charm what it lacked in modern plumbing or wiring.

Between her job, her mother's campaign, and the Judge's deteriorating condition, Carly hadn't given the cottage the time or attention it demanded. Bit by bit, however, the necessary renovations were getting done. A sweating electrician had spent three weeks re-wiring the place to bring it into compliance with current fire and safety codes. Carpenters had torn out acres of wood flooring and paneling eaten by rot. The kitchen still lacked cabinets and generally looked about as inviting as a war zone, but the newly installed central air-conditioning purred like a Siamese kitten.

Its cool air slapped at Carly's lungs as she let herself in through the attached garage. Tossing the irises into the chipped enamel sink the workmen hadn't gotten around to removing yet, she pushed through the swinging doors and put the kitchen chaos behind her. In the rest of the house, at least, she could justify her insanity. Here, she found tranquillity.

Heart-pine beams polished to a golden hue by time and loving hands timbered the hallway. The same mellow pine framed the square arch leading into the high-ceilinged living area, created by knocking down two walls. French doors flooded the spacious area with natural light and exposed the potted geraniums and the heavy wisteria shading the walled patio.

Kicking off her shoes, Carly curled her toes against the smooth wood. A quick click of a remote turned on the high-tech sound system that took up one whole wall. The newscaster on her favorite FM station cut through the quiet of the dusk.

". . . forecasting more thunderstorms for tomorrow and Friday, with the possibility of flash flooding throughout the weekend."

Oh, no!

"The director of emergency services has issued a statewide alert. In addition, the governor has ordered evacuation of the farms below the Jones Bluff Reservoir to allow worried officials to open the flood gates."

Frowning, Carly headed for the stairs. Her grandfather's farm lay above the spill from the reservoir, but the river cut through the south pasture. She'd better get out there tomorrow to make sure the young couple who worked the place had moved the horses . . . and that blasted mule. It certainly wouldn't break Carly's heart if the damned thing floated downriver and out into the Gulf, but she knew better than to say so around the Judge.

Her uniform jacket came off before she hit the narrow, curving stairs; her blouse halfway up. She dropped both items on her bed. Her skirt followed a moment later. She'd just peeled off her panty hose when the doorbell chimed. A quick peek out the front window showed the gleam of a black Jag.

Parker.

The little ripple of irritation that hit her took her by surprise. She hadn't seen Parker since the cocktail party at her mother's house last week. Long enough to have forgotten her annoyance over his call to the warden. Certainly long enough to be ready for an hour or two of agreeable companionship . . . or Parker's skilled brand of lovemaking. Yet she threw on a pair of cutoffs and an old University of Alabama T-shirt and went downstairs with something less than enthusiasm.

When she opened the door, the tanned, smiling assistant DA held up a six pack of dew-streaked Corona and a brown paper sack reeking with the luscious aroma of fresh steamed shrimp.

"Hello, beautiful. Have you eaten yet?"

"Hello yourself, and no, I haven't."

"Care to feast on warm Gulf shrimp and cold beer?"

"Mmmm, sounds delicious."

"Not as delicious as you look."

With a smile and a sureness that came with familiarity, he bent to take her lips.

It was her second kiss of the day. Warm. Sexy. Inviting. Even as her senses registered the contact, a shocked Carly realized that she was comparing Parker's touch to McMann's, searching for the same burning heat, the same electricity.

No! No way she was going there! Deliberately, she slammed the door on the thought. Still, she couldn't bring herself to lean into Parker's kiss, to wrap her arms around his waist and welcome him with the spontaneous warmth he obviously expected.

His disappointment showed when he lifted his head, but he didn't comment on her restraint. Making himself at home, he strolled inside.

"The shrimp are getting more aromatic by the moment. Why don't we eat outside?"

"As long as you don't mind wisteria hanging down around your ears."

It was a standing joke between them. At five-three, Carly considered the tiny, walled-in patio just off the living room a perfect blend of beauty and function. At six-one, Parker had to stoop to avoid banging his head on white-painted arbor crossbeams and the twisted wisteria vines they supported.

"The vines and I are becoming best friends," he returned with a grin. "You get the cocktail sauce and some lemon. I'll start peeling."

By the time Carly carried out a tray loaded with plates, napkins, cocktail sauce, and thick wedges of lemon, her erstwhile guest had created a respectable pile of translucent pink skins on an outspread newspaper. A mound of succulent peeled shrimp was taking shape on the flattened brown paper bag.

"I tried to call you this afternoon," Parker mentioned as she elbowed the French door shut behind her. "The clerk said you'd gone to a funeral. Anyone I know?"

"I doubt it." She slid the tray onto the table and reached for the beer he'd opened for her. "Just some-one I met briefly during—"

"What in the hell!"

Startled, Carly jerked her head around to find Parker staring at her wrist. His brows snapped to-gether, his expression at once concerned and fiercely protective.

"Where did you get those bruises?"

CHAPTER NINE

Carly hadn't even noticed the purple smudges ringing her wrist. Absurdly, she found herself fighting the irrational impulse to cover the finger marks with her other hand. It was too late to hide them . . . not that she had any reason to. Too late, as well, to avoid the explanation Parker waited for.

For a moment she was tempted to lie, to say she tripped and one of the mourners caught her wrist to break her fall. That shocked her even more than the realization that she'd measured Parker's kiss against McMann's. Carly admitted to a lot of faults. Lying wasn't one of them.

"I got the marks at the funeral I attended this afternoon."

"How, for God's sake?"

She lift a shoulder in a deliberate shrug. "Accidental contact with one of the mourners," was her technically accurate lawyer's response.

"Accidental?"

Dusting the shrimp peels off his hands, Parker reached out and grasped her arm gently above the wrist, turning it to the light to get a closer look at the marks.

"I see a lot of battered women in my line of work," he said slowly. "These don't look accidental to me. Who did this to you?"

"No one you know." She slid her arm out of his grasp. "Let's drop it, okay?"

"No, it's not okay. Who made these marks? What's going on, Carly?"

Irritation washed through her again, stronger this time and more piercing. This was why she kept resisting Parker's attempts to wring a commitment from her. She'd been her own woman for too long now to appreciate this kind of well-intentioned but unsolicited involvement in matters she preferred to handle herself.

"I ran into Ryan McMann at the funeral," she began coolly. "We—"

"McMann did that?"

Disbelief flashed over his fine-boned features. His chair shoved back, metal legs scraping against brick with an angry cry.

"That son of a bitch! I'll destroy him."

"No, you won't!"

"No ex-con is going to lay hands on you and live to—"

"It was an accident!" she insisted sharply. "A misunderstanding."

"What the hell kind of misunderstanding gives him the right to touch you?"

"He thought I was going to slap him and grabbed my wrist to stop me."

If anything, her explanation fanned the flames of his anger. Red surged under the layer of carefully cultivated tan. "What did the bastard do that deserved a slap in the face?"

"Oh, for . . ." Gritting her teeth, Carly fought for patience. Dammit, she didn't need this. Didn't want this.

"He made one of the usual cracks about lawyers. This one got to me, and I raised my hand. *I* intended to put on my flight cap and march away. *McMann* thought I intended to smack him a good one."

Her listener raked his hand through his blond waves. "I'm not getting any of this. Why was McMann there? Whose funeral was it, anyway?"

"One of the inmates from the prison."

It took him only a moment to process that. Professional interest leaped into his eyes, edging aside both anger and concern over the bruises.

"I take it this inmate is somehow connected to the Dawson-Smith murder and your investigation."

She busied herself by emptying the tray she'd carried out to the patio, hoping Parker would take the hint from her refusal to discuss the matter further. The DA in him just wouldn't let it go.

"Talk to me, Carly. Tell me what's going on."

The plate of lemon wedges hit the table with a thump.

"Why? So you can make another phone call?"

His head reared back, brushing against the low-hanging wisteria. In an automatic reflex, his hand came up to smooth his hair.

"I've already apologized for that," he said stiffly.

She bit back a sigh. "Yes, you have. Now, it's my turn. That was uncalled for. I'm sorry, Parker ... sorry I snapped at you, and sorry I'm not particularly in the mood for company tonight."

As irritated now as she was, he took a swig of his beer. The bottle hit the table top with just enough force to set her teeth on edge.

"Fine." He ducked under the vines. "Call me when you are in the mood."

Carly let him find his own way out, wincing when the front door closed with a thud. At least he'd left the shrimp, she thought with a spurt of selfish satisfaction. Plopping into one of the high-backed patio chairs, she grabbed a lemon wedge and spurted juice over the pile Parker had peeled.

When the door chimes rang some minutes later, she was tempted to ignore them. An icy beer and a dozen warm shrimp had worked their magic. She felt relaxed and mellow for the first time today . . . but not quite mellow enough for the requisite kiss-and-make-up scene.

The chimes poured out their golden notes again. Sighing, Carly pushed out of the chair.

The realization that she'd have to end things with Parker followed her from the patio through the living area. She liked him, a lot, but she didn't love him. A small, grudging corner of her appreciated his concern, yet the stubbornly independent streak that formed her core resented his growing possessiveness. He couldn't seem to understand that she neither needed nor wanted anyone to fight her battles for her.

Well, better to break it off now, before either of them got in too deep. Steeling herself for the discussion to come, she tried for a smile and opened the door.

"If you've come back for the shrimp, you're almost too late. I . . ."

Her words stuck in her throat. Stunned, she stared at the dark-haired figure on the stoop.

Ryan turned slowly, his senses alive with the riot of colors and scents crowding in on him. This was the South he'd experienced only peripherally during his enforced stay in Montgomery, a South of gracious architecture, generous textures. Even in the rapidly descending darkness, his engineer's mind noted with precise detail the dark green ivy shimmering on terra-cotta stucco, the ancient, twisted vines climbing over the attached garage, trailing wisteria and perfume and some little pink flower he didn't recognize. Plank shutters in a gray washed pine stood ready to be closed against the darkness or the hurricanes that roared up from the Gulf. The shutters reminded him of the French Quarter in New Orleans, with its narrow alleys and private courtyards and seductive night sounds.

The woman captured by the light spilling through the open door reminded him of nothing he'd ever seen before, however. In uniform, she could stop any man in his tracks. Out of it, she hooked him right around the throat.

He hadn't expected that loose tangle of hair. Or those thigh-skimming cutoffs. Hell, he hadn't expected anything except maybe a door slammed in his face.

That might still happen. She didn't look particularly thrilled to find him on her doorstep. He wasn't particularly thrilled to find himself there, either. Cursing the gut-deep shame that had driven him out of his rented apartment and onto the streets, he offered a gruff explanation.

"I got your address from the phone directory. I just came by to apologize . . . again."

"This seems to be the night for it," she muttered, still rattled by his unexpected appearance but recovering fast. "Just out of curiosity, what exactly are you apologizing for? The crack about lawyers, the stranglehold you laid on me, or the kiss you dropped on my wrist?"

Get it out of the way, Ryan told himself grimly. Tell her you're sorry, climb back in your car, and find the nearest bar. What he needed was a few stiff shots to dull the loneliness, the nagging regret over Billy. But what he wanted was a few moments more with Carly Samuels.

"Just out of curiosity," he countered, "do you always think in threes?"

"Excuse me?"

She didn't see it. Didn't have a clue that she stiffened up, flashed fire from those slanted, thick-lashed eyes, and counted off each of his infractions with the precise articulation of a metronome. The fact that she seemed completely unaware of the annoying little habit made her human. Far too human. He'd better remember who she was. What she was. And why he was here.

"One," Ryan enunciated with a small, mocking smile, "I can't say I'm sorry for expressing my opinion of members of the bar. Two, I'll cut off my hand before I lay another hold on you, hurtful or otherwise. And three . . ."

"Yes?"

Three, he wanted to kiss her again. So badly he hurt with it.

"Three, you'd better get back to those shrimp you mentioned."

He was halfway to his Bronco when her voice floated to him on the darkness.

"I've stuffed down all I can eat. Would you like to finish them off?"

Carly heard herself issue the invitation, saw McMann hesitate, and royally kicked herself. Of all the impulsive, idiotic, irresponsible . . .

"Do they come with strings attached?"

"Just shells," she drawled.

He couldn't just accept or decline. Not McMann. He had to get in a little dig first.

"If you're asking whether I'm going to interrogate

you while you eat," she added coolly, "the answer
is no."

"And afterward?"

"Look, McMann, you're a big, tough jock. You can
handle whatever comes afterward. Do you want the
shrimp or don't you?"

Carly saw the refusal in his face and breathed a relieved sigh, only to have it snag halfway out.

"I used to be a big, tough jock," he threw back at
her. "Now I'm a big, tough ex-con. You sure you can
trust me inside your home?"

She couldn't back out now, not with that half taunt,
half challenge hanging on the air between them.

"I'm sure. Come in."

He filled the quiet spaces in the carriage house in a
way Parker never had. Maybe it was his size. Or his
lithe, graceful moves. Or the appreciation in his eyes
as he took in the smooth pine flooring, the white-
washed walls, the mantel cluttered with framed
photographs.

Carly waited while he acclimated himself to the
place, and she acclimated to his disturbing presence
in her island of tranquillity. He wore the same dark
slacks and pale yellow dress shirt he'd worn at the
cemetery, minus the coat and tie. The shirt gaped
open at the neck. Its rolled-up sleeves gave him a
casual, but no less elegant, air. With his black hair,
intent eyes, and tanned skin, some fanciful souls
might have described him as a modern-day Lucifer
come to call.

Carly didn't consider herself particularly fanciful,
but the simile stayed with her as she joined him in
the living area.

"Who's this?"

She moved closer to get a look at the silver framed
photo he indicated. "My grandfather."

"The Judge?"

She nodded, surprised that he remembered.

"That's Clarissa he's riding," she added dryly, "the sorriest excuse for a mule God ever put on this earth. She took more bites out of me when I was a kid than I want to remember."

He shot her a sideways glance. "I'll bet you got in a few licks, too."

"A few. We called it a draw about the time I got big enough to swing a baseball bat."

He tilted another photo toward the light, this one of Carly and her mother on the east steps of the Capitol. The Mall stretched behind them, with the Washington Monument gleaming white and straight in the distance. Congresswoman Samuels laughed into the camera, still high from the thrill of having taken her seat for a second term, her arm looped around a much younger, much skinnier Carly.

"You take after her around the eyes and chin."

"Thank you."

McMann probably hadn't intended the casual observation as a compliment, but Carly took it as one. Both Adele Samuels and her daughter possessed what the portrait painter who'd later captured them together in oils had described as character-defining chins. Adele masked her strong features and equally strong will with a natural charm and elegance. Carly didn't even try to disguise hers.

"And this?" His blue gaze slid to hers, measuring, assessing. "Friend, or lover?"

"My brother . . . not, I might point out, that it's any of your business."

He replaced the photo. "The Chinese have a saying, something about inviting a stranger into your soul when you invite him into your house."

"I'll remember that the next time my doorbell

chimes." She gestured to the French doors standing open to the night. "I left the remains of the feast on the patio."

All too conscious of his step behind hers, Carly led the way through the doors and into the puddle of light thrown by the carriage lamp mounted on a tall black-painted pole. Thankfully, the soggy spring hadn't yet produced the bumper crop of mosquitoes the old hands were predicting. Just enough breeze slipped over the walls to make the night air cool and comfortable.

McMann picked up immediately on the empty plate and half-downed beer across from Carly's. "Am I interrupting something?"

"No."

The clipped response earned her a quick look, but he took the hint with better grace than Parker had. Either that, or he didn't really ascribe to the Chinese saying and consider himself invited into her soul. In any case, he didn't pry, merely reached for her chair to pull it out for her at the same time she did.

"Jesus! Did I put those marks on you?"

She wasn't doing this scene. Not again. Calmly, Carly slid into the bentwood chair.

"Yes, you did. It was an accident, you've apologized, and I didn't even notice the bruises until . . . until a little while ago. So sit down and help yourself to a beer while I peel the rest of the shrimp."

He stood wire tight and unmoving for so long she wasn't sure what to expect next. Finally, he conquered whatever inner demons had brought him here to apologize once again. The chair next to hers scraped back.

"I'll peel them."

With a tug on the brown paper, he pulled the last of the shellfish to his side of the table. Fascinated, Carly watched his strong, nimble fingers pull off the tails, shuck the skin, and pop the meat free in one smooth movement. He peeled a dozen or more in the time it had taken her to do half that number.

"Where did you learn to do that?"

He took his time answering, as if reluctant to share anything of himself. "One of my buddies from high school talked me into hitchhiking down to Boston one summer. We bummed around until our money ran out, then got jobs with a seafood wholesaler."

"You went out on the fishing boats?"

"No such luck. We worked in the warehouse, cleaning the catch."

"Sounds like hard work."

"Hard, and smelly." He relaxed a bit, his lips curving with the memory. "Neither one of us got a date the entire summer. We couldn't scrub off the stink."

That was probably the last time McMann failed to score, Carly thought, mesmerized by that almost-smile. If the newspaper stories held even a grain of truth, he'd had to fight off women with his hockey stick. And if she didn't tread carefully here, very carefully, she'd fall under the spell of that dark voice, those strong, sure hands herself.

Maybe she already had.

The queasy feeling that had curled in her stomach this morning struck again. This time, she didn't try to deny the source. This time, she admitted the inescapable truth. McMann fascinated her . . . professionally, personally, in other ways she had yet to assess.

She didn't trust him. Still wasn't completely convinced he'd seen Michael Smith's vehicle on River Road. She needed to get into his head, wanted to know the person behind that shuttered face, and the best way to accomplish that was to keep him talking.

"Funny," she mused. "I don't associate shrimp with Boston. Lobster and clams, but not shrimp."

He hooked a brow. "Ever been up East?"

"If you mean to Boston, no. I pulled a tour of duty in D.C. and vacationed with my mother in the Hamptons for a couple of weeks."

"The Hamptons don't qualify. Neither does D.C. People talk funny down there."

"And they don't in Boston?"

"Not to a New Englander."

"Tell me about that summer in Boston."

His busy hands stilled. The suspicion and wariness that never quite left his eyes rekindled into hard pinpoints of light.

"Why, Carly? Why did you invite me in? What do you want from me?"

"I don't want anything from you except what you know about Elaine Dawson-Smith's murder."

"I've told you what I know."

Maybe, she thought. Maybe not.

"So tell me about Boston."

Slowly, reluctantly, Ryan found himself opening doors that he'd kept shut for too long. Between bites of shrimp washed down with beer, he told her about those months spent up to his armpits in scrod and halibut and shrimp. About Burlington. About the rivers of red and gold that poured down the mountains behind his home in fall and the ice that coated Lake Champlain in winter and the first tapping of syrup from the maples. About everything but hockey, and prison, and the woman whose body was found sprawled under a pine.

She listened. With a cool, contained reserve at first. Then she, like Ryan, seemed to pass through some invisible gate. The barriers came down, at least the superficial ones. She smiled, and once she even laughed, the sound a ripple of silvery notes on the night. And she, like Ryan, seemed shocked when the mantel clock inside the house bonged on and on.

He swiped a look at his watch, saw it was ten o'clock. Abruptly, he shoved back his chair. "Looks like I owe you another apology. I didn't mean to go on like that."

She rose as well, waving a dismissive hand when he started to clean up the litter on the table.

"I'll get that."

He took that to mean she wanted him gone. Now that he was on his feet, he wanted to go. He was shaken by the hunger for human contact that had kept him in that patio chair for almost two hours. Shaken, too, by the need that clawed at his gut when Carly walked him to the front door.

He didn't trust her, couldn't quite figure what kind of a game she was playing with him, but he wanted her. Jesus, he wanted her. Almost as much as he was coming to hate her.

What little pride Ryan had left chafed more each moment he spent in her company. She made him ache for things he used to have. No, she made him want things he'd never had, even with his wife. Especially with his wife.

He left with a curt good night and a silent, savage promise to keep his hands and his mind off Major Carly Samuels in the future.

A subdued, thoughtful Carly watched the Bronco's taillights disappear around the end of the drive.

Two hours. She'd spent two hours in McMann's company, and still couldn't decide whether he was the slickest con man she'd come across in a long time, or the smartest. He'd fed her curiosity instead of satisfying it, answered her questions without giving her a shred of real information or insight.

Absently, she folded her hand over her wrist and made her way back inside. Halfway to the patio, the briefcase she'd left on her desk caught her attention. Another quick look at the mantel clock had her changing directions. It was late, but not too late for the phone call she still wanted to make. Fishing the Montgomery phone directory out of the center drawer of the graceful turn-of-the-century marquetry table she used as a desk, she skimmed the listings.

As anticipated, she found only one listing for Matusinak. Dr. and Mrs. Matusinak, 524 County Downs Road. The listing below the residence gave a business number and a twenty-four hour answering service.

A teenager answered Carly's call, shouting over the blare of the TV when she asked for Mrs. Joy Matusinak.

"Mommmm! It's for you."

He dropped the receiver with a careless clatter. The TV shot up a few more decibels. To a chorus of canned laughter, a nasal-sounding character ordered someone to scrape the eggs off the ceiling. Carly heard an annoyed exclamation and an exasperated request to turn that thing down, both of which were ignored by the teen.

"Hello?"

"Mrs. Matusinak?"

"Yes?"

"My name is Carly Samuels. Major Carly Samuels."

"Yes? Brian! Turn down the TV!"

The background chatter didn't lessen. If anything, it seemed to pick up.

"I'm a legal officer at Maxwell," she continued, pitching her voice to be heard over the din. "I've been appointed to conduct an investigation into a death that occurred on base."

She thought she heard a small gasp. With the characters on TV shrieking, she couldn't be sure.

"I'd like to talk to you at your convenience."

"Me? Why do you want to talk to me?"

"You sent some flowers to the funeral of Billy Hopewell. I'm trying to determine—"

"You've got the wrong number. I don't know any Billy Hopewell."

The phone slammed down, cutting off another chorus of raucous laughter.

CHAPTER TEN

Carly lay awake well into the night, chewing over the odd phone call, the unanswered questions, the loose strands she couldn't quite tie up. As if her lack of progress on the Article 32 weren't enough to keep her tossing, McMann's odd visit wove in and out of her thoughts with maddening frequency.

Consequently, she greeted the alarm that buzzed in her ear the next morning with a growl and a slap on the snooze button. She sank back into the pillows, face down, but the clock radio had done its damage. Her mind picked up where it had left off well after midnight. Grumbling, she threw back the sheets. As long as she was awake this early, she might as well try to catch a few worms.

Weak, slanting sunbeams were just breaking through the low-hanging clouds when she turned into the landscaped subdivision she'd driven out to yesterday afternoon. Luck was with her this morning. She'd no sooner parked the MG at the curb of the Matusinak residence than the garage door rumbled up and a fire-engine red Mercedes convertible with an elegantly coifed blonde in tennis whites at the wheel backed out.

The woman's reaction when she swung the two-seater around and spotted Carly in uniform left no doubt as to her identity. She stomped on the brake, squealing the Mercedes to a halt on the pebbled drive. Her eyes went huge above the smudges of dark purple beneath them. In the hazy sunlight, she looked fragile and tired.

And terrified, Carly saw with a sudden leap of her pulse. She tried to disguise it behind the polite mask she now pulled on with obvious effort, but her red-tipped nails dug into the steering wheel and her skin drained of all color, until it showed almost as white as the sweater knotted loosely around her shoulders.

"I'm Major Samuels." Carly started up the curving drive. "I called you last night. I'd like to speak to you, please. Just for a few moments."

"I told you, I don't know this . . . this person you mentioned."

The blond shoved the gear shift from reverse into forward, her motion jerky, her grip on the wheel deathlike. Diamonds flashed a rainbow of color from her left hand.

"His name was Billy Hopewell."

"I don't know him!" The cry rang with more desperation than denial. "I've never heard of him!"

The electric, searing certainty that she'd stumbled onto something kept Carly walking up the center of the drive. The woman would have to run over her to get away without answering a few questions.

For a few startling seconds, Joy Matusinak seemed to be considering just that possibility. The engine pitched again. The car rolled forward. Carly didn't pause. Her heels loud on the paving stones that threaded the pebbled drive, she walked forward.

At the last moment, the Mercedes shuddered to a stop, its fender brushing Carly's skirt hem. Coldly, she lifted her gaze from the gleaming chrome and lasered into the woman at the wheel.

"I'm here on official business, Mrs. Matusinak. If it isn't convenient for you to speak to me now, I'll come back later with a copy of my letter of appointment and a stenographer to record your statement."

She was stretching her authority about as far as it would go. As an Article 32 investigating officer, she couldn't compel a civilian to provide a statement or a deposition. The woman in the red convertible didn't know that, however.

"My . . . my statement?"

"About your relationship to Billy Hopewell."

For long moments, Carly thought her bluff had failed. Joy Matusinak stared at her through the windshield. Her teeth bit down on her lower lip so hard the skin turned white around the skillfully applied gloss.

Then suddenly, startlingly, she fell apart. Like a piece of expensive sculpture dropped at just the wrong angle, the woman simply shattered. A sob tore out of her throat. She dropped her forehead onto the backs of her hands. Her shoulders shook under the tennis sweater.

"I only did it once!"

The wrenching wail resonated with anguish, fear, a guilt that went soul deep.

"Mrs. Matusinak . . ."

She lifted her head, her eyes wild. "I went once! Only once! Elaine tried to get me to go again, but I wouldn't. Oh, God, I need my pills."

Carly's system shot pure adrenaline. So there was a connection between the inmate and the murdered officer! Her pulse pounding, she fought to keep her excitement from showing as Joy Matusinak tore her hands from the wheel and fumbled frantically in the

Coco Chanel purse on the seat beside her. Sunglasses, lipstick, a wallet bounced onto the leather. A brown plastic container followed. She clawed at the lid, moaning piteously when her shaking hands scattered the white pills into her lap.

Alarm raced through Carly, hard on the heels of her pulsing excitement. For all she knew, the woman had a heart condition and needed to pop a nitro. She scooped up the container to check the prescription at the same moment the older woman pushed a pill into her mouth.

Tranquilizers, Carly saw with relief. Industrial strength, according to the label. She handed the plastic bottle back to the driver.

Diamonds flashed again as Joy Matusinak's trembling hand closed around the bottle. Tears runneled down her cheeks, leaving a trail of black mascara. She looked so haunted, so hunted, that Carly's heart twisted. Even after all these years at the bar, the human pathos behind every desperate act still affected her.

"Wouldn't you feel more comfortable talking inside?" she suggested.

The other woman stared at her, unseeing. The agonizing tears continued to roll down her cheeks.

"Mrs. Matusinak. Joy. Do you want me to call someone? Your husband? Your doctor?"

Her vacant stare clicked into focus. In the depths of her tear-drenched eyes shone a scathing resentment.

"My husband *is* my doctor. He's the last person I'd want you to call."

"Why don't we talk about it inside?"

The entryway of the house matched its impressive exterior. Plantation shutters angled against the morning filtered the hazy sunlight. Terrazzo tile floors echoed their footsteps emptily.

Joy led the way to a formal living room done in grays . . . gray walls accented with glistening white woodwork, plush gray carpeting, and matching gray love seats filled with chintz throw pillows. Carly took one of the love seats, separated by a glass coffee table from the woman who sank into the other.

The tranquilizer hadn't kicked in yet. Joy Matusinak still shook like a leaf. Carly could only watch and wait while she wrapped both hands around her waist and rocked back and forth. Seconds slipped by before she began to pour out the same disjointed phrases.

"I only went once. Just once."

"Went where?"

"To the club. Elaine talked me into it. She said . . . She said . . ."

"What, Mrs. Matusinak? What did she say?"

"She said he was beautiful." A dry, wrenching sound that might have been a sob or a laugh tore out of her throat. "Big and beautiful and stupid, just the way men were meant to be."

"She was referring to Billy Hopewell?"

At Joy's nod, the less than favorable impressions Carly had gathered of Elaine Dawson-Smith segued into acute dislike.

"I wouldn't go at first," Joy whispered. "Not for a long time. Then Paul flew up to Atlanta. Another medical convention, he said, but I knew he went to see that little bitch he's been fucking for almost a year. And Brian . . ." She rocked forward, back, her movements small and quick and hurtful to watch. "His teacher called me in for another conference."

"Mrs. Matusinak . . ."

"Brian's failing three of his classes. It's my fault. I

don't make him study enough. His teacher said so. Paul says so. I try, God knows I try." She pleaded for understanding. "I can't get him to turn down the TV without a major confrontation, much less turn it off to open a book."

Making vague, sympathetic noises, Carly steered her back on track. "Your husband was out of town, you were feeling desperate, and you went with Elaine Dawson-Smith to meet Billy Hopewell."

"I didn't go with her. She had class that afternoon. She told me where and when and how much . . . how much to pay."

Carly sat back, her stomach clenching as the pieces dropped into place. Two women, one a bright, brittle lieutenant colonel with a well established sexual appetite and a contempt for the man who satisfied it. The other a bitter homemaker, resenting the husband who kept his wife in diamonds and his mistress in Atlanta. Between them, they shared a golden-haired Adonis.

"How much did you pay to have sex with Billy Hopewell?"

"One hundred dollars."

The sobbing admission sent Carly's mind off at warp speed. Did Michael Smith know his wife had paid to play sex games with an inmate? Did Smith follow her, shoot her in a rage of jealousy and disgust? Had Billy Hopewell witnessed the killing? Or . . .

The inmate could have snatched the gun from Elaine Dawson-Smith's purse and shot her through the heart. Then returned back to the scene of the crime, as so many perps loved to do, the afternoon Carly had stumbled into him.

The possibilities, the unanswered questions, stormed through her with hurricane force. If Michael

Smith didn't kill his wife, what was he doing on
River Road at the time of the murder? *Was* he on
River Road at the time of the murder? Like a rat running in circles, it came back to that. Smith's word
against McMann's. With Billy's death, there were no
other players in the drama.

Or were there? Surely some of the other inmates
had known about Billy's meetings with Elaine,
maybe even participated in the games themselves.
Air force investigators had questioned the men
working in the area on the day of the murder, but
maybe they hadn't asked the right questions. She'd
go out to the prison, talk to the men on work detail
that day . . .

A small, pathetic sigh snapped her attention back
to Joy Matusinak.

"I paid him, but I didn't have sex with him."

The air seemed to go out of Joy's lungs. She folded
in on herself, shoulders hunching, head limp on her
neck.

"I wanted to. God knows, I wanted to. I took off
my blouse, my skirt, let him touch me. *Made* him
touch me," she amended dully.

The pill was taking off her edge. She still rocked,
still shook, but more slowly, less desperately.

"He was so beautiful. Just like Elaine said. So big.
His skin felt like silk against mine. And his hair, I've
never seen hair like that on a man. I've never seen a
man cry, either."

Another sigh slipped out, achingly small in the
quiet of the house.

"I held him against my breasts. Like I used to hold
Brian when he was a baby. I rocked him, and whispered to him, and took his fears into me. For a moment, I felt needed again. Almost . . . almost loved."

"That's why you sent the white carnations?"

"Yes. I saw the death notice in the paper." Her gaze lifted. Eyes red from tears and torment tried to focus on Carly. "I felt sorry for him. He was so lost, so confused. He knew his momma would say that what he was doing was bad. I . . . I agreed."

So had McMann!

Carly searched her memory, trying to recall the words Billy Hopewell had stammered to her.

Joy said it wasn't right.

Ry said so, too.

Damn him! McMann knew about Elaine Dawson-Smith, knew about Joy Matusinak. The possibility that he'd even played their games himself thinned Carly's mouth to a tight, hard line.

"Elaine laughed when I told her what happened. She said there were others. If Billy didn't punch the right buttons for me, there were others who would."

Right. Like Ryan McMann, Mr. God's Gift to Womankind. Mr. Big-time Hockey Hunk, with the bedroom blue eyes, world-class buns, and a conviction for statutory rape. Suddenly, his twice-a-week return visits to the prison took on added dimensions. Carly's stomach clenched.

"Did Elaine give you names or descriptions of any of the others?"

"After Billy, I wasn't interested."

"What about before Billy? Did she mention anyone else?"

"I don't . . . I can't remember anyone specific."

Absolute certainty and searing doubt battled like Titans in Carly's chest. Forcing herself to put aside the question of McMann's possible involvement, she searched for other answers.

"Your name wasn't listed among Elaine's close friends and associates. How did you know her?"

"We have . . ." With a hitch in her voice, Joy corrected herself. "We *had* our hair done at the same salon in Eastdale Mall. We started talking one day. About tennis, the school she's attending, things to do around Montgomery. We had drinks a few times, once with our husbands, usually without."

She smoothed the pleats in her short white skirt, first one, then another, until they lay flat against her trim, tanned thighs.

"Elaine saw right away how miserable I was. I told her about Paul, and she needled me about the way he was treating me every time we met. Said I was stupid for letting him have all the fun."

"Can you confirm that Colonel Dawson-Smith had sex with Billy Hopewell?"

"She said she did. She described his . . ." Her hand lifted, dropped. "She said he was hung like a Clydesdale."

Elaine ought to know, Carly thought with a cynical twist to her lips. According to her husband, her horse was the only creature she really loved.

"Did her husband know about her trysts in the woods?"

"I don't think so. I don't know."

"Did she tell you how she got involved with Billy?"

"I don't remember." Joy scraped the heel of her hand across her forehead. "One of the members of the club probably told her about him, I suppose."

"Club? The riding club?"

"No." A thin, painful smile pulled at Joy's lips. "The Afternoon Club. That's what the girls called it. The Afternoon Club."

"I need to see Colonel Dominguez."

The base JAG's secretary smiled a refusal. "I'm

sorry, Major Samuels. He's in conference, reviewing a case file that has to go up to the Air University commander by noon. He doesn't want to be disturbed."

"Disturb him."

Her brow arching, the secretary reached for the phone. She relayed Carly's presence to her boss, then passed on a query.

"Is this in reference to your investigation?"

Impatience bit at Carly. What else would she want to see the man about? "Yes."

Dominguez came out a moment later, radiating equal parts pleasantry and annoyance at being rousted from his inner sanctum. He waved Carly to his deputy's office and shut the door behind them both.

"Have you completed the Article 32?" he asked, hiking a hip on the corner of the desk. "I appreciate that you wanted me to hear the findings firsthand, although I would . . ."

"I haven't finished the investigation, sir. In fact, it's about to blow wide open."

Dominguez stiffened. "What are you talking about?"

Carly paced the office. She'd dissected her thoughts during the drive in from Joy Matusinak's house, distilled them to their stark, unpalatable essence, but they still rushed at her, black and whirling, like storm clouds pushed up from the Gulf.

"Elaine Dawson-Smith allegedly engaged in sexual intercourse with at least one, perhaps more, of the inmates at the prison."

"What?"

"So did a number of other women. They call themselves the Afternoon Club."

The colonel's swarthy face took on a yellowish hue. Carly could understand why. The headlines shouting out the woman's murder had been lurid enough. She could imagine what the media would do with this bombshell.

GENERAL'S DAUGHTER SERVICED BY INMATES.

KINKY SEX FOR MONEY.

LOVE IN THE AFTERNOON ON MAXWELL.

"What evidence do you have to support this allegation?" he asked sharply.

"One of the participants in the club provided a statement of fact this morning. Although she never actually witnessed Colonel Dawson-Smith or any of the others having sex with inmates, she gave me enough details to support widening the investigation."

Dominguez raked two fingers through his mustache, digesting the implications of what he'd just heard. From the look on his face, it didn't go down easy.

"Is this witness suggesting that one of the inmates put a bullet through Colonel Dawson-Smith's chest?"

"No, sir. This woman swears she doesn't know anything about the murder. She hadn't spoken to Elaine for almost a week before her death."

"Dammit, why didn't the OSI pick up on this . . . this damned club during their initial investigation?"

Carly didn't attempt to speak for the Office of Special Investigations.

"We've got a whole new scenario here," the colonel grumbled.

"Or we could have exactly the same scenario, with a clearer motive," she pointed out tightly. "Assuming Michael Smith found out about his wife's activities, rage might have driven him to follow her into the woods and put a bullet through her heart. At this point, the preponderance of the evidence still points to him."

"Unless McMann lied about seeing Smith on River Road. He could have been protecting one of his own, the inmate Elaine went to meet. Hell, maybe she went to meet McMann himself. The celebrity stud. The famous jock. Given his reputation, the odds are he humped more than a few of these so-called club members."

Stone faced, Carly nodded. "I've considered that possibility."

"We ruled him out as a suspect based on the results of the polygraph, the tight time line from his arrival on base to the time he signed in at the prison, and lack of any motive or apparent connection to the victim. We'll have to revisit all of the above."

"Yes, sir."

"All right." The colonel pushed off the desk. "Make me a copy of this witness's statement."

"I already have."

She dropped several Xeroxed pages into his hand.

"It's unsworn," she advised as he flipped through the handwritten pages. "I took her statement at her home and got her to review it before I left, but she was in no condition to swear to it."

Actually, Joy Matusinak could barely hold her head up by the time Carly finished scribbling down the facts as she'd related them. Carly couldn't ask the woman to swear to a statement given under the influence of those powerful tranquilizers, of course, nor would she try to introduce such a statement in a court of law. Under the looser rules of evidence that governed the pretrial investigations, however, she could and would consider any such unsworn statements that had bearing on the case.

"You'll have to provide copies of this to the accused," Dominguez reminded her, scowling over the closely written pages.

"Yes, sir."

"We need to read in the Office of Special Investigations," he continued, half to himself. "And the Bureau of Prisons."

"I've already talked to the assistant warden once regarding the case. I planned to go back out there this afternoon and—"

"Brief the OSI first. Get them to review their case notes in light of this information, put another spin on the interviews they conducted with the inmates. In the meantime, I'll take this to the wing commander, He'll probably want to give the warden a heads-up personally, so they'll be expecting you when you get there."

Carly could imagine her reception when she arrived. The colonel skimmed the handwritten notes again, his mouth curling in disgust.

"The Afternoon Club. Christ!"

The same refrain echoed in Carly's mind as she headed back to the conference room assigned to her for the period of the investigation.

The Afternoon Club.

The acid irony of the name ate at her. It conjured up images of dainty porcelain teapots and white lace gloves, of genteel ladies tittering over the latest gossip. This particular group of women had tittered, all right . . . over the physical endowments of the studs they paid to service them.

Carly had prosecuted people accused of far worse offenses against society, but it disgusted her to think that a woman who wore the same uniform she did had participated in this so-called club. Lieutenant Colonel Dawson-Smith had dishonored not only herself but, by the inevitable association that would follow, all other women officers. Her acts would raise all the old, hackneyed doubts about females in the military. The pundits would shake their heads. The hard-liners would moan about lowered standards and fraternization and inappropriate conduct in the ranks. The Phyllis Schlaflys of the world would take to the podium with a vengeance to sing their never-ending women-belong-at-home chorus.

It wouldn't matter that Joy Matusinak was a stay-at-home wife, that most of the others who allegedly participated in the afternoon sessions were townies, not associated with the base. They counted among their numbers a doctor's wife, a real estate agent, a stewardess, a boutique owner, all well-to-do, all bored, all seeking that added edge, that thrill of forbidden sex.

From what Joy had told Carly, the members of the club experienced no difficulty gaining access to Maxwell or to the inmates. They came to visit friends, to apply for a job at civilian personnel, to deliver a gift or flowers or a birthday cake, or so they told the gate guards.

The whole scenario disgusted and angered her, but Carly didn't kid herself. A good portion of her fury was directed squarely at herself.

She'd sat with McMann for almost two hours last night, listening to his voice with its distinctive Yankee cadence, seeing the pictures he painted in spare phrases. In the process, she'd allowed him to skirt the real issue, the only issue, that lay between them.

Elaine Dawson-Smith had paid to mount a young, muscled Adonis who knew what he did was wrong.

Joy said so.

Ry said so.

Now Elaine Dawson-Smith was dead. And so was Billy Hopewell.

At this point, Carly couldn't decide who she held in more contempt. McMann for keeping to the code of silence surrounding the events in the woods, or herself for feeling somehow betrayed.

CHAPTER ELEVEN

Her blood still at a simmer over the Afternoon Club, Carly put herself on autopilot and set up an appointment to meet with Special Agent Derrick Greene, chief of Detachment 405 of the Office of Special Investigations later that day. The OSI chief, Carly suspected, wouldn't like what she had to tell him.

Her next call was to Michael Smith. When his answering machine clicked on, Carly requested a meeting with him and his attorney as soon as possible.

She grabbed a late lunch at the Officers' Club, then logged onto the computer to detail the sequence of events that had led her to Joy Matusinak. Just before leaving for her meeting with the OSI chief, she put in another call, this one to the prison. Warden Bolt was out of town, his secretary advised her, but Assistant Warden Preston was expecting her call.

Fayrene Preston wasted no time on polite preliminaries. "The wing commander called. I understand we've got a problem."

"It appears so."

"When do I get the details?"

"I'm just heading over to brief the OSI now. It's going to be a long session. I can come see you first thing in the morning."

"That won't work. The warden's out of town and I

have to be downtown at eight. FEMA has called an emergency session of the Federal agencies' disaster response force. The Coosa's broken through its banks and flooded half of Chilton County."

"I heard about it on the radio."

"Let's say two o'clock, just to be safe."

"Fine."

The assistant warden hung up with a noticeable absence of the polite friendliness she'd displayed during their previous meeting. Carly wasn't surprised by the chilliness. She was, after all, the bearer of bad tidings. In former centuries, such messengers had been stoned to death.

She still hadn't heard from Smith or his lawyer by the time she left the wing headquarters and drove against the late afternoon exodus of traffic to the Office of Special Investigations. The OSI detachment was housed in a two-story stucco building just south of the aircraft hangars. Like most of the other buildings on the historic base that was once home to the Wright Flying School, the long, low, cream-colored hangars carried touches of art deco in their metal window frames and corner pillars.

In no mood to appreciate either art or architecture, Carly pulled the MG into the parking lot. Special Agent Greene met her at the door and escorted her to his office. After a brief preamble that detailed the sequence of events from the encounter with Billy in the woods to her visit to the woman who sent flowers to his funeral, she handed over Joy Matusinak's unsworn statement.

Greene read through the statement twice. His boyish face wore a grim cast when he laid the handwritten pages aside.

"Beats the hell out of me how we missed this."

"I only stumbled onto it by chance."

He grunted, obviously less than happy with his detachment's field work. "We'll follow up on the list of names Mrs. Matusinak provided. Maybe some of these other women can give us a better idea of the scope of this little operation." His eyes hardened. "We'll also go out and have another chat with the inmates."

Carly skimmed the computer-generated list of inmates he'd pulled off for her. She'd read the official case files, but this list included all contacts, even those whose statements didn't make it into the case file for lack of any pertinent information.

"I don't see Billy Hopewell listed here."

"We didn't interview him." Greene tabbed through several dog-eared pages of information on Bureau of Prisons letterhead stationery. "The work roster for the day of the murder shows Hopewell pulled road and grounds detail that morning, but he remained at the prison compound that afternoon. Looks like he was scheduled for some kind of class."

Carly knew exactly what kind of class. A tutoring session with his friend, his buddy, Ry. As McMann had explained in his original statement, the standing commitment brought him back to the prison twice a week.

Or did it?

Unbidden, her mind flashed an image of McMann's powerful body pinning Elaine Dawson-Smith to a tree trunk, his hips driving into hers, her head thrown back as she gasped and clawed at his shoulders for support, for leverage, for the sheer, carnal joy of scoring his flesh with those long-tipped crimson nails.

Her teeth clenching, Carly banished the searing image. She'd uncovered no evidence that McMann participated in the orgies in the woods. Yet. But he'd known about them, and before she finished with him, he'd damn well tell her everything he knew.

"The tutoring sessions Hopewell attended didn't begin until three," she pointed out to Greene. "We need to account for his whereabouts between the time he returned from his morning detail and the start of that session."

"We'll check it out." He scribbled a note beside Billy's name. "Damn, I wish we'd gotten to him before he took the long way down that short slope."

"So do I."

Greene sat back, his pen tapping on the stack of files. "What does this do to your Article 32 investigation? Are we putting the case against Michael Smith on hold?"

"No, I'm pressing ahead. At this point, we have no proof that his wife met with any of the inmates the afternoon she was shot. Unless and until we do, the evidence still points to her husband as her killer."

"Even more so, if Smith knew about her little trysts in the woods," Greene murmured.

"Exactly."

Carly left the OSI detachment to a flurry of wind and unusual activity on the flight line across the street. Aviators in green flight suits had lined up to dump gear bags in the back of a truck before heading for the blue crew bus waiting patiently. One of the aviators waved and broke out of the line.

"Hey, Major. I thought I recognized your MG."

Captain Jo West crossed the unused apron. Her neck-to-ankle Nomex flight suit clung to her trim figure like a second skin. Honey-colored tendrils had escaped the clip that held back her hair and whipped around her face.

"What's going on?" Carly asked.

"The front moving our way took a swing to the south. Fort Rucker is expecting golf-ball sized hail and possible tornadoes later tonight."

"Oh, great! That's all they need."

The sprawling helicopter training base in southeastern Alabama had already lost a hangar and two aircraft to the vicious spring storms.

"Rucker's commander isn't taking any chances this time. He's put out a call for instructor-qualified pilots to help the students ferry the birds up here to sit out the storm."

"And of course you volunteered. Anything to get out of class, right?"

Grinning, Jo flipped out her hands. "Can I help it if they asked for the best?"

Carly's laughter joined hers, easing the tight knot of anger she'd carried in her chest since morning.

It was only after she'd wished the helo pilot a swift flight ahead of the storms and watched her stride off that a belated realization struck. The hand Jo had held up a moment ago was bare. Only a pale band of flesh marked her ring finger. Unless flight regulations required removal of all jewelry, Jo West had shed her diamond engagement ring sometime between pizza at Tony's last week and this afternoon.

Sympathy tugged at Carly as she walked to her car. She'd ended an engagement once herself. It had hurt, even with the passion dulled and the dreams faded.

Nor did the ending get easier, even without an engagement ring. Carly hadn't forgotten her decision to call things off with Parker. With a sense of shock, she realized she'd made that decision only last night. It seemed longer, probably because so much had happened after he stalked out of her house . . . not

the least of which were those stolen hours with
McMann.

Her anger jolted back. Damn him!

The force of her fury brought her to a halt beside
the MG. She needed to get a grip here. She'd gotten
too involved, she decided grimly, with McMann,
with this investigation. The unanswered questions,
the half-cloaked truths, had eaten into her thoughts
and robbed her of too many hours of sleep. She
needed to relax, to regain her balance and per-
spective. Which wouldn't be easy considering the
Pandora's box she'd just pried the lid off.

Sighing, she wished she hadn't agreed to attend
the hundred-dollar-a-plate fundraiser tonight, but
she was too much her mother's daughter to miss this
key campaign appearance. Besides, Parker would be
there. He never missed the opportunity to mingle
with the movers and the shakers. She'd talk to him
afterward, Carly decided. That part of her life at least
she could put in order.

As it turned out, Parker made the putting far
easier than she'd anticipated.

She arrived late at the hotel where the function
was being held, only to find Adele Samuels had canceled. The congresswoman had choppered up to
view the flooding in Chilton County, which included
a portion of her district, and had sent her chief of staff
to urge her daughter to the podium in her place. Luckily, Carly was dressed for the spotlight. She'd swung
by the carriage house to change out of her uniform.
Always careful to avoid even the appearance of military support for a political candidate, she'd opted for
a sheath in a red silk layered with flame-patterned
chiffon.

With a wave across the crowd to Parker and a

smile for the friendly faces thronging the banquet hall, she allowed Mozell Denton, her mother's senior legislative aide, to usher her to the head table. The short speech that followed dinner presented no real challenge. Carly had campaigned for her mother often enough to speak glowingly of Adele's past accomplishments and honestly of her current platform.

The problems began at the end of the speech, when pro-lifers crashed into the hall, waving placards and shouting strident protests against Adele Samuels's stand on abortion. One of her mother's more ardent supporters grew incensed at the taunts and launched a dinner roll. Before Carly or any of the function's organizers could stop it, a full-fledged food war erupted.

Adele had trained her daughter and son for just such contingencies. Instead of giving the demonstrators a target and the TV cameras a vivid visual of a food-draped Samuels for the ten o'clock news, Carly made a dignified exit.

Her dignity quickly raveled around the edges when Parker pushed through the swinging doors to join her in the corridor a few moments later. Anger darkened his handsome features, reminding her all too vividly of his expression when he'd stalked out of her house last night.

"What happened to security?" he snapped at the harried chief of staff. "How did those people get in?"

Mozell raked a hand through his short, curly hair. "I don't know."

"Well check it out, for God's sake! We came close to a riot in there."

The Harvard-educated, native-born Alabamian who'd advised Adele Samuels on issues affecting

Afro-Americans for almost a decade didn't take kindly to Parker's curt order. Neither did Carly.

"Back off," she advised shortly. "Mozell knows how to handle a hostile crowd."

The assistant DA swung toward her, his flush deepening. "Then he'd better handle it."

The appearance of her mother's PR director pre-empted Carly's scathing retort. Seething, she folded her arms and held her fire until the chief of staff had hurried away with the PR rep to handle media.

"If you're thinking of walking in my mother's shoes someday," she said icily, "I suggest you watch yourself around Mozell. He can make you . . . or break you . . . with the party."

"Is that right?" The flush on Parker's face deepened. "Maybe you'd better watch yourself, Carly, or I might have to run for your mother's seat sooner than either of us expect."

"What are you talking about?"

"Your private little tête-à-tête with Ryan McMann last night, that's what I'm talking about. What do you think it would do to Adele's anticrime platform if word got around about your association with a convicted felon?"

Shocked, she dropped her arms. "How . . . ? How did you . . . ?"

"How did I find out?" He shoved his hands into his pockets, his whole body rigid with disapproval. "I didn't want to leave things like they were between us last night. I came back to try to patch things up and saw a Bronco parked in front of your house."

"So you ran the tag," she bit out, incensed.

"Yes, I ran the tag." He didn't even blink at the admission that he'd used his police connections for personal reasons. "Smart, Carly, real smart, inviting an ex-con into your home at night like that."

"Who I invite into my home and when is none of your business."

Her acid retort added fuel to a fire that had obviously been simmering all day.

"Yeah, well, I figured that out. What I can't figure is the connection between you and McMann. You let him put his hands on you, then he shows up at your door. Given the guy's reputation, some people might think you invited him in for more than a chat."

"Are you . . . ?" She struggled for breath. "Are you one of those people?"

A waiter rumbled a cart laden with dishes down the corridor, giving them a curious glance as he passed. Carly ignored him, ignored the hubbub just beginning to die away inside the ballroom.

"Are you, Parker?"

He had the grace to drop his eyes and look away. "No."

"Thanks for that much at least."

"Carly . . ."

"See you around, Counselor."

If the scene in the hotel corridor hadn't completely sabotaged Carly's ability to get any work done that night, the call from her mother some hours later certainly did the trick. Still prickly with irritation, she snatched at the phone on her desk and answered with a bite to her voice that Adele picked up on immediately.

"Hello, sweetie. Sorry you were a target for mashed potatoes tonight. Did any hit their mark?"

"Never even came close. You taught us to duck at the first sign of flying food, remember?"

Adele's musical chuckle floated over the wire. "That's the first skill a politician acquires." She paused, then probed delicately. "I understand you had to dodge more than hard rolls."

A small puff of laughter worked through Carly's irritation. She might have known Adele would have heard about the contretemps in the corridor. She maintained and operated an intelligence network that put the Pentagon to shame.

"Care to tell me what you and Parker were arguing about? Or isn't it something a mother needs to get in the middle of?"

Maybe not a mother, but a congresswoman up for re-election was a different proposition. Grudgingly, Carly conceded Parker's point on that matter.

"We were arguing about the fact that Ryan McMann stopped by my house last night," she said slowly.

"McMann . . . McMann . . ."

With an almost audible efficiency, Adele clicked through her formidable list of acquaintances, colleagues, contributors, and connections.

"I know the name but . . . Of course! The hockey player. I met him once, years ago, at some charitable function or another." She made another pass through her memory bank "Didn't he confess to a sex crime? Statutory rape, as I recall?"

"Yes. He served time at the prison on Maxwell and is now on parole."

"I take it Parker objected to McMann's presence at your house last night."

"He did."

"I hope you told him to take a flying leap."

"Who? Parker, or McMann?"

"Parker Stuart, dear. He's not your type. Too pushy. Too possessive."

The laughter came more easily this time. How like her mother not to ask the obvious, like what the heck

McMann was doing at her daughter's house. Carly
had to tell her, however, had to share those aspects of
the investigation she could without compromising
either the air force or herself.

"McMann is a witness in the Article 32 I'm running on the Dawson-Smith murder."

Without going into too specific detail, she touched
on Joy Matusinak's startling disclosures this morning.

"Wonderful," her mother groaned. "Another sex
scandal. Just what the air force needs."

Any other politician running for re-election might
have jumped on the Afternoon Club and trumpeted
it into a clarion call for military reform, for stricter
standards, for a return to the moral values of the
past. Particularly a politician whose district included
both the base and the prison.

One of the things Carly admired most about her
mother was her sense of fair play. She wouldn't trash
Maxwell or the military just to grab some headlines. If word leaked about McMann's visit to her
daughter's house, however, the headlines might just
grab her.

Granted, Carly hadn't known about the club when
she invited McMann in last night. Nor did she know
for sure that he'd participated in the sex-for-money
activities on the base. She'd be blowing smoke if she
tried to convince the media of that, though. They'd
eat up the fact another air force officer had developed an intimate relationship with an inmate, albeit
a former inmate. Denials would only fan the flames.

With a tight curl of dismay, Carly realized just
what she'd put on the line last night. Her appointment as an Article 32 investigating officer, for one
thing. Her professional reputation, for another. And,
as Parker had so bluntly pointed out, her mother's
political standing at a critical time in her campaign.

"We need to talk this through," she said with a tight swallow. "McMann's visit last night could produce some fallout . . . for both of us."

Adele didn't sound particularly concerned by the possibility. "Why don't you come over for dinner tomorrow night?" she suggested cheerfully. "We'll talk about it then, and get the Judge's take. Dave's, too, if he and Allie aren't busy."

Carly tried to work up some enthusiasm for a family caucus. Right now, her feelings about both McMann and her investigation were too raw, too angry, and too damned confused to look forward to laying them out for Dave and Allie and the Judge to dissect. The Samuelses had always solved their problems that way, though. From the time Carly could remember, they talked over their concerns at the dinner table.

Murmuring an assent, she hung up. Maybe by tomorrow night, she'd know what she was dealing with. Dragging a yellow legal pad in front of her, she went back to jotting down the questions she wanted to ask Michael Smith and Fayrene Preston.

She didn't expect much from the accused. Smith might have suspected his wife's extracurricular activities, but his attorney would no doubt advise him not to admit to that knowledge. No sense in handing the prosecution a gold-plated motive.

Hopefully, the visit to the prison would yield more results. Once Preston understood the exact nature of Joy Matusinak's allegations, she might have some insights into the inmates involved. If Carly could get to one of them, convince him that it was just a matter of time until the other women Joy had identified started naming names and providing descriptions, she might just get the answers she was looking for.

And then there was McMann. This time, Carly swore, he'd talk to her. One way or another, she'd pull his secrets out of him.

Grimly determined, she tugged on her favorite UA sleepshirt and fell asleep to the rumble of distant thunder.

CHAPTER TWELVE

Howling winds buffeted the Bronco as it splashed along River Road. Lightning cracked across the black sky.

Cursing, Ryan used both hands to fight the gusts that fired rain at the windshield like bullets. The damned storm the forecasters had predicted would swing south had turned back on its heels and now pounded central Alabama with a vengeance.

It was bad enough Ryan had to return to the prison for these twice-a-week tutoring sessions. Driving through tornado-spawning winds and blinding rain to get to them didn't exactly improve his mood. The fact that Billy wouldn't be there to agonize over every word, every syllable, didn't help either.

Ryan couldn't shake his guilt, couldn't dodge the remorse that snuck up on him and yanked at his conscience at unexpected moments. It ate at him from the inside out that he hadn't helped the kid when he needed it most.

The Bronco plowed into a low spot in the road and threw up a blinding sheet of water. With a vicious oath, Ryan kept the vehicle from sliding off the asphalt. God, he wanted out of this town, this state, this damned rain! He wanted away from everything and everyone who reminded him of his own failings as a man, as a friend.

Away from everyone except Carly Samuels.

The caveat jumped into his mind before he could stop it. So did the picture he carried from those hours he'd spent at her home. Slender legs displayed all too seductively by crotch-hugging cutoffs. Trim hips. Burnished auburn hair. Skin so warm and creamy he'd had to restrain himself from licking it to see if it tasted as good as it looked.

He gripped the wheel, wondering how the hell she'd invaded his head like this. Wondering, too, how he'd get her out of it. Two months. *Less* than two months, and he was gone. It irritated him to think he might take some memory of Montgomery away with him despite his determination to wipe it—

"Hell!"

With a stomp on the brakes, Ryan brought the Bronco to a shimmying stop only feet from the dump truck that rumbled out of the side road. Shoving in the clutch, he shifted into reverse and backed up enough to give the truck room to turn onto the road. It was empty, he saw, on its way back to the civil engineering yard to pick up another load of sand, no doubt. His jaw tight from the near miss, Ryan sent a quick glance skimming down the side road to the mounded earth breastworks in the distance. Driving rain almost obscured the chain of men in camouflage fatigues and drenched prison greens atop the high bank.

The air base had turned out some of its own personnel to sandbag shoulder to shoulder with the inmates. Not many months ago, Ryan would have been slinging the sand-filled bags right alongside them. It gave him a perverse sense of satisfaction to shove the Bronco into forward and leave the rain-lashed crew to their labors. Personally, he wouldn't care if the Alabama jumped its banks and the whole damned base floated down river—which seemed more possible with every passing hour.

If he'd had any sense, Warden Bolt would have canceled such noncritical activities as these tutoring sessions, maybe even started evacuating personnel from the low-lying prison facilities. Ryan didn't like the angry roar coming from just beyond the breastworks. He liked the idea of getting stranded at the prison for an indefinite time while river waters lapped at the raised foundations even less.

Another curse slipped out when he pulled into the parking lot of the prison and saw no signs of unusual activity, much less evacuation. Just the predictable handful of cars huddled against the storm like forlorn ducks. Including, he saw with a sudden kick in his veins, a white MG.

He parked in the row behind the little sports car, letting the Bronco engine idle while he considered the implications of Carly's presence at the prison.

She hadn't mentioned Billy or Elaine Dawson-Smith during those hours at her house the other night. Nor had he. But Ryan hadn't doubted for a moment they were the only reason she'd let him into her home.

Now she was here.

Why? What was she after now?

His gut crawling, Ryan signed in at the gate and waited while the guard checked his ID with careless indifference to the downpour. Shoulders hiked, the collar of his blue windbreaker pulled up against the driving rain, Ryan made for the kitchen first. If there were any rumors circulating, particularly any involving Carly, that's where he'd hear them.

Wind gusted in with him, whipping the pages of a

newspaper. The guard hunched over a cup of coffee slapped a palm down on the sports section to hold the rattling pages and arrowed an annoyed look at the newcomer.

"Close the damned door, McMann."

The outer screen thumped shut, followed by the sturdier inner door. Shaking off the water, Ryan shoved back his wet hair and nodded to the inmate scrubbing down the tables before helping himself to a mug of the coffee kept available to the prison staff.

Blowing steam off the strong, chicory-flavored brew, he let his gaze settle on the guard seated comfortably at the long tables near the windows. John Murphee. One of the old hands. Nearing retirement, lazy as they came, and eminently bribable.

To give Warden Bolt his due, he'd weeded out most of the Murphees over time. Only a few remained, protected as much by the inmates as by their own seniority and devious skill at bending the rules. Those few—a good ole boy who looked the other way at convenient times; a church-going, reputedly devoted husband and father who took special pleasure in body cavity searches; a white supremacist with a legal license to hate—represented the bottom layer of scum in a system Ryan despised.

Which was why his gut tightened when Murph picked up his mug and strolled over to join him at the coffee pot.

"How long you got to keep coming back to tutor these boys, McMann?"

"About two months," he said shortly.

"That right?" Upending a container of sugar, Murphee poured a long stream into his mug. "Two months, huh? Me, I got three years. Three years till I go fishing full time. I might make it, too," he muttered, "if Bolt don't get any wild hairs up his butt."

Ryan's gaze slid sideways. "The warden starting to lean on you, Murph?"

"Nah."

The denial was too quick, too bluff. Its heartiness didn't quite match the lines that snaked across Murphee's sun-weathered brow.

"Bolt doesn't have anything on me. He's just got his wind up 'cause the base commander called him. Seems some major done heard nasty rumors 'bout Billy and that colonel who got herself shot."

The coffee Ryan had just downed hit the back of his stomach. Slowly, carefully, he turned to face the guard.

"What kind of rumors?"

With a little smirk, Murphee stuck his forefinger into his mug and stirred. "I think you got a good idea, boy."

"Maybe, maybe not. Why don't you tell me so I know for sure?"

Shooting a look at the inmate swabbing the tables, Murph lowered his voice to a conspiratorial whisper.

"We both know Billy was diddling the colonel. Some other women, too." His finger stirred faster, creating a small whirlpool. A gleam lit his black pupils. "Hopewell ever tell you about humping those rich broads in the woods, McMann?"

"No."

"Aw, com'on. You were his buddy. The only one he ever talked to, if you could call his stutterin' and stammerin' talk. He got out a few words once in a while, though. Didn't he ever tell you about peelin' down them bitches' panties and sticking it to them?"

Ryan's lungs squeezed. Billy had *wanted* to talk to him. God knew the kid had tried to force the words out, but every time he got close to what Ryan suspected was the truth, he retreated into stammering incoherency.

Then blonde, beautiful, voracious Elaine Dawson-Smith had died of a gunshot wound to the chest. From that fateful day on, Ryan had stopped urging Billy to talk . . . to him or anyone else.

"Bet they got wet soon's as they saw him," Murph said with a salacious grin. "Young stallion like that, they probably lined up to climb onto his dick. Damn, wish I'd seen it. Seen it, hell! Wish I'd had *me* some of that fancy pussy."

His face alive with vicarious lust, Murphee leaned closer. "Bet they was lining up for you, too, McMann. Com'on, boy, spill it. Did you get you some of that high-class stuff while you were in? Is that what's been bringing you back all these months since you been out?"

Ryan slapped his mug on the counter. "No."

"Hell, you wouldn't tell me if it was," the guard complained. "You're even less of a talker than Billy was. It's a wonder to me why Gator always wanted to work alongside him like he did."

Ryan's heart slowed, then thumped so hard against his ribs he had to clench his jaw to keep from grunting.

"Gator wanted to work alongside Billy?"

"Guess we know why now, don't we?" Murph answered slyly. "He was probably getting the kid's leftovers. Or taking the stud fee, more like. Damn, I should of figured something when he slipped me . . . when he asked me to put him and Billy on the same detail after you left."

Suspicion burned an icy hole in the pit of Ryan's stomach.

"Did you?"

"Sure, why not?" A defensive note crept into the guard's voice. "No skin off my nose who worked with who. 'Sides, someone had to look after the kid once you checked out. He was big, but so damned stupid. Look at the way he turned that mower over on himself."

"Was Gator working the same area as Billy the afternoon the kid died?"

"Yeah, sure. He was the one reported him missing."

The ice spread from Ryan's stomach to his chest, searing in its white hot intensity. A slow, sick certainty gripped him. All these months, he'd suspected. All these weeks since Elaine Dawson-Smith's death, he'd gnawed over the awful possibilities. But until this moment, he hadn't connected Billy's accident with Gator Burns.

"Where's Burns now?"

The question was so low, so deadly, that Murphee just blinked.

"Where is he?" Ryan snarled.

"Hell, I don't know. Working with the sand-bagging crews, I'd guess. That's where everyone else is."

Murphee was still slogging back coffee when the door opened again some minutes later. He thumped his palm down again to keep the crossword puzzle he was working from blowing across the table and threw another disgusted look at the newcomers. His expression altered instantly when he identified the assistant warden under a yellow slicker that streamed water onto the linoleum. A soggy looking female in a blue air force raincoat came in on her heels.

"What are you doing here?" Preston snapped. "I

thought I sent all available personnel out to help with the sand-bagging."

"You did." Murph lied with the ease of long practice. "I came a few minutes ago to dry out and shag some coffee.

"Well, finish your coffee and get back to the detail."

"Yes, ma'am."

No way Murph was letting the bitch send him out into the rain. He took a leisurely swallow, eyeing Fayrene Preston over the rim. She was a looker, with them long legs and that sweet, tight ass, but too damned bossy for his tastes. When he'd started with the prison system three decades ago, they didn't hire females to boss men. He couldn't say much for the changes that had come about over the years.

Preston swept the deserted dining area with a quick glance. "We're looking for Ryan McMann. He was supposed to report to the education center at three, but didn't show up there. Have you seen him?"

The cunning that had saved Murph's job on more than one occasion put up its antenna.

"What do you want with him?"

"The major has some questions for him and a few of the inmates," Preston said impatiently. "Have you seen him?"

The guard ruminated over the query, trying to decide if lying would benefit him, then shrugged.

"He came in for some coffee a few minutes ago. Left kind of in a hurry."

"For where?"

No way Murph was going to pass up the opportunity to get the assistant warden out of the camp long enough to let him finish his coffee and his crossword in peace.

"He asked for Gator's whereabouts."

"Gator?"

The air force major rolled the name around in a soft, honey-filled voice that Murph highly approved of. Not barbed, like Fayrene Preston's, not naggy, like his wife's.

"Harry 'Gator' Burns," the assistant warden supplied, her gaze sharpening as it met the major's. "You just looked at his file."

The major's brown gaze swung around to Murphee. "You said McMann left in a hurry to find this Gator Burns. Did he tell you what he wanted to talk to him about?"

Murph had a damned good idea. With the animal-like survival instincts he'd honed over the years, he sensed that the business with Billy and the women in the woods was about to bust wide open. Well, they couldn't track nothing back to ole Murph. He didn't know anything, not for a fact, hadn't seen anything. Probably wouldn't hurt him none to display his ignorance to the assistant warden, either. Scratching his head, he made a show of thinking back.

"Well, I don't recall as McMann said exactly what he wanted with Gator. He was heated up, though. Seemed to think Burns knew something about him and his friend, Billy Hopewell, something McMann didn't want to tell me about."

The two women exchanged swift glances, then started for the door.

"We'll take my vehicle," Fayrene said. "It has four wheel drive and a radio, which might come in handy if we hit high water."

"Right."

Satisfied that he'd put the hounds to bayin' up another tree, Murph ambled to the coffee pot and refilled his cup.

* * *

"Where's Burns?"

Fayrene Preston pitched the question loud enough to be heard above the roar of the river and the pounding rain. The guard supervising the crew strung along the breastworks swiped a hand over his cheeks and shouted a reply.

"He took a ton-and-a-half back to the civil engineering compound. You should have passed him on the road."

"We didn't."

Standing beside them, Carly felt the earth shudder beneath her feet. From the vantage point of the road carved atop the breastworks, she eyed the churning water. It rushed south, then west, then south again, digging a sinuous, ever-changing course through cotton fields and peanut farms all the way to Mobile. Swollen and muddy, it had taken on a snarling character far different from its normal, placid flow. Uprooted trees and debris and what looked like a small, bloated pig pulsed along with the rushing waters. The carcass tumbled and dipped in the muddy river like one of the fishing bobbins the Judge used to tie on Carly's line for her.

The Alabama was going to break. Maybe not here, where long, snaking lines of green sandbags reinforced the raised earthen banks, but somewhere, and soon.

"Try the road to the boat ramp," the guard shouted. "We had another crew working there earlier, helping shore up the dock."

Carly slogged alongside the assistant warden to the utility vehicle that sat with its engine idling and wipers slashing back and forth like sabers. Mud churned up by the trucks splashed onto her pant legs.

Her slacks were already so wet below the hem of her raincoat that the reddish slime slid right off. The door slammed, cutting off the rain and plunging both her and Fayrene Preston into a steamy dampness.

"We'll try the boat ramp," the slicker-clad assistant warden said grimly "Then I'll have to put you and your inquiry on hold."

Before shoving the vehicle into gear, she jerked the radio from its dash mount and instructed central control to put her through to the base civil engineer. They reached him at the command post activated to deal with the worsening situation.

"I don't like the looks of things down here," she informed the colonel tersely. "What's the situation upriver?"

His reply crackled over the radio. "Not good. We've got reports of flash flooding and downed power lines around Clanton. A bridge washed away about three miles south of the town and took a section of I-65 with it. We launched some of our choppers to help the state police locate and evacuate stranded motorists."

Carly pushed her wet bangs off her forehead. She'd bet Jo West was piloting one of those birds. The captain wouldn't want to miss out on the action.

"What about the base?" Fayrene asked the colonel. "Any flooding yet?"

"The fairways east of Cottonwood are pretty much under water, but nothing that worries me too much right now. How about at your end? Your command post rep says you've already completed the preliminary steps in the evacuation op plan."

"I've had central control contact all our off-duty people and put them on standby for recall," she confirmed. "We've also requested extra buses from

the motor pool to transport the inmates to Hangar
Twenty-one, if and when evacuation becomes
necessary."

"What about the warden's family?"

"We'll move them, too. Mrs. Bolt has been notified
that she might have to . . ."

Preston broke off, ducking instinctively when
lightning cracked through the black clouds.

"Mrs. Bolt knows she might have to evacuate," she
continued when the booming thunder faded. "She's
getting her things together. The kids are in school."

"Well, it's your call when to move them, but I
wouldn't wait too long."

The assistant warden flicked another glance at the
reinforced bank, obviously weighing the necessity of
getting a handle on the scandal about to break
against the storm wreaking havoc upriver. Indeci-
sion showed on her face, in the lower lip she worried
between her teeth.

Carly bit down on her need to find McMann and
Gator Burns. Ever since the guard at the dining hall
had linked Billy Hopewell, McMann, and Burns in
the same sentence, her heart had drummed a furious
beat. Hopewell was dead. McMann, she believed
with more certainty each passing moment, knew
more than he'd admitted to either the military investigators or to Carly. Burns, she hoped, would prove
the catalyst that finally, irrevocably unraveled the
mystery of Elaine Smith's death.

She couldn't urge the assistant warden to continue
the search for them, though. Not with everything
else pressing down on the woman at the moment.

Preston hesitated a few seconds longer before in-
forming the civil engineer that she'd be on mobile for
another twenty minutes or so. "I'm going to swing

by the boat ramp," she told him crisply, "then head back to the prison compound."

"Roger that."

Her decision made, she snicked the radio back onto its dash mount and shoved the vehicle into gear.

CHAPTER THIRTEEN

Gator saw them coming.

Through a pinwheel of pain, he caught a flicker of yellow as it rounded the corner of the shed that housed the base's pleasure boats. The assistant warden, his screaming brain registered. Someone else was with her, an indistinct figure in a belted raincoat. He barely had time to identify the figure as female before McMann's left connected with his jaw again.

A fireball of red exploded behind his eyes. Teeth cracking against teeth, Gator staggered back against the fender of the ton-and-a-half, throwing out hands still encased in rough work gloves to keep himself from sliding into the mud.

He needed a weapon, any kind of a weapon! The closest was an iron tie-down rod, designed to secure the truck bed's canvas top if one was used. He lunged for the rod, only to snarl in fury as the grease-smeared pin slipped through his gloved hand. McMann snatched it out of his grasp, tossing it into the truck bed as he closed on Gator, his eyes murderous.

"I should use that rod to beat what I want out of you, Burns, but the feel of my fist in your face gives me a whole lot more pleasure."

"Bastard!"

"I may be a bastard, but you're a dead man. Today, tomorrow, however long it takes, you're dead."

The right fist that plowed into his solar plexus doubled Gator over. He dropped to his knees in a swirl of water, wheezing bloody bubbles.

Above him, lightning cracked across the sky. In the blinding flash of white light, he saw the assistant warden break into a run. While thunder and pain boomed with equal violence, he searched frantically for a way to save his skin, to turn the accusations McMann had thrown at him with every punch back against his accuser.

"Fuck you . . . McMann," he wheezed through the fire igniting his intestines. "You can . . . kill me, just like you killed that Smith woman, but . . . they'll get you. This time, they'll get you!"

"You miserable, twisted son of a bitch, we both know who shot that woman, and why."

Desperate now, Gator cringed against the truck's tires. "Billy told . . . me what you made him do . . . before you was sprung. He told me 'bout money you collected every time you came out to the prison."

McMann straddled him, wrapped a fist in his shirt to haul him into his face.

"Give it up, Burns. You know damn well you're not walking out of here, so you might as well . . ."

"Hold it right there!"

The shrill command barely pierced the rage that had driven Ryan into the storm to find his quarry. His right fist balled, raised, readied to smash into the ugly mug just inches from his face.

"I said hold it!"

Ryan jerked his head around. Rain and blood from the cut over his left eye blurred his vision, but he could see well enough to identify the assistant warden.

"Back away from that prisoner! Now, McMann!"

Beneath him, Gator's split lips peeled back in a sneer. "Looks like we got company, pretty boy."

Just in time, Ryan remembered that the inmate played by street rules. With a twist of his hips, he took the knee aimed at his groin on the inside of his thigh. The bony knee hit with enough force to knock Ryan off balance for a moment, just the moment Gator needed to slither away and stagger to his feet.

"Jesus! Good thing you got here, warden." Burns leaned a shaky hand on the tire of the massive truck and spat a stream of blood. "He tried to kill me, like he killed them others. That Smith woman and Billy Hopewell. He's crazy, fuckin' crazy."

Chest heaving, Ryan turned around to face the warden. Only then did he see the woman standing just behind Preston. Carly's wide, accusing stare slashed like a straight razor through the rage still screaming in Ryan's veins.

She'd heard Gator. Did she believe the bastard?

Did Fayrene Preston?

Although none of the officials at the minimum security facility carried side arms, they were trained to handle volatile and potentially dangerous situations. Keeping a safe distance from the combatants, the assistant warden snarled an order over her shoulder.

"Get back to the vehicle, Major. Radio central control, tell them I have McMann and one of the inmates involved in a situation here. Tell them to dispatch the E-Squad immediately."

Carly gave Ryan a look that ripped out his heart, then spun around. A moment later, she disappeared behind the corner of the shed.

"You boys want to tell me what's going on here?" Fayrene Preston demanded.

"McMann come after me." The words spewed out of Gator, fast and furious. "Damned near drove me off the road. He's crazy, I tell you. Crazy. He done accused me of whoring with women in the woods."

He spat again and dragged the back of his arm across his mouth. Water streamed down his shaved head and squat, bull-like neck, sloughing off the mud that clung to his face like a dirty beard.

"As if any women would pay money to get it on with me," he sneered. "Why should they, when they had studs like Billy Hopewell and McMann here to stick it to them?"

The assistant warden had spent too many years of dealing with the dregs of society to let anything show on her face, but Ryan felt her withering scorn.

"That's a good question. You want to answer it, McMann?"

"He's lying."

"The hell I am. Ask him why he keeps comin' back twice a week, even after he got sprung. Ask him why a big, smart university man like him done got so close with that halfwit, Billy Hopewell. They was gettin' money from those bitches, I tell you, and havin' themselves a time doin' it. You don't have to take my word for it. You can talk to Pauly Rich and Jimbo Johnson."

A product of the streets, Gator knew his word didn't hold any more weight than McMann's. Less, perhaps, since his rap sheet ran to three pages.

Which was why, Ryan guessed grimly, he played his last, desperate card.

"Me 'n Jimbo 'n Pauly ain't the only ones what knew what was goin' on. Ask Murphee why Hopewell always wanted to work the woods by them stables, why he whined for his buddy McMann all the time."

The guard would have to back Burns up, Ryan realized with a twist to his gut, or admit to taking bribes.

He stood rigid, pummeled by rain and the shattering knowledge that it was about to start all over again. Another investigation, possibly another trial. Hordes of media descending on him, dogging his every step, creating sensational fiction when the facts weren't salacious enough to suit their tastes.

The open road that beckoned continually in the back of Ryan's mind shimmered for a moment on a silvered screen formed by the driving rain, then went dark. He'd come so close, so agonizingly close, to anonymity, to freedom. Maybe even a little peace.

Still keeping a watchful distance, the assistant warden instructed Ryan to move away from the truck and from Gator.

"I want you over there, McMann, until the E-Squad arrives. Then we'll . . . Shit!"

Another bolt of lightning cracked out of the black clouds. Preston hit the ground, diving face first into the mud, as it struck the pines only yards away. With a report like a rifle crack, a trunk split halfway up. Blinding white light lit up the entire area. Electricity leapt from tree to tree.

Gator threw up his arms to protect his head and

flung himself down beside the truck. Ryan's first instinct was to do the same. In that heartbeat, he saw Carly coming around the shed.

She froze at the awesome sight, then threw herself down as one ear-shattering thunderclap after another followed the strike and the top half of the pine came crashing down.

Like a big budget disaster movie, nature's wildness played out before Ryan's eyes in vivid, heart-stopping Technicolor. The decapitated pine dragged a another tree down in its wake. The second pine upended, pulling its root ball clear of the river bank that had anchored it. A small gap sprouted in the bank and filled instantly with a rush of angry, churning water. Before Ryan's horrified eyes, what began as a stream exploded into a torrent.

Huge sections of bank crumbled. More trees toppled. Red clay and brown, rushing waters raced toward the shed, toward the boat ramp, toward the woman stretched flat on the ground.

"Carly! Look out!"

She pushed up on one elbow, then onto a knee. A look of terror came over her face as she saw the wall rushing right at her.

Ryan didn't stop to think. Didn't try to gauge his chances of reaching her before the angry water. Using every ounce of speed, every agile move, every defensive countermeasure he'd developed during ten years in the world's most brutal sport, he launched himself across the sodden ground. He scooped her up on the fly, bending to drag her out of the mud, and raced toward the illusive safety of the shed.

For a single, wrenching moment, he thought

they'd make it. Only a few yards separated them from the structure when the force of the onrushing water knocked his feet out from under him. He tried to throw Carly clear, fought to lift her out of the muddy swirl and propel her sideways. He couldn't get any purchase. She was fighting him, fighting the swamping water, thrashing in his hold. He lost her, somehow tangled an arm in the belt to her raincoat, found himself anchored to her as they tumbled and twisted alongside tree branches and brush that stung at his face and neck.

Just when Ryan thought they might ride the beast to safety, it devoured them whole. Like a wild animal with a nose pushed through the door of its cage, the river roared free of its banks. Ton after ton of water poured over and through and around the breastworks, until long sections of earth disappeared and the swirling, crashing water turned back on itself.

Ryan fought its pull, went under, came up beside a choking, spitting Carly. He saw Gator drag himself into the bed of the ton-and-a-half, thought he caught a flash of yellow slicker, before the rampaging brown river sucked him down again. Concrete scraped one side of his face as the rushing vortex dragged both him and Carly down the boat ramp and into the main current.

Ryan had never imagined anything as monstrous as the force of that current. It drove him down, down, into water thick with silt, captured him, weighted him. His lungs bursting, he kicked, scissored, clawed upward with one hand. Carly was a dead weight at the end of his other arm, tethered to Ryan by the raincoat's belt. He dragged her up with him, felt his arm almost tearing from its socket with the strain.

He burst to the surface, heaved Carly up beside him. Gasping, thrashing, she hacked out a stream of brown water.

"Swim!" he shouted, knowing it was useless but determined to try anyway. "Kick!"

"I . . . am!"

Fighting the raging current, Ryan tried to angle toward the bank, or what used to be the bank. The ramp, the shed, were gone. Muddy water spread at warp speed, gobbling up the landscape like an insatiable beast. The ton-and-a-half sat in the middle of a spreading lake, an immovable island in a sea of brown.

"The truck," Ryan shouted. "Try . . . for . . . the . . . ."

"Oh, God!"

Carly's horrified cry snapped his desperate gaze from the ton-and-a-half to the river. What little air he'd been able to suck into his lungs left on a curse.

A downed pine tree rode the vicious crosscurrent. Bristling with broken branches, it hurtled toward them like a deadly projectile fired by a malevolent hand. Ryan knew they had one chance, just one chance, to dodge those ragged spikes. He dove straight down, dragging Carly by her belt, grabbing her arms, rolling her under him to protect her body with his.

Sharp stakes ripped along his back, tore through his jacket. Something snagged on the windbreaker's collar. He fought the stranglehold, twisting, jerking, trying to reach behind him with one hand as he was dragged along with the racing current. Water filled his nostrils, his lungs. He felt Carly's frantic hands on his just before the muddy water turned black.

Spread-eagled on the roof of the truck, Gator clung to the rim of the open window. Ragged breath whistled through his broken teeth. His heart slammed against the metal roof with all the fury of the river pounding against the truck's sides.

Through streaming eyes, he watched McMann and the woman disappear under the branches of a fast moving tree. The pine swept toward the river's bend. Gator held his breath, watching, hoping. Seconds passed, five, ten, a minute and more. When neither McMann nor the woman came up again, his lips pulled back in a vicious smile. Still smiling, he watched the pine swoop around the bend.

He hoped McMann suffered. He hoped the bastard saw his whole life cartwheelin' in front of his eyes as he swallowed half the mud in Alabama. With any luck, Gator would be there to see it when they found his bloated carcass, stuck in the mud like a dumb cow.

He didn't feel even a twinge of sympathy for the woman who'd gone down with McMann. He figured she was the officer behind the rumors that had been flying around the compound like wildfire yesterday, the woman who was investigating Billy-Boy, else why would she have been out in the storm lookin' for him and McMann? It would suit Gator just fine if McMann had taken her to the river bottom with him.

Now if only the Alabama had swallowed that tight-assed bitch of an assistant warden, too! Gator didn't know how much she'd heard of McMann's accusations, couldn't be sure whose story she'd believe.

He bellied around on the roof and raised his head, turtlelike, to search the lake that already spread for a good quarter mile or more. Preston had washed right past him into the trees and scrub beyond what used to be the boat shed.

She was still there, he saw to his profound disgust. Her yellow slicker was like a flag, torn half off her back, trailing in the water as she clung with both hands to the top of a bent-over sapling. Her brown hair rat-tailed down her face, and her blouse was plastered to her like a second, muddy skin. She spotted him almost the same moment he saw her.

"Burns!"

She shook her head, trying to throw her hair out of her face and clear her vision. The movement bent the sapling even more. The bitch went under and bobbed up a moment later, spitting and grabbing frantically at the slender, slippery limb.

"Is . . . Is there a radio or a squawk box in that truck?"

Gator took great pleasure in the tremor that shook her voice. She was scared, scared and soaked and surrounded by still surging water.

"Yeah," he shouted. "A squawk box."

"Can you get to it?"

"Maybe."

He could, Gator thought with a twist that pulled at his split lip, but he didn't think he would. Nossir, he didn't think he would. Not right yet, anyways.

"Do it!" she shouted, as though she still exercised

authority over him. "Tell whoever you raise to alert
the E-Squad to the flooding. Tell them to get us some
help out here!"

Yeah, sure. As if he gave a flying fuck whether
the emergency response squad drove into a wall of
water.

"Do it, Burns! Now!"

He decided to let her think he was cooperating. Keeping a wary eye out for any critters that
might have swum into the cab with the raging waters, he lowered himself gingerly through the open
window.

Back bent, boots on the seat and ankle deep in the
muddy swirl, he fished around for the switches on
the rusted box bolted to the dash. It was one of
those old-fashioned jobbies, connected only with
the civil engineering roads and grounds shop, the
kind you could call in to request water or more
sand.

The box was silent, minus its usual, scratchy static.
The water must have shorted it out. Still, Gator
wasn't taking any chances. He flipped the switch
to off.

He wasn't quite sure how he was going to use
this situation to his advantage. Maybe Preston
would get tired of hanging on to that tree. Maybe a
nice, accommodating cottonmouth would swim up
her pant leg and take a bite out of her ass. Hell,
Gator wouldn't mind taking a bite out of that ass
himself. She shook it around the compound often
enough.

The idea grabbed at his gut, sent hot streaks
straight to his groin. She was scared, half drowned.
A couple of fists to the jaw would knock the fight
out of her. He could bend her over the edge of the

truck bed, peel down her pants, have at her. He'd have to make sure she didn't tell anyone about it, though. Make sure the river got her, too, like it did McMann.

Almost salivating with eagerness, he swung through the window into the back of the truck. Water sloshed calf high, lapping over his boots and climbing his legs. His eyes glued to the figure clinging to the bent-over sapling with straining arms, he started for the rear of the truck. It wasn't until his boot toe clunked against iron that he remembered the tiedown rod . . . and the fact that McMann was the last person to touch it.

A sudden, visceral excitement leapt into his gut. Would the river water have washed off McMann's prints? Gator searched through a lifetime on the streets, trying to remember bits and pieces of police lore learned the hard way. He didn't think so. Hell, he knew so!

The rod was filmed with black grease. The damned thing had slipped right through Gator's gloves. Grease didn't mix with water, but it should make for nice, fat prints.

Satisfaction pricked into him sharp and fast, like the jab of a good needle. He shifted his narrow gaze to the Preston bitch.

"Burns!" Her thin, strident cry cut across the muddy water. "Did you raise anyone on the box?"

"Yeah," he lied. "The CE yard. They're sendin' help. May take some time, though."

"How much time?"

Longer n' you got, lady. "Didn't say."

She spit out a curse that raised a smile in Gator's heart. Setting her jaw, she tried to work her way up the sapling, hand over hand. The more she clawed and climbed, the more the young tree bent into the water. She gave it up, frustrated and still hanging chest high in swirling, muddy water.

"That trunk's gonna break," Gator shouted. "You'd better let go and swim over here while you still got some strength left."

He could spot the mistrust in her face even across the newly made lake. She'd seen him and McMann going at it, heard something, Gator didn't know what. He would, though. Before he finished with her, he'd know exactly what she'd heard. She'd sob it out, he promised himself with mounting excitement. She'd sob more than that out.

While she stewed and hung with straining arms from her tree, Gator slowly, cautiously shuffled his boot toe from side to side, feeling, searching. When his sole rolled onto the smooth round rod, his hands fisted inside the wet work gloves.

McMann's prints were on the tie-down rod, but not Gator's. Christ, it was like being handed the keys to the bank. Whatever he did, whatever he made Fayrene Preston suffer, he could lay squarely on the man who bashed her head in before he himself drowned.

And if McMann hadn't drowned, Gator thought with savage glee, he'd surely wish he had. Yessir, when Bolt and company got through avenging the brutal assault on one of their own, McMann would surely wish he had.

First, though, Gator had to lure the rabbit into the snare. Cupping his hands around his mouth, he shouted across the water.

"Better haul yourself up some, Warden. I just seen a cottonmouth swim by."

He could hardly hide his grin when she twisted

and thrashed at the end of her sapling like a hooked bass.

"Jesus! There's another one." He managed a credible display of repugnance. "The water's crawlin' with 'em! Get over here fast . . . if you can!"

CHAPTER FOURTEEN

"McMann! McMann, please! You have to ... help me. I can't ... I can't ..."

Carly's plea ended on a sob. Exhausted, too weak to move her arms or legs, she lay on her back and stared at the sullen sky. Water lapped at her calves. Something crawled across the back of her hand. She couldn't summon the strength to shake it off.

Eyelids encrusted with mud drifted down, shutting out the sky. The black clouds were gone. The storm that had spewed such destruction had passed. Blown east, Carly thought numbly, where it would rain down more havoc, more violence. More death.

No. Her sluggish brain registered the protest. Not death. McMann wasn't dead. She'd heard him groan a while ago, after she'd used the last of her strength to half drag, half swim him to the only island of high ground in this endless sea of river. It took almost all she had to break the mud's suction and open her eyes once more.

"McMann."

The hoarse croak got no response from the inert form beside her. Almost weeping with the effort, Carly slid an elbow deeper into squishy Alabama clay and levered up the top portion of her body.

Lungs still on fire from the long, terrifying ride down the river wheezed out a strangled gasp. Sweet Lord above! If she hadn't heard that groan, hadn't felt McMann's chest rise against hers when she'd collapsed on top of him a few moments ago, she'd swear the river had claimed him. Like Carly, he sprawled half in, half out of the turgid water. His black hair was plastered to his skull. Slime coated his face and neck and what remained of his shirt, scored to tattered strips by the pine that had almost drowned them both.

Just the thought of that spike-branched tree suffocated her with panic. If the trunk hadn't turned, if it hadn't lifted them both clear of the water for the precious seconds it took for Carly to rip McMann's windbreaker free of the jagged spear that had gone through it, they would have died, tangled together by her belt, in the dark, silt-filled waters. The terror of those moments rushed back. Carly whimpered, digging into the mud like a frantic crab to escape it.

It was the sound of her own mewling that shocked her to her senses. She blinked and waited for her galloping pulse to slow once more. She'd survived, she reminded herself with a gulp that scratched her raw throat. She'd pulled herself and McMann out of the water.

Almost out of the water. The river still lapped at them, still wanted them. Well, it wouldn't get them, she vowed fiercely. Not today.

Willing her brain to shoot some neurotransmitters to her aching arms and legs, she pushed out of the sucking mud and onto her knees. The effort started a buzzing in her ears. Watery earth and watery sky spun dizzily. Panting, she waited for the world to right itself.

When at last it did, she planted a hand on McMann's shoulder, another just under his ribcage. Grunting, she shoved at his bulk, let him rock back, shoved again, until she managed to roll him over.

Too weak to fight the force of her own momentum, Carly rolled with him. She hung across his middle, gasping, while seconds slipped by. Long moments passed before the insistent, slapping water forced her onto her hands and knees. She was gathering her strength for the next move when McMann gave a raspy cough.

She turned her head to find him staring at her with red-rimmed eyes.

"I . . . wondered . . . if that . . . was you."

She didn't bother to reply to the obvious. She couldn't. Her breath still needled painfully through her lungs just from the effort of turning him over.

He ran his tongue over caked lips, grimacing at the taste of mud, and tried again. "Are we . . . still tangled . . . together?"

"No." Using the butt of her hand against his stomach, Carly pushed back on her haunches. "I shed my . . . raincoat right after I got you . . . out of your windbreaker."

He thought about that for a long while. Too long for Carly, who felt the water oozing between her legs.

"We have to move," she got out wearily. "You have to help me. I can't . . . drag you. I had to float you this far. Me and the pine."

"The pine." A shudder started at McMann's shoulders and shook its way down his chest. "I thought it had us."

"It did."

Her throat was scraped too raw from the water

she'd coughed up to tell him that the same pine that had almost killed them had, in fact, saved them. She had no idea how long she'd clung to its rough-barked trunk, how long she'd kept her body wedged against McMann's so he wouldn't slide through the branches into the angry river. The tree and the raging current must have carried them a good five miles before the storm passed, the drumming rain ceased, and the river broadened into a lake where acres of rich farmland used to be.

The sight of that endless expanse of drowned earth had clutched at Carly's heart when she'd first seen it. The only signs that humans had once inhabited the area were a line of telephone poles in the distance, the tin roof of a submerged house, the upper half of a barn. They'd floated on, the current less savage but still relentless. She'd grown weaker, McMann more heavy. Panic had started to claw at her when she spotted the farmhouse perched atop a hill that rose out of the muddy sea. Using reserves of strength she didn't know she possessed, she'd kicked and thrashed and tried to propel the tree toward the tiny atoll, all the while shouting for help.

Her feeble cries hadn't raised any signs of life, much less of rescue. The pine wouldn't turn or angle closer. It had almost swept them past the island of safety when sheer desperation gave Carly the courage to abandon her hold on the trunk and drop into the water, dragging McMann with her. Finally she'd crawled onto oozing red mud and collapsed.

Now she needed to tap into the last of her reserves. Hands on her upper thighs, she pushed off her haunches.

"We need to get higher. Out of the water. Can you move?"

McMann lifted an experimental hand. The small effort put white brackets on either side of his mouth.

"I can move."

Carly could only guess what it cost him to roll over and stagger to his feet. She knew what it cost her. Exhaustion pulled at her like an anchor as she hooked an arm around his waist.

"I'll help you. You help me."

Together they stumbled up the steep incline toward the row of pecan trees that formed a windbreak around the house. From the way the stately trees reached almost to the eaves of the two-story dwelling, it was obvious they'd been there for decades.

So had the house. White paint peeled in strips from the trim on brick and stone facade. Even from halfway down the hill, Carly could see that the porch sagged a bit on its cinder-block supports and the screen door hung at a comfortable angle. Despite the evidence of age and hard use, however, the farmhouse represented a sanctuary that had her almost sobbing with anticipation.

There was a barn in the fields beyond the house, she saw as she wove an unsteady path beside McMann, a weathered structure that had also seen a few decades of use. The river had burst through its doors and flooded the lower regions, but she caught a flutter of movement through the open hatch of the loft.

McMann saw it, too. He halted abruptly and pulled free of her. Lifting his hands to cup his mouth, he shouted hoarsely across the water.

"Hey! In the barn! Is anyone there?"

The only response was a flurry of straw from the upper story. Thin stalks drifted down to float on the water. McMann chewed on the inside of his cheek, staring at the puddle of straw.

"Chickens?"

"Or barn cats," Carly answered.

His little grunt spoke volumes. Not a cat lover, apparently.

He slid an arm around her waist again, and the welcome support made her realize that he'd regained far more of his strength than she had. Her legs would hardly hold her. Her lungs still wheezed with each step. She'd lost one of her shoes as well as her raincoat to the river.

The first time her heel came down on a sharp rock, Carly winced. The second time, McMann bent and lifted her into his arms. She didn't protest. She'd gone beyond caring how she reached shelter, as long as she reached it.

She couldn't even hold her head up. She sagged against McMann's shoulder, letting her body absorb the heat and movement of his. What remained of his tattered shirt and windbreaker cushioned her cheek. The river's stench clung to him as it did to her. The wet, rusty smell grew more potent in the crook of his neck, where his skin had warmed with the effort of walking up the hill, but Carly had breathed and swallowed too much of it now to care. Her lids swept down again as exhaustion claimed her.

She didn't open them until the wooden steps leading to the front porch squeaked under their weight. When McMann set her down on the white-painted porch, the toes that stuck through Carly's shredded hose curled against the smooth-planed wood.

Propping her against one of the roof supports as he would a rag doll, McMann pulled open the screen and hammered on the front door. His forceful thuds echoed emptily inside the house. He pounded again, then again for good measure, before rattling the doorknob. He gave up after a few tries.

"Looks like they were smart enough to get out before the river jumped its banks."

"Either that, or they were evacuated," Carly said, scraping back her tangled hair. "I heard on the news last night—I think it was last night—that county co-ordinators were evacuating some of the farms south of the city. Just in case."

"Good planning on someone's part," McMann muttered as he worked his way along the porch, testing the windows. Their sturdy bolts held.

"Stay put. I'll try the back door."

Carly couldn't have moved if she'd wanted to. Still, his brusque assumption of command put a crease between her eyes. She stirred a little, not enough to surrender the support at her back, then sank against it again.

It was some moments before she could process thoughts and memories through her bone-deep fatigue. For the first time since the river sucked them into its maw, she thought back to the scene she and Fay Preston had stumbled onto. Slowly, the images resurfaced. Bit by bit, the pieces clicked into place. She could hear the inmate, Burns, screaming accusations, see once more the fury in McMann's expression as he leaned over, fist raised to smash his accuser's face.

Her sense of victory at having cheated the river died. Twisting her head from one side to the other, Carly swept another look over the bleak vista that stretched in every direction. Nothing moved except the water. No boats chugged across the horizon. No helicopters circled overhead. Unless McMann's pounding on the back door raised a response, she was alone with a man Gator Burns had identified as Elaine Dawson-Smith's killer.

And Billy Hopewell's.

A chill crawled down Carly's skin. Oh, God! Was it true? Had Billy fallen victim to a killer?

Setting her teeth, she forced herself to examine the possibility that the handsome young inmate ended up under that mower by design, not accident. Her lawyer's mind sorted through the facts. Hopewell's death was ruled an accident, but there had been no witnesses. The mower rolled over him sometime on Friday afternoon, after Carly had stumbled into him in the woods. The same afternoon, she recalled with a sudden closing of her throat, that she'd taken McMann to a barbecue stand to grill him about Billy . . . and a person named Joy.

No!

The denial ripped from deep inside her, erupting from instincts that disregarded facts and possibilities.

No!

He didn't kill Billy. Ryan McMann was capable of violence. Carly acknowledged that. His chosen profession proved it beyond any doubt, for heaven's sake, as did the brutal beating she'd seen him administering to Burns such a short time ago. But the man who'd stood alone in a southside cemetery, his face closed and stark, couldn't have engineered Billy Hopewell's death. He couldn't have!

The sudden rattle of the front door made Carly jump. Her head swung around, her gaze colliding with McMann's as he unhooked the screen door.

"There's no one here. I got in through a back window. Guess I'll have to add breaking and entering to my list of crimes."

She couldn't speak through her tightly-closed throat. He caught her silence, his eyes narrowing as he weighed it and her rigid stance. His shoulders shifted, squared.

Ryan needed only one look at Carly's face to guess why limbs that had shaken like Jell-O only moments ago were now stiff as boards. She'd had time to think during his short absence, to remember the accusations Burns had screamed, to regret the fact that she'd pulled a murderer out of the river. Now she was alone with the killer she'd saved.

Weariness and a sense of defeat ate into his soul. He wouldn't defend himself to anyone, including Carly.

Especially Carly.

"The electricity's out," he told her, holding her eyes with his. "I checked. So is the phone."

The look on her face nearly destroyed him. He didn't blame her. He couldn't. Yet his heart felt weighted with lead as he pushed the screen door wider and held it open for her.

She didn't move, except to wrap her arms around her waist. Ryan swallowed the bitter dregs of pride and offered her the only assurance he could.

"I don't know how you managed it, but you got that tree branch out of my jacket collar and dragged us both out of the river. I owe you, Major, and I always pay my debts. You're safe here."

"Am I?"

"As long as the river doesn't rise any higher," he answered quietly.

Under her wrapped arms, Carly's fists clenched. He knew what she was thinking. He had to know. Yet he didn't even attempt to deny Burns's accusations.

How like him, she thought on a whip of anger. He

convicted himself of one crime and refused to file an
appeal that any first-year law student could see
would result in a reversal. Now he refused to defend
himself against charges of another, far more heinous
crime.

Well, she wasn't a first-year law student. Nor, she
decided with a tight set to her jaw, was she going to
gain anything by huddling out here on the porch.
Whatever was going to happen between her and
McMann might just as well play out inside the house.

She pulled a long breath in through nostrils still
clogged with river silt and slowly, carefully, un-
clenched her fists. Pushing herself away from the
porch support, she ordered her wobbly legs to carry
her past McMann and into the house.

Stale, unused air greeted her, along with the odor
of mildew from the rains that had plagued the area
all spring. Beneath those scents, though, she picked
up a hint of furniture polish and carpet cleaner and
old cooking . . . all the hidden layers that turned a
house into a home.

The farmhouse was laid out like so many others in
the fertile lowlands fed by the Alabama. A hall pa-
pered in faded pink roses bisected the downstairs
rooms and ended in the eat-in kitchen. Narrow, functional stairs led to the upstairs bedrooms. Carly gave
the front rooms only a cursory glance as she passed.
The one on the left was what her grandmother
always referred to as the parlor, stiff with formal
furnishings and used only on Sundays when the
preacher came to call.

The room on the right was obviously where
the family gathered. A green and yellow plaid
couch sagged against one wall. Two recliners sat
side by side, facing a large-screened TV. Magazines

overflowed the cherrywood rack between the recliners . . . *National Geographic*s and *Readers' Digest*s
and old issues of *People*. Bookshelves crowded with
family clutter flanked the brick fireplace.

Add a scarred, rolltop desk, another wall of bookshelves, and bound copies of the Alabama statutes,
and Carly might have thought she was a little girl
again, waiting with childish impatience for the
sound of the Judge's heavy tread on the porch and
the outrageous stories he would tell her of his days
on the circuit.

Those weren't the Judge's footfalls behind her,
however. They belonged to a man who not long ago
had stood on the opposite side of the bench, at the
defendant's table. A man who might stand there yet
again.

Her chin angled, Carly strode past him into the
kitchen. Having lived with the ever-present threat of
hurricanes blowing up from the Gulf for most of her
life, she didn't even blink at the dozen or so plastic
milk jugs filled with water that crowded the counter-
tops and white-painted pine table. The owners had
prepared for the worst, including the loss of electricity and water. Then the worst got worse and
forced their evacuation. Still, there was always a
chance their water pump operated on a small, self-
contained generator, like the one the Judge had installed after Hurricane Hugo had taken down power
lines out at the farm for more than a week.

Heading straight for the double-basined sink set under the window looking toward the half-submerged
barn, Carly twisted the tap. Water gushed out. Clear,
unmuddied water.

"Thank God! The river hasn't contaminated the
well yet."

With greedy hands, she splashed her face. her throat, her straggling hair. Red silt ran like rust into the sink. Blindly, she groped for the paper towels hanging just below the window. She felt almost human again when she turned and leaned her hips against the counter.

McMann watched her from across the round pine table, his eyes still rimmed with red, his manner still closed and careful. In the weak light slanting through the kitchen windows, he looked even worse than he had before she scrubbed the mud from her eyes. His shirt hung in tatters. His hair had dried in matted clumps. A long tear in his jeans bared his right leg from thigh to calf.

She didn't have to glance down at her uniform shirt and slacks to know she didn't look much better. They both wore the trappings of a creature who'd crawled out of a swamp. At the moment, however, her appearance constituted the least of her concerns. The quiet thundered between her and McMann for long seconds before he broke it.

"What do we do now?"

She gripped the counter behind her. "I'm thinking."

"One?" he asked softly.

"One?"

"You always think in threes. What's number one on your list of possibilities?"

A flush warmed her just-washed face. How had he come to know her so well?

"One, I'm going upstairs to clean off. If the sink works, the shower should, too."

"Two?"

"I'm going to raid the owner's closet."

"And three?"

"Three, I intend to wait right here while you complete steps one and two." She dug her ragged nails into the counter and went with the gut-deep instincts that were rapidly cementing into certainty. "Then I'm going to listen while you tell me why Billy Hopewell shot Elaine Dawson-Smith."

CHAPTER FIFTEEN

Carly left McMann rooted in silent shock. She half expected him to put out an arm to bar her way and demand an explanation before her still wobbly legs carried her through the kitchen door. Thankfully, he did neither.

She couldn't have given him an explanation at that moment, couldn't have summoned either the strength or the coherency to explain what was basically a matter of instinct. McMann didn't kill Billy Hopewell. She believed that with every fiber of her being. Nor was there any evidence to indicate he'd killed Elaine Dawson-Smith. But he knew who did, or maybe he just suspected.

In any case, he'd protected someone with his silence, and it didn't take an F. Lee Bailey to deduce that someone *wasn't* Gator Burns. The hate flaming between the two men had torched the air around them. No, McMann wouldn't keep silent to protect Gator. Nor would he have any reason to shield Michael Smith. He didn't even know the officer accused of killing his wife.

Which left the troubled youth McMann had tutored . . . and subsequently buried. By a process of elimination, Carly could only conclude he'd been protecting Billy Hopewell. Whether McMann would confirm or deny that, though, was a matter she intended to take up *after* she sluiced away the rest of the river mud.

The wooden stairs groaned under her weight, as though they'd borne a few too many climbers in their years of use. Grayish light slanted through the windows at the west end of the upstairs hall. With a start, Carly realized it was still just the middle of the afternoon. She felt as though she'd been in the river for half a lifetime.

Aching with weariness, she limped one-shoed down the hall, glancing through the open doors as she passed. The three bedrooms and small, functional bath all showed signs of recent occupation and hasty departure. Closets stood open. There were empty spots on dressers where precious pictures and possessions had been snatched up.

Two rooms obviously belonged to kids. Michael Jordan posters and a whole shelf of basketball trophies decorated one; the second was crowded with a frilly-skirted dressing table, teddy bears, and young girl's clothing scattered in colorful heaps on every horizontal surface.

The third was the master bedroom. Carly didn't waste time looking around, but headed straight for the closet. If the river continued to rise, it could contaminate the well at any minute or flood the pump's backup generator. With silent apologies to the owners for invading their privacy, she grabbed a man's work shirt and a pair of woman's shorts. The shorts could have circled her twice around, but the drawstring waist would keep them from sliding off her hips. Feeling like a thief, she rifled through the dresser drawers for equally large but clean underwear.

A few scrubs with a wash rag, one smear of shampoo worked into her scalp, a quick rinse, and she was done. Grimacing at the multitude of scrapes and bruises that mottled her arms and legs, she toweled off and let the blue work shirt swallow her whole.

Like the shirt, the undies and shorts were far too big for her, but the clean, soft cotton felt wonderful against her skin. Letting the shirt tails dangle over the shorts, she rinsed out her dirty clothes, then searched the medicine cabinet above the sink for antiseptic cream. She'd doctor herself downstairs, she decided, while McMann took his turn in the bathroom.

When she returned to the kitchen, she saw that he'd recovered enough from her parting bombshell to do some salvaging while she bathed. A flashlight and several boxes of candles had joined the milk jugs on the table. The cupboard doors stood open, as if for a visual inventory. The array of canned goods that stocked the shelves told Carly they certainly wouldn't starve.

"The bathroom's yours," she said with a briskness that barely skimmed the surface of her exhaustion. "Make it quick, then you'd better fill the tub with water, too, in case the pump goes down."

She brushed past him to dump her wet clothes in the sink. She'd hang them outside later. When she had the energy to lift her arms.

She might have known McMann would ignore her brisk instruction. A small sigh escaped her as he closed the distance between them. She could have used a little more time to regroup before he confronted her.

To Carly's surprise, he shoved a glass at her. "Here, drink this."

She took a cautious sniff of the syrupy-sweet odor. "Peach brandy?"

"I couldn't find anything stronger."

"You're in the heart of the Bible belt, remember?" She tried to hand him back the glass. "I'll pass. I can't take this stuff on an empty stomach, or any other time for that matter."

"You're white as a sheet without your layers of mud. Drink it."

"McMann . . ."

"One, you drink. Two, I clean up. Three, we talk."

Her eyes narrowed. Was he mocking her? Did she really count off like that?

"I don't like peach brandy," she said with a snap to her voice that wasn't there before.

"Drink it, Carly, or we don't talk. That's the deal."

She gave in to the quiet ultimatum with a distinct lack of grace. "It's too late for deals, but I'll drink the damned stuff if it makes you feel better."

After the first, eye-watering punch, the potent concoction licked at her belly with a heat that spread with astonishing speed to assorted portions of her anatomy.

Carly sipped cautiously while McMann showered. She was beginning to feel the brandy's effect when he came back downstairs a short time later. Warmth suffused her limbs and added to the mugginess that came with the lack of electricity and any means of stirring the air inside the house. Carly had opened the downstairs windows in hopes of catching a breeze while she spread antiseptic ointment on her various scratches.

When McMann appeared in the doorway, cream squirted through her fingers and squiggled down her leg. Amazing what a little unmuddied water and a comb could do. He looked almost human again, with his black hair slicked back and his face scrubbed clean. She wished he'd put on the shirt he carried in one hand, though, and lessen the impact of that muscled chest, wide and hard-ridged and lightly dusted with dark hair that tapered to a V just above the waistband of his appropriated jeans. Like Carly's borrowed shorts, the jeans skimmed dangerously low on his hips.

Annoyed, she realized she was staring at the flat belly revealed by that sagging waistband. She scooped the squiggle of antiseptic onto a fingertip and offered a cool suggestion.

"You had better spread some of this on your scratches."

"I will, when they stop oozing." At her quick frown, he shrugged. "The shower opened up some of the cuts on my back."

"Let me see."

He tossed the shirt on the table and reached for the chair opposite hers. "They'll heal."

"Let me see." Cream in hand, Carly rounded the table. "Lean forward, McMann, and I'll ... Good Lord!"

Horrified, she stared at the raw, vicious welt that traced diagonally from the right side of his neck across his spine and lost itself in his left ribs. A sluggish liquid too thin for pus and too clear for blood weeped from the wound in several spots. Swallowing, she probed the worst spot with a cautious fingertip.

"This looks like it might need stitching."

"Just put some antiseptic on it."

"It's going to leave a scar."

"One more isn't going to matter."

"No," she murmured, "I guess not."

Her gaze moved from the angry welt to the older, more faded battle marks imprinted on his tanned flesh. A jagged white line showed just above one rib. A longer, neater one followed the curve of his right scapula. The same tracery showed just above one elbow. He'd been cut and stitched more times than a quilt.

"Did you collect all these scars playing hockey?"

"Most of them. You get slammed into the boards often enough, you break a few bones."

"Wonderful sport," she muttered.

"Yeah."

The clipped response shut the door of that subject in Carly's face, but not before she'd caught a glimpse of the emptiness behind it.

He missed the brutal game. Just as he missed the cold, the ice that coated the lake behind his house, the bursts of fall color he'd described to her that night at her place. Hockey was his life, or it had been before he confessed to the crime that brought him to Alabama . . . where he might stand accused of yet another crime if he couldn't refute Gator Burns's allegations. Carefully, she daubed ointment along the raw welt.

"Tell me about Billy Hopewell and Elaine Dawson-Smith."

She felt him flinch under her fingertips.

"Burns said you killed them. Both the assistant warden and I heard his allegations, as I assume we were intended to. You'll have to answer her when we get back. You might as well answer me now."

Back stiff, face away from her, he didn't answer. Her fingers glided over his skin, soothing, insisting.

"Tell me about the Afternoon Club. Tell me how Billy got in, and why he had to kill to get out."

Still he didn't answer. Dammit, didn't he realize how much was at stake here?

"Were you part of it?" she probed insistently. "Did you . . . ?"

He moved then, jerking away from her hand, surging to his feet. He turned, his blue eyes glacial.

"Did I screw those women for money? Or just for the hell of it? Is that what you want to know?"

"I want to know everything, McMann."

He hissed, moving forward just enough to crowd her against the table.

"Every twisted detail, Carly? Every mewl, every grunt? How many times I made them come? How much they paid for each orgasm? Is that what you want?"

She lifted her chin. "If those details will explain Elaine Dawson-Smith's death, yes."

"And what if I tell you that I never provided any of those women stud service?"

"Did you?"

The answer dragged out of him, low, rough, ripped from the core he kept so private, so shielded.

"No."

The woman in her wanted to sag in boneless relief. The lawyer remained cool and relentless.

"Then we're back to the same question I asked a few moments ago. How did Billy get in so deep with you watching out for him the way you did, and why did he have to kill to get out?"

The anger, the scorn in his face died, drowned by an agonizing guilt.

"I didn't watch out for him."

He turned away from her, reached for the shirt he'd tossed on the table. His moves were jerky, lacking his usual coordinated grace. Shoving his arms into the faded blue denim, he moved away. The window over the sink drew him, or maybe it was the bleak watery landscape outside. Bracing his hands wide on the Formica counter, he stared through the curtained panes.

"I knew the kid was in trouble. He wanted to tell me, tried to tell me, but I didn't have the skill to draw it out of him. Every time I got close, every time I thought he'd open up, he'd get to thinking about what his momma would have said and retreat into misery. That was before I started hearing rumors. About inmates and some local women."

She thought of a dozen questions. Why didn't he try to get professional help for Billy? Why didn't he take his worries over the kid to someone in authority? Why did he keep these rumors to himself?

The answer stared her in the face. McMann didn't trust the system that had imprisoned both him and Billy to help either of them.

"I shrugged off the rumors at first," he said slowly. "The whole time I was in, someone was always whispering in his bunk about the hot piece of snatch they'd spotted somewhere on base that day, fantasizing about ways to get into her pants. Even after I got out, I'd hear about them when I came back twice a week. The honey-pot wives playing golf in tiny little skirts or riding their horses in skintight jeans; the secretaries out sneaking a cigarette break and flashing some thigh as they crossed their legs; the female officers jogging along River Road in skimpy little shorts and sweat-slicked T-shirts."

The images made Carly angry, bringing with them as they did the unspoken implication that every woman should shroud herself from view, but she tried to be fair. "I suppose it's only natural for men denied regular contact with women to fantasize about them."

"You think so?" He turned then, knifing her with a glance. "I saw you once, when I was driving out to the prison. You were crossing Chennault Circle,

walking over to one of the academic buildings. The
sun set your hair aflame."

His gaze skimmed down her bare legs. When he
brought it back to her face, Carly's heart bumped.

"Your hair wasn't all that was on fire that day. I
started to burn, too. You were wearing black high
heels. I remember wondering how the hell you could
balance yourself on those thin spikes . . . and how
those incredible legs would feel wrapped around
me. I'm still burning, Carly."

Air clogged her lungs. She couldn't breathe,
couldn't squash the thrill that centered in her belly,
any more than she could tell Ryan McMann that he'd
ignited a few late night fires in her blood, too. This
wasn't the time or the place for such admissions.

Ruthlessly, she shoved aside the thought that they
might not ever have another time or another place. It
cost her, but she managed to keep her voice cool and
impersonal.

"When did these vague fantasies, these general rumors, start to take on substance?"

Jesus! Ryan swung away again, ripped in half
by stinging anger and grudging admiration, and
damned if he was going to let her see either. He'd just
admitted that she turned him inside out, and she sat
there cool and composed and lawyerly right down to
her toenails.

Not for the first time, the savage need to shatter
that composure gripped him. He wanted to snatch
her out of her chair, cover her mouth with his, de-
vour her whole. The urge left him shaking. The vow
he'd given not to touch her again, not to hurt her, left
him aching.

"About three months ago," he ground out.

He forced his mind from Carly and what she did to
him, took it back to that January day. Chill had

nipped at the air. An early darkness had draped around him like a cloak when he stepped outside the education center to find Gator waiting for him. He'd walked right past Burns, ignoring the inmate's presence, ignoring, too, the salacious, audacious proposition Burns put to him as they cut across the compound through the deepening dusk.

There was this little club, Gator had sniggered, this handful of rich bitches who got their secret thrill by having sex with inmates. They'd heard about McMann. They wanted him to join their afternoon fun. They'd pay big bucks to climb onto his superstar cock. These weren't no trulls, Burns had assured him. No twenty-dollars-a-trick street whores. They was clean, clean and hot. McMann could take his pick, and Gator would expect only a small cut for setting it up.

"When did you begin to suspect that Billy Hopewell was being forced to . . . entertain the members of the club?"

"I don't think he was forced," Ryan said slowly, his vision locked on the gray lake surrounding their hilltop sanctuary. "I think he probably enjoyed it at first. He had the mind of a child, but he was a man, with a man's body and a man's needs. He would've been scared, would have had to be coaxed the first time or two, but that hot spill of pleasure would have seduced him, just as it would most men."

"But not you."

It wasn't a question, just a soft echo of his previous denial.

"Joy said Billy sobbed in her arms," Carly continued after a moment. "What changed him? What made him realize that having sex with those women was wrong?"

A vile taste filled Ryan's throat. He swallowed the gall and pushed around to face his inquisitor.

"I did."

To her credit, Carly didn't blink.

"Isn't that rich?" he asked on a snarl of laughter. "Me, giving advice to the lovelorn. I don't even know what I said to the kid, exactly. I've tried to think back. God knows, I've tried. All I can remember is that he was reading one of his books, a second grade picture book, and something, some picture or word, triggered a thought. He asked me about girls, or that's what I thought he asked. He was stammering so badly that day I could barely understand him."

His mouth twisted with disgust.

"I think I fed him some crap about learning from my mistakes. I know I warned him to be careful who he had sex with, said he should know his partner and be gentle with her. Like a damned fool, I even suggested that his momma would want him to wait for the right woman to love."

He read neither pity nor condemnation in her face. Only that cool, detached calm. God, he hated it. Hated her at that moment. He folded his arms to hide the fact that his hands had balled into fists.

"Billy seemed to retreat inside himself after that. I couldn't get two coherent words out of him, couldn't even get him to look at me half the time. Once, I saw fingernail scratches on his neck, the kind a woman makes when she wants to mark a man. When I asked him about them, he cried."

Across the quiet of the kitchen, Carly watched him. Just watched him. He let out the air that was hurting his lungs.

"Then Elaine Dawson-Smith was shot, and I stopped trying to get Billy to talk at all."

"Why did he kill her? Why didn't he just walk away?"

"She wouldn't let him," Ryan shot back savagely.

"How do you know?"

"I pounded the truth out of Gator this afternoon, before you showed up on the scene and he started singing a different tune. He told me your colonel refused to let a big, dumb inmate balk at playing the games she'd taught him. She insisted that Billy continue to meet her in the woods, seemed to delight in proving that she could make his body do what his confused mind had decided was wrong."

"God, that sounds like her."

From the quick, irritated way Carly clamped her mouth shut, Ryan gathered she hadn't intended to let that comment slip out.

"Yeah, just like her, if half of what Gator said is true. She'd taunt Billy, threaten to say he raped her. She'd even dig the barrel of the gun she carried in her purse under his chin and warn him she could make it look like self-defense if she put a bullet through his brain."

Carly tried to imagine how Billy could perform to Elaine's satisfaction with a gun under his chin. The woman must have followed her threats with an erotic stimulation that would raise the sap in a tree stump.

"She played her sadistic games with the kid once too often," McMann continued grimly. "He snapped, wrestled the gun away. I don't know if he meant to kill her. We'll never know. At the sound of the shot, Gator came running. He wiped the prints off the gun and hustled Billy away."

"Then he had to find a way to keep Billy from confessing and blowing the lid off his moneymaking schemes," Carly said slowly.

"You're quicker than I am, Counselor." Bitterness clawed at Ryan's gut. "I suspected Billy might have been involved in the colonel's death, but I didn't question the accident that killed him. Not until today, when one of the guards let drop that Gator had bribed him to put Billy on the same crew the day he went under the mower."

The silence in the kitchen deafened him. Ryan felt the weight of his own culpability in Billy's death crushing down on him. If he hadn't kept silent, would the kid be alive today? Carly's relentless questioning only added to his inner torment.

"Why didn't you tell the agents investigating Elaine Dawson-Smith's murder your suspicions?"

"I answered every question the cops asked me."

"Don't give me that bullshit, McMann. You knew about the Afternoon Club, but you kept quiet about it. You suspected that your friend was involved in it, that he might have killed Elaine Dawson-Smith, yet you let her husband take the rap for her murder."

His eyes went hard and flat. "You charged him, Carly. You, and the system you represent. Not me."

Incensed, she sprang out of the chair. "Based on evidence you provided. Unless you lied about seeing Smith's car on River Road."

"I didn't lie. He was there. For all I knew at the time, he could have killed his wife."

"He could have, but you suspected differently, didn't you, McMann? Didn't you?"

His stony silence made her see red.

"How far would you have let it go?" She strode up to him, the air around her vibrating with the fury that the river had temporarily washed away. "If Billy hadn't died, would you have let the system you despise so much crucify Michael Smith?"

"Come off it, Counselor. You and I both know that

it's doubtful Smith's case would ever have come to trial. If it had, he would have walked. It was his word against that of a convicted felon."

"Is that right? What if I tell you that the prosecutor would have suppressed your conviction under the rules of evidence?"

"Yeah, sure. Just like the judge in my trial suppressed the past sexual activities of the girl I took up to that hotel room. It doesn't matter what the rules say, Carly. Lawyers can find a way around them."

"I can't speak to the incompetency of the judge who presided over your trial, nor to the ethics of your defense team," she said icily. "I *can* tell you that if you'd completed your rehabilitation, the military justice system wouldn't allow evidence of your prior conviction."

A frown slashed across his forehead. "The jury wouldn't have needed evidence," he argued after a moment. "In most people's minds, my name brings an instant image of sordid sex and a young girl's death."

"You flatter yourself, McMann. Not everyone knows either your name or your past. *I* never heard of you until I started this investigation. Think about that the next time you decide to hold to your own code of silence and play God with another man's life!"

Scooping the sodden bundle of clothes out of the sink, she strode past him to the back door. The screen banged shut behind her.

CHAPTER SIXTEEN

Hammered by Carly's parting shot and his own bitter regrets, Ryan was driven by a savage urge to do something, anything. He needed occupation. He needed to keep busy while he regained a measure of control over himself and the jagged guilt that ripped through him whenever he thought of Billy's needless death.

He made his first order of business a search of the detached garage, where he collected everything that might come in useful, including a gallon of dark green paint and a brush. Leaving the paint on the back stoop, he went upstairs to appropriate a sheet from the girl's room. Stunned by the mounds of garments apparently necessary to clothe one young girl, he dragged a daisy-trimmed sheet off the bed.

It took only a few strokes to outline a giant S O S on the flat fabric, a few more to fill the letters in. The last rays of a hot, traitorous sun burned his back as Ryan climbed out onto the eaves. With the sureness he'd gained from his months of wielding a staple gun, he crawled up the steep roof to nail the distress flag in place.

That done, he sat back on his heels and took a 360-degree inspection. His stomach ratcheted tighter with each quarter turn. Jesus! They might be sitting in the middle of a lake or a vast, flooded reservoir. Patches of green showed here and there, but for the most part there was only water, endless water.

Turning his back on the low-hanging sun, Ryan squinted to the east, searching for the city's skyline, for the red-checkered water tower that marked Maxwell, for anything that might give him an idea of how far they'd come downriver. He couldn't find any familiar landmarks.

The sun was an orange-red ball afloat on a lake of gold by the time he crawled off the roof. He didn't need the visual reminder of the time. His rumbling stomach had already made itself heard.

Not knowing how long the electricity had been off, he wouldn't trust the contents of the refrigerator. Nor could he trust himself to talk to Carly without a return of the anger that had seared them both earlier. Stiff and silent, they shared a dinner of canned chickpeas, canned asparagus, and canned tuna. Dusk was falling when Carly shoved back from the kitchen table. She still wore the marks of her fight with the river on her body. Bone-deep exhaustion ringed her eyes and gave her face a grayish cast. The scrapes on her arms showed raw against her creamy skin.

"I'm going upstairs to get some rest. I'll take the boy's room."

"Fine."

"Do we need to take turns mounting a watch, in case the rescue choppers or boats come looking for us?"

"If they come looking, I'll hear them."

"Are you sure?"

"I'm sure. Get some sleep."

She left with a curt nod. Ryan let her go.

He wasn't ready to admit she was right, that he shouldn't have tried to protect Billy with his silence.

The truth he'd pummeled out of Gator this afternoon was still too raw. Pushing away from the table, he decided to make another sweep through the house for items to add to their store of emergency supplies.

His earlier search of the garage had turned up a coil of rope, rubber hip boots, a small hand ax, and a box of traffic flares in addition to the paint. Now he took time to go through cupboards that he'd only skimmed through the first time around. From the kitchen cabinets he extracted more salves, liniment, and a snake-bite kit. A shelf in the living room yielded a high-powered boom box, but no batteries to operate it. Ryan took the radio to the kitchen on the off chance that the batteries from the flashlight he'd discovered earlier would fit.

They didn't. Rolling the two D-cells back and forth on his palm, he frowned at the silent radio. He'd take a look at that little auxiliary generator that powered the water pump tomorrow. Maybe he could hook it up to the boom box instead.

He didn't like being cut off like this, didn't like not knowing the forecast or the situation upriver or how long they'd have to wait until the waters subsided enough to walk out of here or help arrived. If the assistant warden had survived the wall of water that crashed down on her, she would have started the search by now. If not . . .

Ryan's fist closed over the batteries. Gator sure as hell wouldn't want them rescued. He'd probably climbed into the back of that ton-and-a-half praying the river would swallow McMann whole. That way he could pin the Afternoon Club on a dead man. Elaine Dawson-Smith's murder and Billy's "accident," too.

A shudder passed through Ryan when he thought of what would await him when he got back. The accusations. The denials. The inescapable fact that he'd withheld all knowledge of the happenings in the woods. That alone could bust his parole, put him back under Bolt's control.

Christ! He'd been so close, so damned close, to shaking Alabama's red clay off his boots and hitting the road to nowhere.

With a savage oath, Ryan shoved the batteries back into the flashlight. Cupboard doors slammed as he searched through them again, one by one, until he found the bottle he was looking for. Peach brandy. Not exactly his drink of choice, but at this moment he didn't care what kind of coating the kick wore.

A small, muzzy sound dragged Carly from sleep. Groggy and disoriented, she blinked at the wall-sized poster of Michael Jordan. The basketball star's ten-megawatt smile flashed down at her through the moonlight streaming in the open window.

She lay still for long moments, awash in boneless lethargy, contemplating that smile. A small corner of her mind listened for a repeat of the sound. The larger, more sensible portion pushed her back toward sleep. She'd almost drifted off again when she heard it again, a thin, distant cry.

A bird? An animal trapped by the rising water? Unbidden, the hairy muzzle and yellowed eyes of her grandfather's mule flashed into her mind. Carly couldn't bring herself to hope the animal had been swept away, but it certainly wouldn't break her heart if the river took some of the pure, cussed meanness out of her.

Which led her to wonder how far and how fast the flood had spread, and to worry about the young couple working the Judge's farm. Were they safe? Had they moved the horses to high ground? Would they think to cart the family albums and the Judge's law books upstairs?

And what was happening with her family? The river had broken through its banks west of the city, bypassing the heavily populated areas. Still, Carly couldn't help worrying about her mother and the Judge, about Dave and Allie and the kids. Only now, with her body slowly regaining its strength and her mind working free of its exhaustion, did she realize how worried they must be about her, too. The last sight anyone had of her was just before the river claimed both her and Ryan.

Thoroughly awake now, Carly tried to think of some way to let her family and officials at the base know she and McMann were safe. Unless some carrier pigeons came home to roost, she didn't see how she could communicate with anyone outside their water-shrouded world.

Rolling over, she punched the pillow. She wished she knew how far downriver they'd come. Would the searchers look this far, miles from the base? Would anyone? The area below the dam had already been evacuated, but patrols would still run checks for stranded livestock or trapped motorists. Surely someone would see their SOS.

She was still trying to reassure herself when the cry came again, small and sad, like the wind whispering through winter branches. Sighing, she pushed off the bed. She had to see what it was.

Her bedroom looked over the pecans and hackberry trees shading the front of the house. The sound, Carly discovered after a few moments of listening at the screen, came from the back. Tugging on her borrowed shorts under the rumpled shirt she'd slept in, she made for the hall.

Following the breeze to the open window, Carly

swallowed a gasp at the moonlit vista spread out below. Beyond the windbreak, the all-encompassing river eddied around their hilltop sanctuary, white gold and shimmering in the moonlight. The farmhouse and its yard seemed to float on an endless sea.

The scene held a wild sort of peace, a beauty all its own. Carly might have been seduced by the rippling water if not for the debris that dotted its surface. An uprooted tree floated by in the distance. Closer in, the main current carried several old tires on its swift moving back . . . and carried as well the sound of that tiny, mewling cry.

Kittens.

Her eyes went to the barn, half submerged in the sea of liquid gold. The loft doors where Carly and Ryan had spotted movement in the straw earlier this afternoon yawned wide and dark. The water lapped just below the open loft.

Hopefully, the owners had moved their livestock as well as themselves to safety. They'd probably tried to round up the barn cats, too, but Carly knew a nursing momma would have hidden herself and her kittens in an out-of-sight corner. Well, they were safe and dry . . . for now.

She'd started to turn away when a shift of shadows in the backyard caught her eye. It took a moment to separate the solitary figure from the darker patches thrown by the pecans crowding the house. He was sitting on a stump near the water's edge, one ankle hooked over a knee, staring across at the barn as Carly herself had done.

She leaned a shoulder against the window frame, absorbing the play of light and dark as the breeze rustled through the pecans. Absorbing McMann's still, silent grace. Seconds slipped by, then minutes.

Carly chewed a tender spot on her bottom lip.

Common sense told her to go back to the narrow twin bed and leave him to his solitary vigil. She still hadn't forgiven him for withholding vital evidence, or for choosing to protect Billy Hopewell at the expense of Lieutenant Colonel Michael Smith.

Although . . .

Here in the moonlit silence, she could understand Ryan's choice. Billy was already a victim twice over, once of the judicial system that should have recognized his limitations, then of Elaine Dawson-Smith. He wouldn't have stood a chance if charged with her death.

Unlike Michael Smith, whose testimony would have been weighed against that of an ex-con.

Sighing, Carly shoved a hand through her tangled hair. She could understand Ryan's choice, but she couldn't accept it. She'd tell him that much, at least.

Hoping to avoid any close encounters with critters that might have crawled or slithered out of the waters onto their small island, Carly slid her bare feet into the high topped rubber boots McMann had brought to the kitchen. The boots thumped across the linoleum, then squished on the damp grass of the backyard.

He swiveled slowly at her approach. His shirt hung open, the tails trailing his hips. With the moonlight water shimmering behind him, his face was in shadow. She couldn't tell if he welcomed the intrusion or resented it.

"I heard the kittens mewling," she said. "They woke me."

He regarded her for long moments, his eyes hooded and midnight dark.

"I didn't think anything would wake you," he said at last, his voice tipped with a mocking sting that told Carly he'd recovered from his bout with the river . . . or the bout with his conscience. "When I checked, you were sleeping the sleep of the pure and righteous."

The idea that he'd looked in on her while she was sunk into oblivion disturbed Carly a whole lot more than his sarcasm. She could only hope her big shirt had covered her borrowed panties, which had a tendency to slide off her butt.

"There's something to be said for pure and righteous, McMann. You should try them sometime."

He gave a little snort. "I'm way past pure, sweetheart. Oh. Sorry. I forgot. I'm not supposed to call you that."

He rolled the last few words just enough to make Carly suspicious. She stepped closer, sniffing. Sure enough, the sticky sweet odor of peach brandy hung on the air around him. She skimmed a quick glance around the stump and spotted the dull glint of moonlight on glass.

"Good Lord, did you drink the whole bottle?"

"I made a damned good try at it."

"Without puking it all up?"

He snorted again. "That's still a distinct possibility."

She shook her head, torn between amusement and sympathy. She could still remember the time her brother had snitched a bottle of home-brewed sheepshower wine, a gift to the Judge from a neighbor. Of course, Dave had dared her to taste it. Of course, she'd had to do more than taste. She'd thrown up for two days after downing most of the potent, clover-based concoction. Dave, she recalled, had spent the same two days in the woodshed as penance.

She nudged McMann with a knee. "Move over."

He wouldn't be nudged. Slitting his eyes, he peered up at her. "Why?"

"So I can sit down."

"Why?"

"So we can watch the water, or count the trees floating by, or talk."

His jaw jutted out. "I'm done talking."

They both knew he wasn't. He'd have to talk to a whole army of people when he left this farmhouse. Air force investigators. Prison officials. His parole officer, to name just a few. None of them would appreciate any more than Carly had the fact that he'd tried to shield Billy Hopewell by keeping his suspicions and his knowledge of the Afternoon Club to himself.

"I'm awake now, too," she pointed out unnecessarily. "But if you don't want me to share your tree stump, just say so and I'll go find my own."

"Go find your own."

"Oh, for . . ."

He sounded so much like Dave in one of his surly, go-away-don't-bother-me big brother moods that Carly dusted his shoulder with an irritated slap. The instant her hand made contact, she realized her mistake. He moved then, surging to his feet with that dangerous, athletic ability and a dark fire in his eyes.

"Go away," he snarled. "I swore I wouldn't touch you again, and I won't." He raked her face, her tangled hair, her legs. "But I want to. I've been sitting here thinking about just how much."

A string of warning beacons burst into flame under her skin. Do as he says, her instincts shouted. Turn around and walk away. Now!

She tried to do just that. She might even have made a dignified exit if the muddy grass hadn't sucked at one of her rubber bootheels and refused to let go. She came half out of the oversized boot, felt it knocking at her shins, pitched over.

She fell sideways into McMann, digging a shoulder into his chest with a force that staggered him. He brought his arms up to steady her and fought to keep them both from tumbling over the stump behind him. The awkward dance had Carly twisting in his hold, grabbing at his unbuttoned shirt for balance.

Arms wedged against the wall of his chest, she found her footing. Her hips, her stomach, her knees made clumsy contact with his. With a ripple of shock, she discovered he was rock hard, straining against his jeans, pressing into her belly. A sudden, vicious stab of lust hit her in exactly the same spot he did. She must have gasped, made some small sound. His arms fell away instantly.

Hers wouldn't move. The feel of him against her was like a brand, white hot, icy cold.

She hadn't planned this physical contact, hadn't intended it. But she wanted it. The realization burst inside Carly like a mortar round, ripping a hole in her pride even as her pulse jumped to a rhythm that matched his. Her head went back, and the woman in her took a shamed delight in the rigid line of his jaw Her fingers curled into his shirt.

"McMann . . ."

"I've told you all I knew, all I suspected. What more do you want from me?"

She couldn't be anything but brutally honest. "I want . . . I want the same thing you want from me."

The admission set Ryan on fire. He fought the pounding need to wrap his arms around her. He couldn't do this, couldn't let her do this. Even with the brandy blazing in his stomach and Carly hot in his blood, he'd hold to his promise not to touch her.

Carly didn't seem to appreciate his restraint. She stared up at him for endless moments, then slowly, so slowly, slid her arms around his neck. Her breasts flattened against his chest. She went up on her toes, wrapped her arms tighter and pulled him down so she could reach his mouth. Her tongue slid along the bottom lip, stealing the fiery residue left by the brandy. Her teeth scraped his, her tongue pushed inside.

Still he didn't respond. Insistent now, Carly played her mouth to his, taking, tasting, stirring more excitement in her blood, more need. She loosed one arm, let her hand roam across his shoulder, slide down his spine, drag up his shirt tail. The skin of his back was slick and damp. Even in her surging heat, she took care not to rake her nails across the welt scored in his flesh by the tree branch.

Short breaths later, she let him know she wanted more than just this one-sided exploration.

"McMann ... Ryan." The words were ragged against his mouth, urgent. "You can touch me."

Still he didn't move.

"I want you to touch me."

"No."

Christ! Didn't she see how tight he was? How close he was to dragging her down and ripping off that oversized shirt? A sick memory rose unbidden in his mind of another night, another girl. He'd killed her. The brandy clogged his veins, fired him with the fear that he'd hurt Carly.

"Yes. Here. Touch me here." She feathered her fingertips across his chest, traced a line to his navel, slid inside the waistband of his jeans. "And here."

His stomach muscles leaped under her fingertips. On a swift, harsh breath, Ryan caught her hand. He had to stop her. Had to halt this insanity. Deliberately, he roughened his voice.

"We better get the terms and conditions straight

first, Carly. Do you pay me before or after I perform to your satisfaction?"

Shock fisted into her. She stumbled back, the glorious, greedy heat snuffed out. "What did you say?"

His face was savage. "Isn't that what this is all about? You're playing the same game the others did. Taking a taste of the same forbidden fruit."

Carly swallowed both her pride and an urge to violence that startled her in its intensity. Only when she could trust herself not to howl out her frustration and her rage did she reply.

"I told you before, McMann. I don't play games. You said you wanted to touch me. For a few, insane moments, I wanted the same thing. If you think that puts either of us in the same category as Elaine Dawson-Smith and her friends, you're more twisted than she was!"

Each scathing word raised a sting of regret on Ryan's skin. She was right. She'd offered him a gift, and he'd flung it back in her face. But he didn't need her gift, and sure as hell couldn't satisfy his cancerous need for her with just a few kisses, a few touches.

"I am twisted," he snarled. "Twisted into knots so tight I hurt with them. I lied when I said I wanted to touch you. I want more than that. I want you, all of you, under me, on top of me, wrapped around me."

She backed away a step, just one step, but Ryan felt the crevasse yawning between them. Ruthlessly, he widened it into an impassable barrier.

"I want to slide inside you, watch your eyes widen with the shock of taking me, feel your breath hot and moist on my skin."

He was sure that would drive her away, fully expected her to spin around and flop back to the house in those oversized boots. He should have known she'd stand her ground and give as good as she got.

"Maybe . . ." She wet her lips. "Maybe I want that, too. I'll have to think about it."

Think about it! Ryan choked. Just the glide of her fingertips over his skin had fried what was left of his brain, not to mention his balls, yet she retained her capacity to process signals and thoughts.

"Yeah, well, let me know when you're done with thinking."

"I will."

She got halfway to the house before he remembered the demons that had driven him out into the night.

"Carly!"

She slowed, turned at the waist, eyed him warily. "What?"

"I wouldn't have let Smith burn."

When she didn't answer, he told himself he couldn't blame her. He hadn't exactly given her a lot of reason to believe in him.

"I didn't know for sure about Billy and Elaine Dawson-Smith. I only suspected. Then her husband was arrested. I figured he could take the heat better than the kid could, but I swear, I wouldn't have let him take the fall."

Her brow lifted. "I'm sure he'll be happy to hear that."

She trudged up the yard, leaving Ryan still hard, still hurting, and wishing like hell he hadn't dumped that last slosh of brandy into the grass. He was strung even tighter now than he'd been before and needed release . . . the kind that only Carly could give him.

But she had to think about it first!

Setting his jaw, Ryan reclaimed his stump and started counting the hoots of a barn owl, the bits of debris floating past, the ripples on the water, anything that might take his mind off the woman who'd just turned him inside out.

The damned cats finally snagged his attention. Their cries scratched at his ears, irritated him with their mewling helplessness. As if he could do anything to help them! Hell, he couldn't even get himself and Carly off this tiny atoll to safety.

He scowled at the shadowy barn, searching for the jagged board he'd decided on earlier as a reference point. When he finally found it, the kink Carly had tied in his gut became a tight, strangling noose. Since he'd last measured it, the river had climbed another foot up the wall.

Chapter Seventeen

Carly woke to the rumble of thunder, faucets that yielded only a few drops of water, and an empty house.

The first sent a jag of worry along her nervous system.

The second had her chewing on the inside of her cheek as she transferred a few careful glasses of water from the filled bathtub to the sink to scrub her face and her teeth.

The third sent her stomach plunging.

Steeling herself for her first meeting with McMann after their session by the tree stump, she walked into the kitchen. She expected to find him there, red-eyed and irritable after swilling the whole bottle of brandy. Instead, she found only the brooding quiet that comes before another storm.

Thinking McMann might have gone outside, she pushed open the screen door. She was hit by a morning far too sultry and sullen for late April and the throat-grabbing realization that their hilltop island had shrunk noticeably during the night. A single glance across the water at the barn brought her heart into her throat. The river had reached the loft doors and now snaked through the upper half of the structure as well as the lower.

The barn sat on lower ground, she reminded herself with a swallow, well below the hilltop that formed their little island. The river would have to rise another fifteen, twenty feet to reach the house. Even then, she and McMann could retreat upstairs.

Maybe he'd already retreated upstairs. She hadn't thought to check the master bedroom before she came down. Or maybe he'd passed out from all that damned brandy and still lay in a peach-flavored stupor.

The stillness of the house pressed in on her as she hurried back inside and up the stairs. A perfunctory rap on the master bedroom door and a sharp demand to know if he was in there brought no response. Frowning, Carly opened the door. The bed hadn't been slept in. Nor was there any sign that McMann had even used the room at all.

She stood rooted on the threshold, fighting a ridiculous flutter of panic as the possibilities marched through her mind. One, he could have passed out and spent the night beside his stump. Two, he could have tripped over something in the dark and hit his head. Three . . .

When she realized what she was doing, she choked out what should have been a laugh but sounded too close to a sob for her comfort. Damn McMann! She couldn't even marshal her thoughts anymore without feeling the weight of him in her mind. She couldn't sleep, either. She'd lain awake for hours last night, remembering the feel of his damp skin under her fingers, the heat of it, listening for his footsteps, worrying about whether he'd come into her room to check on her again. Wondering how she'd welcome him when he did.

She knew now exactly how she'd welcome him this morning, she thought grimly as she headed back downstairs. She'd tear another strip off his back for scaring her like this.

Where was he?

She pulled on the rubber boots and went outside to search. The humidity wrapped around her like a wet blanket. She cut across to the side of the house, her throat tightening when she saw that the stump was gone, buried under muddy gray water. So was the well. The hungry river now licked at the base of a tall sycamore that yesterday had stood high and dry.

"McMann?"

Her shout hung on the heavy air.

"McMann, where are you?"

Prickly with nerves, she wove through the pecans shielding the house and angled toward the water line. Debris had floated onto the slope . . . an old tire and what looked like a chicken coop. The tangle of drowned birds trapped inside had her backing off in a hurry.

Her heart thumping hard now, she made a full circuit, checking the trees and bushes, the sloping yard at the front of the house, the detached garage. With every step, the possibilities tumbled through her mind, each one more frightening than the last.

He'd spotted a boat or something floating past, maybe the chicken coop, tried to swim out to it. The river had sucked him in, swept him away. He'd been drunker than she thought, passed out, woke to find himself miles downriver. He'd been bitten by a water moccasin, died an agonizing death before the river claimed him. Oh, God! Not that! Please, not that.

She burst out of the garage. Fright pumped in great, painful lumps through her veins. She broke into a loping run, the boots slapping at her calves.

She'd make another circuit. He had to be here somewhere! He had to!

She took only three, panicked strides before she
spotted him, rising like a swamp creature from the
water, holding a burlap bag in one fist like some
prize he'd found in the murky depths.

"McMann!"

Panting with accumulated fear, Carly stumbled to
a halt. Her breath came in shallow, wheezing gasps
as he waded through thigh-high water. His black
hair was plastered to his skull. His wet shirt outlined
every line, every curve of his torso.

"Where were you?" she gasped.

"I took a swim, over to the . . ."

"Took a swim! Took a *swim!*" Fear and fury shot
her voice up an octave and a half. "You idiot! Don't
you know the rain's washed every cottonmouth
and copperhead between Birmingham and Mobile
out of their nests? You could have gotten snake
bit! You could have been snagged by another tree!
You could have ended up *swimming* all the way to
the Gulf!"

"I only swam over to the barn, Carly."

In contrast to her screech, his voice soothed, but
she could see he was fighting a smile. Her hands
balled at her sides.

"You think it's funny? You think it's a joke? You
scared the shit out of me, McMann."

"I'm sorry."

"You should be. Damn you, don't do that again!
Don't leave me!"

"I won't," he said gently.

"Without telling me first, I mean," she huffed.

"I won't."

She shoved back her hair, determined to hold on to
her anger a while longer. It was her only defense

against the overwhelming urge to throw herself into his arms. She was still trying to regain her shattered equilibrium when a small, pathetic meow came through the burlap sack in his fist.

Thunderstruck, Carly gaped at the bag. It bulged, bumped a little on one side, cried again. Her incredulous gaze whipped back to McMann.

"Cats?" she got out on a strangled gasp.

He shrugged, his expression at once embarrassed and disgusted. "I listened to them crying the whole night. I should have let the river take the damn things, but, well . . ."

"You swam through a flood for *cats*?"

"They're kittens. Only two of them. Something must have gotten the rest. And the mother. I couldn't find her." He shoved the bag at her "You'd better take them."

Still reeling with the knowledge that he'd risked his life so recklessly, Carly backed away. She'd spent too many years on a farm to feel any burning desire to take charge of half-wild barn cats.

"No, thanks."

"They're pretty weak. They need, you know, nursing."

"You rescued them. You nurse them."

"I always had dogs. I don't know anything about cats."

"The same general principles apply to both."

"Give me a break here, Carly." He sounded desperate now. "I can't stand the things."

"You . . . can't . . . stand . . . them?" she stammered, flabbergasted all over again.

"Just take them, will you?" He grabbed her hand, wrapped her fingers around the burlap. "I saw a cardboard box in the garage. We can put them in there."

He strode off, leaving her literally and figuratively holding the bag.

"I don't believe this!" Her stunned gaze went from the back of his dripping head to the now restless, mewling bundle in her hand, then to McMann once more. "I don't believe him."

Throughout her career, Carly had always guarded against the habit so many cops and lawyers fell into of stereotyping persons convicted of crimes. Until this moment, she'd prided herself on her professional neutrality. McMann had just blown a career's worth of illusions all to hell.

For weeks now she'd viewed him only in the context of her investigation. She weighed his history, his credibility, his careless kindness to Billy Hopewell against the a backdrop of the current case. Even the lust and longing that kept her tossing last night had centered on the Ryan McMann she thought she knew . . . a dark, compelling figure at the center of a storm. Never once had she thought of him as a man. Simply a man. Certainly not as the kind of man who'd swim a swollen river to rescue creatures he detested.

Carly sank to her knees, shaken by the emotions that grabbed her heart and squeezed. Hard. Last night's lust was still there, stronger than before, almost strangling her. But there was also a stirring that went deeper, wider.

Slowly, she folded the neck of the bag back. Two calico kittens untangled their scraggly bodies, then cringed away with a hiss and a swipe of needle sharp claws when she tried to stroke one.

"'Smart cats," she murmured. "Don't trust anyone when you're in a burlap bag and this close to water."

The garage door banged shut. Carly lifted her head and felt the ache around her heart intensify.

"Except him," she whispered. "I'm pretty sure you guys can trust him."

He strode down the sloping backyard with that long-legged grace. He'd raked a hand through his hair, but it still stuck up in spikes, glistening like shiny black coal in its wetness. Two days' growth darkened his cheeks and chin. His sodden shirt tails flapped against his jeans. He looked totally disreputable, and so ridiculously cat shy that Carly knew she'd never forget this moment.

He held out the box, regarding the creatures in the burlap bag warily. "I lined the box with some old newspapers and found a piece of Plexiglas to put on top. Just dump them in here."

Reaching around those sharp little claws, Carly got the first one by the scruff and deposited it in the box. The second, a mottled white and orange and black, hissed and spit and jumped in on his own to join his sibling. McMann slid the Plexiglas over the top.

"They're feisty little devils," he muttered. "I had a helluva a time getting them into the bag."

From the scratches on the backs of his hands, she could believe it. He hefted the box, uncertain what to do with it now that he had it.

"Think we should keep them in the house or the garage?"

"They're barn cats, not house pets, but . . ." She shrugged. "I saw some canned milk in the cupboards. We might as well take them inside and feed them."

While McMann banged through the upper cupboards in search of condensed milk, Carly retrieved a chipped earthenware bowl from under the counter and wiped it free of dust with a paper towel. McMann popped two holes in the can with an old fashioned opener and poured the contents into the bowl.

"Not so much!" she protested. "You'll make them sick."

She knelt beside the box and set the bowl down inside with a careful eye to her fingers. At the first scent of the milk, the calicos' inbred wariness gave way to frantic hunger. One had its front paws in the bowl and was working its tongue before she withdrew her hand. The other pounced and landed facedown in the thick, concentrated milk. It righted itself instantly, lapping nonstop.

McMann hunkered down beside her, observing the frantic feeding. "Greedy buggers, aren't they?"

"They're starving. I guess that's why they kept you awake all night."

"They didn't keep me awake."

"You said they did."

"I said I listened to them all night, but . . ."

"But?"

His glance slid sideways. He measured his words, tested them in his mind, before letting them go.

"You're what kept me awake."

Carly's lungs stilled. The blunt admission cut through the fright of the past few moments, through the shock of seeing him walk out of the water like Lazarus rising from the dead, and left her with that queer little ache again.

"We're even, then. I didn't get much sleep either."

"Were you thinking?"

"Yes."

He crossed a wrist over his knee. "Still thinking?"

The guarded watchfulness in his eyes pulled the truth from her.

"No, Ryan. I've done enough thinking."

"And?"

She wet her lips. "And I want to feel you on me, and under me, and in me."

Her soft echo of his words last night stunned him into immobility for all of two seconds before he surged to his feet, taking Carly with him. Her fingers dug into rock hard biceps still slick and wet under the clinging shirt.

"Are you sure?"

"Yes."

His jaw locked tight. The muscles under her fingers could have been molded from steel.

He wasn't going to live up to all those dark, promising threats, Carly thought on a spasm of disappointment so strong her womb clenched. Damn him, he was going to leave her wanting, just as she'd left him last night. She was tasting the bitterness of her own need when he shoved his hands through her hair and tilted her head back.

"Which do you want first?"

"What?"

"On or under or in?"

She swallowed the egg-sized lump in her throat. "Surprise me."

In one smooth move, he lifted her onto the kitchen counter and used a hip to spread her legs. At her startled gasp, he flashed her a grin that was pure unadulterated male.

"We call that a body check, sweetheart. Using a shoulder or a hip to slow or stop the opponent with a puck."

That crooked grin sucked every molecule of air from Carly's lungs.

"I don't . . . Oh!" She gasped again as his hands attacked the buttons on her shirt.

His fingers stilled on the last button. The same stillness came into the blue eyes so close to her own.

"You don't what?"

"I don't . . . have the puck."

At that moment, Ryan knew he wanted more than sex from this woman. She looked so flustered, so flushed, with her hair spilling down her back like a river of tangled flame and her brown eyes alive with an urgency that matched his own. She didn't try to hide it, didn't play the coy games so many women did. He wanted all that he could have of her.

"You may not have the puck," he answered, his grin now ragged around the edges, "but you have what I want."

He peeled back her shirt, trapping her elbows behind her where she braced on the countertop.

"God, you're beautiful."

Beautiful and perfect, her breasts fuller than he'd pictured during all those dark, sleepless hours. Her nipples were almost as red-brown as her hair. They budded at his touch, then peaked when he bent to tease them with his tongue and teeth. Just the taste of her sent need fisting into him. He felt the slam to his groin, knew there was no going back. Not now. Not ever. His breath speeding, he wrapped an arm around her hips, swept her hard against his pelvis and took her mouth, that full, generous, tormenting mouth he'd wanted for so long.

The crush of his lips on hers destroyed any faint notion that Carly could control him . . . or herself. Her neck bowed. Her head thumped against the upper cupboard. She used its support to take the force of his kiss. He devoured her, consumed her. Some faint corner of her mind recorded that he tasted like toothpaste and smelled like river.

Sandpapery stubble scraped her cheeks until she found that perfect match of lips to lips, chin tucked around chin.

Even then, she couldn't breathe, couldn't concentrate on the dark, erotic play of tongues and teeth. His hands were all over her, smooth and rough and incredibly skilled. He found every nerve ending, every flash point, his palm sliding on her flesh, his fingers rough and tender on her breasts. She fought to get out of her shirt, moaning with frustration when her elbows wouldn't pull free.

"Ryan! I can't . . . I can't . . . get my arms . . . out!"

He dragged his head back, the rise of his chest as fast and hard as hers. "Good."

"Is this . . . ?" She gulped in air and the damp, dank heat of him. "Is this another one of your hockey moves?"

A smile edged the flame in his eyes. "You might call it a power play."

"I don't think I like the sound of that."

The smile slipped into something wicked. "Then I'd better not tell you what we call this."

He flexed his arm, canting her hips high, pulling her harder against him. Carly felt a rush of liquid heat between her thighs and wanted to moan again. She leaned back against his arm, lifted her legs to wrap them around his waist, did some flexing of her own.

She was swimming with need when he attacked the rest of her clothing. The drawstring knot disintegrated. She raised her hips, or maybe he raised them. However it happened, the baggy, borrowed shorts and panties slid down as far as their joined bodies would allow.

"Ryan!" Frantic to free herself of shirt and shorts

and everything else between them but flesh, Carly tried to wiggle out of his hold. "Move back. Move away. Let me get these things off."

"We'll . . . work . . . around them," he growled.

She was still struggling with the shirt when his hand found the damp folds between her legs. Heat jolted through her. The sparks shot all through her body when she felt his fingers slide into her, slide out. Carly felt the first tight waves of an orgasm build, recede, build again, tighter, sweeter. The swiftness of it, the power of it stunned her. She'd never . . . She'd always . . .

Elbows back, body arched, every nerve below the waist on fire, Carly groaned an urgent warning.

"You'd better . . . work . . . fast!"

He did. Fast and sure and so smoothly that she registered only a short separation and the snap of his jeans before he entered her. She felt herself stretch. Felt him thrust, gently at first, then with the full power of his hips and thighs and knees. Mere moments later, her climax raced at her, a rush of white light and dark, searing sensation. She arched back, groaning, as pleasure splintered through her.

His came a few seconds after she did. Or maybe it was minutes. Or hours. Carly was still shuddering with the force of her release when he thrust up and in, bringing her down at the same time.

She was slick with sweat and completely boneless when he eased her back onto the counter. Her fanny slid across the smooth Formica. The cupboard propped her up. With a determined effort of will, she opened her eyes.

"Don't tell me. Let me guess. That was a slapshot, right?"

A groan rumbled up from somewhere and came

out sounding suspiciously like laughter. Chest heaving, he braced one hand on the cupboard and tipped her chin with the other.

"No, ma'am. The slapshot comes later, after the Zamboni."

"You're making that up."

"Think so?" His mouth came down on hers, even more thrilling in its now familiar greediness. "I can see you're got a lot to learn about the sport."

CHAPTER EIGHTEEN

Whenever she looked back on her time with Ryan, Carly would always think of the bubbles her three-year-old niece loved to blow from one of those little plastic hoops. Like the shimmering circles, those stolen moments in the kitchen were fragile and beautiful. And short. So terrifyingly short.

Harsh reality began to intrude while she was still limp and sheened with sweat from her shattering climax. The hazy notion of squeezing into the upstairs shower with Ryan formed in the back of her mind. Only then did she remember that they'd lost the pump to the river's relentless rise.

Evidently Ryan's mind had shifted to the same reality. He dropped another kiss on her swollen mouth and eased away, snapping his jeans. The sleek, smug look of a satisfied male gave way to a carefully casual expression.

"We'd better think about moving some of these water jugs and cans of food upstairs. Just in case."

Carly dragged her shirt together, fighting the wholly irrational and totally female need for a little postcoital cuddling. This wasn't the time or the place for cuddling. That would come later. Maybe. After the flood receded. Or she and Ryan got back to civilization. Or they cut through the tangled ties of murder and deceit that bound them together.

Willing her boneless body to move, she slid off the counter and reclaimed her borrowed shorts and underwear.

"Do you think it's going to reach the house?"

"It could. Doesn't hurt to be prepared." He loaded himself down with two-gallon jugs. "I'll take these upstairs. Why don't you see if you can find some sacks or a box to carry the cans in?"

Carly stole a few minutes and a meager ounce or two of water to clean up before starting a search. She remembered seeing some paper sacks somewhere. Under the sink, maybe, or in one of the lower cabinets. Sliding the box with the now-sleeping kittens aside, she checked under the sink first, then the cabinets beside it. She worked her way almost to the stove before she found them, neatly folded and stacked on a lower shelf. She'd pulled them out and had started to push to her feet when a cigar box that had gotten shoved to the back of the shelf snagged her eye. With one knee on the floor and a shoulder to the narrow cabinet door, she groped for the box.

At first glance, the contents didn't look promising. The jumble included a package of shoestrings, a set of keys, clipped coupons for everything from dish washing detergent to low-fat pretzels, a rusted jack-nife. Just the kind of flotsam that drifted into a kitchen and ended up in a cigar box. Then she spotted the fat, rolling weights at the bottom of the box.

Batteries! She scooped them out, praying they weren't leaking or rusted. The cigar box dropped with a clatter that startled a hiss out of the kittens. Surging to her feet, Carly aimed straight for the boom box Ryan had left on the kitchen table. Excite-

ment and the thought of reestablishing some contact
with the outside world made her clumsy. She fumbled off the plastic battery cover.

Dammit, she never could figure out which end
went which way. Squinting at the squiggly marks inside the battery casing, she jammed the fat cells into
place. Of course, the cover wouldn't go back on. She
pushed and shoved at it, trying to fit the little plastic
tabs in the slots. Finally, the damned thing clicked
shut.

With a silent prayer, Carly tried the power switch.
Static screeched out at her. Sagging with relief, she
fumbled for the volume control, then poked at the
buttons and levers until she found the station selector. Her thumb held the selector down until the digi-
tal display on the front of the boom box flashed the
numbers for her favorite station.

The moment she released the lever, one of the
Statler Brothers' classics filled the air, mellow, melo-
dic, wishin' they could get back to the sweet Atlanta
Blue. Sighing, Carly sank into one of the kitchen
chairs. There was still a world out there.

Funny, she hadn't felt the full weight of their isola-
tion until this moment. Now, the familiar ballad both
reassured and jarred. Why were they playing music?
Why weren't they broadcasting twenty-four hour
emergency information?

The music brought home the telling truth that a disaster really affects only those caught up in it. Rue-
fully, Carly remembered how she'd draped herself in
flame-colored chiffon and driven to her mother's
campaign dinner while half of Chilton County was
under water.

Obviously, the flooding hadn't hit Montgomery. Yet.
Thinking nervously of the rumble of thunder

she'd awakened to this morning, Carly hit the selector again, stopping at each station until she found one with a news broadcast instead of music.

"... assisting state and local rescue efforts. The state director of emergency services has added three more shelters to the list of those up and fully operational. Cots and meals are available at St. Stephens, the First Baptist Church of the Nazarene, and the Lurleen Wallace Middle School on Cloverdale Street. At last count, a little more than four hundred people have taken shelter. More are expected as the flooding south of the city . . ."

Over the modulated tones of the newscaster, Carly heard the clump of McMann's footsteps racing down the hall just seconds before he burst into the kitchen.

"Where did you find the batteries?"

"In a box at the back of one of the cabinets." She worried her bottom lip. "They're not new. I don't know how old they are or how long they'll work."

"Long enough to let us know what's happening, I hope. Did they give the weather forecast or say where they're concentrating rescue efforts?"

"Not yet."

He pulled out a chair and straddled it, his face so intent that a flutter of panic hit Carly's stomach. He was more worried than he'd let show earlier. She attempted a swift mental calculation, trying to compute how far the river had risen during the night, how far it still had to go before it reached the house. She gave up in frustration after the second or third attempt to divide hours into feet. There was a reason she'd loaded her college schedule with liberal arts and pre-law courses. Some people called it math avoidance. Carly called it math anathema.

"Residents of Wetumpka are still without water or electricity," the announcer informed them. "Firefighters have put out the blaze sparked by shorting electrical systems last night at the regional high school. Homeowners threatened by rising water are cautioned to turn off all electrical systems and throw the circuit breakers."

"Flood and fire," Carly murmured. "As if one wasn't bad enough."

"Quiet!"

McMann took charge of the volume control. The announcer continued.

". . . air and river patrols are working those sectors in Autauga and Lowndes counties where the worst flooding occurred. According to the director of emergency services, the farms below the Jones Bluff Reservoir had already been evacuated. Rescue officials state that there are always a few who ignore the evacuation order, however. Stranded residents should display a distress signal—a red or other bright garment tied to a pole or television antenna is suggested—and be prepared to take to upper stories, if necessary."

The announcer's voice took on a solemn intonation.

"With more storms moving in from the north, it could well become necessary. Forecasters are predicting rain throughout the afternoon and early evening."

"Hell!"

"At this time, we'll return to our regularly programmed broadcast. Stay tuned for updates. We will, of course, interrupt with any new bulletins from the governor or the director of emergency services."

McMann clicked off the power and pushed out of his chair. "We'd better save the batteries. Come on, Carly, let's get this stuff upstairs."

She didn't need any further urging. Snapping

open a paper sack, she headed for the cupboard. She dumped the contents of two shelves into bags when her worried gaze flitted to the window above the sink. Sure enough, the clouds scudding low across the sky looked noticeably blacker than they had before. Suddenly, she froze.

"Oh, no!"

Her low, muted cry spun Ryan around.

"What? What's wrong?"

"It's gone."

"What?"

"The barn. It's gone."

He crowded beside her at the sink, his black brows slashing together as he stared at the empty stretch of water. Through her almost paralyzing dismay, she sensed the tension that coiled through his body.

"We didn't even hear it go," she whispered.

The ragged edge to her voice brought Ryan's head around. He saw the way her skin stretched tight across her cheeks, the hollowness in the eyes that stared across the water. Shoving his own, gut-clenching thoughts aside, he summoned a lazy smile.

"I'm not surprised, given what occupied us for the past half hour or so. The house could've gone, too, and I wouldn't have noticed."

"Oh, that's reassuring to know!"

His smile slipping into a grin, he tucked a strand of tangled auburn behind her ear. "The sun could have exploded, Carly, and I wouldn't have noticed. The sky could have dropped into the sea. The . . ."

She gave a little huff that came close enough to a laugh to satisfy Ryan. "If you're trying to say that the earth moved for you, I get the message."

He waited. "Well?"

"Well what? Oh."

The fear that had darkened her eyes a moment ago was harnessed now, put in check for a few moments, a few hours perhaps. Ryan only hoped they had that long.

"All right," she admitted with a cool lift of one brow, "it moved for me, too."

He lifted a hand, slid his palm around to cup the back of her neck. "Want to make it shift again?"

Her head cocked. Those cinnamon brown eyes took his measure, stripped away the forced playfulness, found whatever she was looking for.

"Yes."

The soft reply had Ryan wondering what had happened to the air in the kitchen. One moment, he was breathing. The next, he was sucking for oxygen. He still hadn't found it when she pushed up on her toes and brushed a kiss across his lips.

"Let's get this stuff upstairs, and we'll talk about it."

"Talk, hell."

She was the one with the grin now. "I'll take the grocery sacks. You bring your cats."

"They're not my cats. Hey! Carly!" He snatched up the box with the kittens, two more plastic water jugs, and the radio. "They're not mine!"

They were on the third trip ferrying supplies when McMann went still. Her arms full, Carly turned in surprise to find him frozen halfway up the stairs.

"I hear something."

He dumped his armload on the stairs and raced back down. Carly unloaded hers and scrambled over the bags after him. The screen door was bouncing on its hinges when she got to the kitchen. She rushed outside, her heart hammering, and cut through the pecan trees that surrounded the house to what was left of the sloping front yard. There she heard the faint drone that had caught McMann's ear.

"It sounds like a plane. A small one. Single engine. Coming from . . . Yes! There!"

She pointed to a speck that was either a very large hawk or a very small plane making circles in the darkening sky.

"Looks like a spotter aircraft," Ryan muttered. "Too light for rescue."

"It's probably a Civil Air Patrol bird. Their national headquarters is at Maxwell. They've probably got the whole staff in the air in addition to the local wing."

She gnawed on her lower lip, willing the speck to grow larger, swing closer. It did neither.

"They're too far away," she wailed. "They won't see us or the S O S on the roof."

"They'll see this." His jaw tight, Ryan tore open the slender box of traffic flares he'd snatched from the kitchen table on his way out and extracted one. "Here, hang on to these. Don't let them get wet."

Carly clutched the box to her chest, breathing in cordite and heavy, still air while he yanked at the tape and twisted off the cap. It took several scratches of the cap against the exposed end to ignite the flare. Within seconds, the narrow red stick was spitting bright sparks.

"There should be a metal holder in the box," Ryan told her, keeping the flare at arm's length.

"Here!"

He slipped the holder onto the cylinder and ordered her back. "This thing could explode and ignite the other flares."

Hastily, Carly backed away from the shower of sparks. Her heart in her throat, she searched for the distant aircraft while McMann waved the incandescent wand in a slow half circle. To her dismay, she couldn't find the plane again against the dark clouds.

She could hear it, though, that faint, steady drone audible even over the spit and sizzle of the flare. It was up there, dodging the clouds she guessed. Chewing on her lip in earnest now, she checked the box to see how long the flare would burn.

Fifteen minutes! Surely, the pilot would bank his aircraft, look this way, spot the bright white/red light within the next fifteen minutes!

The time slipped by, one agonizing minute after another. Two, three, five, each one feeling like a year or more. The flare burned lower and lower. Cautiously, Ryan pushed it forward another inch in the metal loop.

Neither of them could say afterward whether it was the last sputters of the flare that finally caught the pilot's eye or the lightning that sliced through the sky out over the water. The flash came out of the clouds a good distance away, several miles if the old saw about counting the seconds until thunder boomed was right, but Ryan dropped into an instinctive crouch. Carly wasn't as proud. She went flat, spread-eagled on the ground.

"He's spotted us." Grim relief laced Ryan's voice. "He's turning."

Carly lifted her head a cautious few inches and held her breath while the small plane banked. Not until the plane was clearly visible did she raise up off the ground and wave like mad.

The pilot made two circuits over the house, coming in so low the second time he almost skimmed the tops of the pecans. Carly danced in a circle, waving furiously, and had to swallow her bitter disappointment when he wagged his wingtips and flew off.

Obviously, he couldn't land. He'd mark their location and radio for helos or river craft to come in. Still, it gave her an odd sensation to watch the dark clouds swallow the tiny single-seater.

"How long do you think it will be before we can expect a rescue craft?" she asked McMann.

He eyed the evil-looking sky. "If they don't get here before the storm breaks, they won't risk flying through it. My bet is they'll either send a river craft or wait the storm out."

Carly nodded, resolutely refusing to sweep a look over her shoulder at the empty spot where the barn had stood. The farmhouse was higher, sturdier, anchored to a concrete foundation. It would weather one more storm, defy one more attempt by the river to claim it.

It had to.

The rain hit almost as soon as they got back in the house. A soft patter against the windows at first, it quickly gathered both force and volume. Within minutes, a steady torrent drummed down on the roof.

They waited it out in the kitchen. A half hour passed, an hour. The rain eased to a drizzle, but the black clouds hanging low over the farmhouse promised more, and soon. Ryan took advantage of the brief respite to check the river's level. When he returned, he wore a mask of unconcern, but Carly knew him well enough now to spin around on her heel and head for the living room. Grimly determined, she went through the shelves one by one. Ryan followed, frowning at the jumble she'd collected.

"What are you doing?"

She shoved a stack of photo albums into his arms. "Trying to save the things that insurance can never replace. We owe the owners that much, at least. Take those upstairs."

"Yes, ma'am."

She gathered framed photos, a family portrait from what looked like the '40s, a display of World War II medals, a basket of souvenir matches, a cross-stitched Lord's Prayer, anything and everything that might have sentimental value.

She sent Ryan up and down the stairs six times before she admitted defeat. Every worn area rug, every needlepointed throw pillow, every old, comfortable piece of furniture would be a loss to the people who had lived with them for years. Sighing, she joined Ryan in the kitchen for another meal of tuna, canned peas, and cold beans.

The cheery room was dark, far too dark for mid-morning. Or was it afternoon? Carly had no idea what time it was. She pushed the beans around on her plate and tried to count back, to fix the hours and events in her mind. There was the plane. The shock of finding the barn gone. Those incredible moments with Ryan here in this same room.

She slanted him a quick look. The lean, stubbled cheeks, the black hair looking like it hadn't seen a comb the past month, the blue eyes startling against his tanned skin. They all seemed so familiar to her now that she couldn't remember a time when they weren't part of her life.

With a shock, Carly realized that she felt as though they'd spent a week here together instead of a mere, what? Eighteen? Twenty hours? How many more would they have together before they abandoned their precarious sanctuary.

*   *   *

She got her answer as soon as Ryan checked the boom box for a situation report. The announcer's voice jumped into the dim, quiet kitchen.

". . . advising all persons south of the Jones Bluff Reservoir to evacuate immediately. Those above the reservoir are advised to move to high ground. More than three inches of rain has been recorded at Danley Field in the past two hours. Flash flooding north of the city has brought the Alabama to within a foot of its banks."

Carly felt the cold beans congeal in the pit of her stomach.

"Stay tuned for further instructions from the director of emergency services."

While the announcer ran down an updated list of shelters, Ryan moved to the window to survey the encroaching water. Without a word, he gathered those emergency supplies they hadn't yet moved upstairs. The rope he looped over one shoulder. The box of flares he jammed in his back pocket. With the flashlight tucked under his arm, the rubber hip boots in one hand, and the snake-bite kit in the other, he gave Carly a smile she was sure he intended as reassuring.

"Bring the radio, will you? We'll keep it on as long as the batteries last."

Nodding, she reached for the box's plastic handle. A silence settled between them as they walked down the dim hallway, broken by the steady stream of announcements.

"The Alabama National Guard has been put on Code Two status. All members are to report to their companies. Units from Maxwell Air Force Base have joined the search and rescue effort, augmented by helicopter crews from Fort Rucker and Hurlburt Field, Florida."

If she'd had anything on her to bet with, Carly would have taken odds that Jo West was out there in that black soup. The helo pilot wouldn't miss out on the fun. A strained smile played at her lips as she took the stairs.

"In a related story, a ham radio operator intercepted a transmission from a Civil Air Patrol pilot. WHYK has learned that the pilot reported sighting two people. One fits the description of Air Force Major Carly Samuels, daughter of Congresswoman Adele Samuels, reported missing yesterday afternoon."

Carly jerked to a halt at the top of the stairs. "Did you hear that?"

Ryan crowded past her. "I heard. Turn it up."

She fumbled for the volume control.

". . . the description of Ryan McMann, a former inmate at the Federal Correctional Facility at Maxwell, currently wanted for questioning in connection with the brutal slaying of Fayrene Preston, assistant warden at the prison."

"Oh, my God!"

Ryan ignored Carly's stunned whisper. His eyes, his whole being were focused on the boom box.

"An eyewitness allegedly saw McMann bludgeon Preston with an iron rod when she confronted him with evidence linking him to the murder of Lieutenant Colonel Elaine Dawson-Smith. Our sources confirm that McMann's prints were found on the murder weapon."

Carly felt her lungs squeeze painfully. Unable to choke out a single word, she stared at the stark, unremitting face of the man opposite her.

"The former hockey great then reportedly abducted Major Samuels with the intent of using her as a hostage. A prison spokesman would confirm only that McMann is wanted for questioning, but warned that he is considered extremely dangerous. Congresswoman Samuels could not be reached for comment.

"Turning now to an update on the situation in Chilton County, on-scene disaster relief . . ."

The rubber boots dropped with a thump. Ryan reached out and stabbed the power switch. An awful, suffocating silence descended, broken only by the rattle of rain on the roof.

CHAPTER NINETEEN

"... Would confirm only that McMann is wanted for questioning, but viewers are advised that he is considered extremely dangerous."

Her flight helmet dangling from one hand, Jo West gaped at the picture of Ryan McMann that filled her TV screen. Stunned, she listened to the tail end of the story she'd just walked in on after three long, grueling missions.

"Congresswoman Samuels spoke with reporters only moments ago. We take you now to channel nine's Tara McKinley at the congresswoman's residence."

Gripping the chin strap of her helmet, Jo watched a small, elegant woman who looked remarkably like her daughter hold up a hand to quiet the reporters throwing questions at her like hand grenades.

"At this time I can only say how relieved and thankful my family and I are to know Carly's alive. I have every confidence the authorities will bring her and the man with her in safely. I'm sorry, I can't take more questions now."

As if they hadn't heard her, the news people launched another barrage.

"What about reports your daughter's being held hostage?"

"Are you in contact with the authorities mounting the rescue attempt?"

With the skill of a longtime politician, the congresswoman kept a smile on her face as she turned away from the lights and cameras.

"Representative Samuels! Aren't you worried by the fact that your daughter's alone with a murderer?"

She stilled. For a second, only a second, the camera caught the strain in her porcelain features. Then her chin came up and she looked the persistent newsman square in the eye.

"At this time the allegations that Mr. McMann murdered anyone are just that, allegations." Her delicate nostrils flared. "And, yes, I'm worried about my daughter. But Carly's a remarkable woman. She can handle herself in any situation. Now, if you'll please excuse me, I have work to do."

She swept out to a chorus of strident questions. Jo's teeth ground together as the camera swung back to Tara McKinley, who solemnly recounted the startling developments.

"Murderer, my ass!" Jo muttered.

She refused to believe any of it. Her brother, Jack, paralyzed from the waist down and still active in hockey thanks to Ryan McMann's Ice Buddies program, sure as hell wouldn't believe it, either.

Nor was Jo about to remain glued to the TV when a friend was down. Snatching her helmet bag from the chair where she'd just tossed it, she ran for the door. Rain pelted her with stinging force as she dashed from the BOQ to her car.

Damn this front! It hung over the base like a mean-tempered dragon, spitting out the wind gusts and lightning strikes that had made her last mission a flight through a black hell. As she tore around Chennault Circle headed for base operations, Jo shook off the mental fatigue that had come from intense concentration and constant division of attention between instruments, visual coordination, and the various communications ongoing during flight. By the time she rushed into base ops, helmet and bag in hand, her adrenaline had fully recharged.

"What do we have that's ready to go?"

The tired major who'd taken her post-flight report just ten minutes ago looked up in surprise. "Didn't I just send you back to the 'Q for crew rest?"

"I'm okay. What's ready to go?"

"You've already flown three missions, Captain. We've got student crews from Fort Rucker who can take up the slack for a while."

"I just heard that a friend of mine is down," Jo said urgently. "Major Samuels. Carly Samuels."

"The JAG?"

"You know her?"

"Yeah, sure, she put together a special briefing for our squadron on the legal issues surrounding our ACUZ problem."

Jo wasn't interested right now in the Aircraft Critical Use Zone issues that had the Maxwell flying community grinding their teeth with frustration.

"What have you got that's ready to go?"

The major swept a quick look down the computerized status board projected onto a wall-sized screen. "A student crew is getting ready to preflight one of Fort Rucker's schoolhouse Huey's right now. Hang loose, I'll talk to the army liaison."

Jo paced in front of his console while he radioed
the harried army officer who'd brought his birds and
crews up from Fort Rucker and plunged instantly
into around-the-clock flood relief efforts. He hung
up a moment later.

"The army's more than happy to have an experienced hand on the stick." He punched a change
into the status board. "All set. You're on as pilot. Tail number seventy-three dash one-seven-
two-one."

The '73 prefix on the tail number told Jo instantly
the bird was a Vietnam-era H-model, single engine,
simple and unsophisticated by today's standards,
but smooth, powerful, and a joy to fly.

"Thanks!"

She dashed for the crew bus just pulling up outside base ops. Scant moments later, she jumped out
and ran across the rain-soaked apron to the squat
UH-1. Jo had flown her first solo in a Huey at Fort
Rucker and logged more hours in the bird during
follow-on air force training at Kirtland Air Force
Base, New Mexico. She knew its capabilities, trusted
its proven record of performance.

A drenched army lieutenant greeted her with a
salute and obvious relief. "Just heard you're taking
the right seat, Captain."

"That's a roge, Lieutenant."

She introduced herself to the crew chief, tossed
her bag into the cockpit, and climbed into the
aircraft commander's seat. While the lieutenant
strapped himself into the left seat, she dragged
on her helmet and fire-retardent Nomex gloves
with leather palms for a tight grip on the controls.
With her copilot calling off the checklist steps and
the crew chief preparing the back of the aircraft

for takeoff, she whipped through the preflight procedures.

The engine wound up with a high-pitched whine. The rotors began their initial whirl, slowly picking up speed as Jo advanced the twist-grip throttle, bringing the Huey to the 6400 rpm necessary for lift off. When the aircraft rattled and shook with an eagerness that said she was ready to fly, Jo gave her copilot a thumbs up.

"All right, Lieutenant," she shouted into the mike of her helmet, "let's get this bird in the air."

With one hand nursing the collective at her side, the other working the slanted cyclic between her legs, and both feet on the pedals, Jo employed the natural coordination all helo drivers had to be born with. Slowly, the Huey picked up to a hover. Countering wind, driving rain, and the helicopter's natural tendency to whirl into a spin, she pushed the cyclic forward and pulled up on the collective to increase both altitude and airspeed. The runway fell away, and soon even the hangars were lost to the haze of rain.

As soon as the Maxwell tower had handed them off to the emergency command center controlling search and rescue operations, Jo got on the radio.

"This is army Rescue one-seven-two-one. Request the coordinates of the two people tagged by a Civil Air Patrol spotter less than an hour ago."

The reply came crisp and clear through the chatter on the radio. "This is Rescue Control. We've already dedicated assets for that operation."

"Roger that, but they may need backup."

"Two police choppers are enroute. They haven't asked for military backup."

One way or another, they were going to get it.

"There's a military officer on the ground, Control. Request permission to fly cover and keep Maxwell advised on military frequencies."

The harried controller came back on a few moments later. "All right, two-one, you're cleared, but for backup only. Be advised this is a police operation."

He rattled off the coordinates, which the copilot hastily grease-penciled on the acetate-covered clipboard strapped to his knee.

"Got 'em?" Jo asked.

"Got 'em."

"What's our ETA?"

He plotted the coordinates, calculated airspeed and distance on the circular navigational slide ruler universally referred to as the whizwheel, and gave her an estimated time of arrival.

"Army Rescue one-seven-two-one enroute," she advised the control center. "We should arrive on-scene in twenty minutes."

With a smooth coordination of arms and legs, Jo tipped the nose forward and opened the throttle. Moments later, Montgomery's rain-shrouded skyline had disappeared from view. Then there was only the wind, the black clouds, and the angry water below.

Jo's stomach clenched as she searched for the terrain features she'd noted on her flight through this sector less than an hour ago. So many had disappeared. Too many.

Jaw tight, Ryan turned away from the half-flooded stairwell. He didn't try to minimize the situation.

"We've got a half hour, maybe less, until we have to hit the roof."

Carly nodded. In contrast to her near panic when she'd found him gone earlier this morning, she was calm now, almost numb.

"We'd better get what we need and stack it by the window," she said quietly.

Ryan cut her a sharp glance, his insides tight and aching. God, she looked so pale, so self-contained. So damned different from the flushed, panting woman he'd held in his arms what seemed like a lifetime ago that he ached with the loss. It was clear that the shock of the radio announcement they'd caught a little while ago still hadn't quite worn off.

He'd give his right arm to turn the clock back twenty-four hours. If only he hadn't decided to beat the truth out of Gator. Carly wouldn't have come after him and been caught in the flood. The assistant warden wouldn't have died.

If only Carly had rounded the boat shed a second or two sooner than she had. She would have seen that Preston was still alive when the lightning stuck. Still alive when Ryan threw himself across the yard in a futile attempt to save Carly from the rushing waters.

If only.

The two most painful words in the English language. Ryan felt their slash as he caught up with Carly in the hall. Snagging her arm, he turned her around. The darkness that had come with the storm shadowed her face, but not her eyes. They lifted to his, wide and clear.

"I didn't kill Fayrene Preston."

He'd already told her, already said the words. He needed to say them again.

"I believe you."

"Why?"

"The radio report said she suffered multiple fractures to the skull and apparent sexual assault. You didn't have time to inflict that on her in the short time I was gone."

"Two?"

"Two, it's your word against Gator's. I've already been down that road, Ryan. I believe you."

"And three?"

"Three . . ." She chewed on her lower lip. "I can't think of a three right now."

She was lying. For the first time she could remember, Carly deliberately and with malice aforethought violated her personal code of ethics and flat out lied. She knew darn well what constituted reason number three.

She believed Ryan McMann because she loved him. It was a shaky kind of love, too new, too scary to even think about right now. But it was there, curled deep inside her chest, waiting for the right time and the right place to unfurl and grow.

She'd suspected it when she stood in the backyard this morning, her mouth agape and a burlap bag squirming with kittens in her hand. She'd felt it flutter beneath the splintering layers of passion Ryan had released inside her. She'd acknowledged it silently when he'd reached out, shut off the boom box, and stared at her, simply stared at her, from the depths of his own private hell.

They both knew what faced him when they got back. If they got back. Another investigation. Another media frenzy. Another incarceration, this time at a maximum security facility, while the Bureau of Prisons shifted through the evidence in Fayrene Preston's horrible murder.

Carly's jaw set. This time Ryan wasn't going to put his life in the hands of a team of high-priced lawyers he didn't trust and an incompetent judge. This time, he'd damn well get the best. A familiar surge of adrenaline shot through her.

"Don't worry about number three," she told him with a brisk smile. "I'll come up with something before we get back to Maxwell. Come on, let's get our gear together."

The silent torment left his face. To her intense relief, he even managed a smile.

"You sound pretty chipper all of a sudden for a woman who may have to crawl out a second story window onto the eaves at any minute."

"At least I'll be crawling along with someone who knows his way around a roof." She started down the hall. "How are you going to carry your cats?"

"They're not my cats! Carly! Dammit, they're not mine!"

Ryan missed his guess by fifteen minutes. The water crept up the stairs faster than he'd estimated. It was calf deep in the upstairs hallway and lapping at the window sills outside when he lifted the sash and punched out the screen. Rain needled his head and body, soaking him instantly. He tested the line that anchored him to the heavy dresser and gave Carly a last, reassuring grin.

"After today, I'm giving up roofing as a second career."

"After today, I'm giving up water in any way, shape, or form. I'm bathing only in milk and drinking only the Judge's corn mash."

"Sounds like a good plan to me." He slung a leg over the sill. "Wait for my signal."

"I will. Ryan!" She grabbed his arm, pulled him back. "Take this with you."

Her mouth came down on his, hard, hot, wet and wild and sweet. He took the taste of her with him into the nightmare of wind and rain that hit him the moment he swung onto the steep-pitched gable.

The composition shingles were as slick as spit under his boots. Only a tight grip on the window frame, a lifetime of balancing himself on the ice, and the skills he'd picked up in the past eight months kept him from sliding off and pitching butt first into the waters swirling around the house. His jaw tight, he swung the hand ax he'd found in the garage. Its blade bit into the shingles, and the handle gave him a grip to hang onto.

"Stay put until I pull on the rope," he shouted to Carly. "Too pulls! Wait for two pulls!"

"Two pulls! Got it!"

She leaned out the window, ignoring the rain that drove into her face and upper body like bullets. Ryan wouldn't let himself look back at her, wouldn't let himself think about the worry for her that clawed at his gut. If he could reach the high-pitched ridge, pull Carly up and anchor them both to the chimney, he might buy them another ten, maybe fifteen minutes. If rescue didn't arrive by then, they'd have to take to the river with only the plastic milk jugs they'd emptied, capped tight, and strung together as life vests. The prospect of another ride down the raging Alabama buoyed only by milk jugs raised a cold sweat that even the rain streaming down his face and neck couldn't wash away.

Testing the rope knotted around his waist to make sure it gave him enough slack, Ryan began the longest crawl of his life. Whacking the ax into the shingles, he hung on to it with one hand and scrabbled in the rough-surfaced shingles with the other. Rather than go straight up, he angled across the roof, sliding his body inch by inch.

His hands were raw and bloody by the time he pulled himself up and straddled the ridge. He caught his breath, swiping his palms down his thighs to clean away the blood and embedded particles, then worked his way backward to the brick chimney. With a fervent prayer of thanks to the farmer who put in a fireplace even in the deep South, Ryan looped the rope around the brick. Then he drew in a ragged breath, said another silent prayer, and tugged on the rope. Once. Twice.

He didn't breathe again until he pulled Carly up beside him, her hair streaming, her shirt plastered to her body. She found a precarious seat on the shingles and eyed the water swirling past them with a deliberate nonchalance that made Ryan's heart ache. Swiftly, he reeled in the rest of the line, hauling up empty milk jugs, a pillowcase holding plastic-wrapped flares, flashlight, and food, and finally, another pillowcase, this one padded with newspaper and occupied by two extremely unhappy kittens.

"I'm going to shorten your line," he shouted to Carly over the roar of rain and river. With a quick twist he looped the rope, shortening the line that tied her to the chimney. "This is a slip knot. It'll give with a single tug if the water . . . If we have to . . ."

"If we have to swim," she finished for him. Incredibly, she flashed him a grin. "We beat the river once, McMann. We'll do it again."

They almost did.
Not five minutes later, Ryan heard the choppers.

Using the rope looped around the chimney as a safety line and the embedded ax as a handhold, he surged up. He had a flare out and sparking before Carly managed to find her feet on the roof's ridge. Hanging on to the rope, she shoved her hair out of her eyes and searched frantically for the source of the distant *whump whump whump*.

"There they are!" she shouted. "Over there!"

Afterward, Ryan could never say how it happened. Maybe she knocked against his arm. Maybe he jerked too hard on the ax handle.

However it happened, the ax came free and Ryan twisted frantically to avoid slicing Carly. She jumped back, lost her footing. With a yelp of sheer terror, she hit the roof on one hip. Hands and feet scrabbling, she tried desperately to stop her slide, but only succeeded in pulling loose the slipknot in the shortened rope.

Terrified that the knot around her waist might give, too, Ryan threw himself down and caught her flailing wrist. For long, panicked seconds, they sprawled head down on the roof, Ryan anchored to the chimney by his rope, Carly anchored to him by the bruising grip around her wrist. With a grunt, he managed to swing the ax and bury it in the roof for added support.

He tried to drag her up, but the shingles caught at her shirt, her shorts. "Flip over! Carly, can you flip yourself over?"

"I . . . I think . . . so."

She used her feet and hips and shoulders, flopping like a stranded dolphin. Ryan gritted his teeth and held on to her rain-slick wrist with all the strength he had. Finally, she twisted onto her stomach.

"Take a breath," he ordered, "then reach up with your other hand and grab my wrist."

She stretched and pushed with toes that couldn't find purchase on the slick shingles. They were both grunting with effort by the time she got a hold of his arm and took some of the strain off hers.

"All right. You're still roped to the chimney," he reminded her, praying the remaining knot had held. "It's a safety line, but we won't need it. We're going to inch back up the roof, like a crab."

"Got it," she panted. "Like a crab."

"Okay. I'll pull. You push with your toes."

The stark terror at seeing Carly slide down the roof had driven everything else from Ryan's mind. Only now that he had her hands wrapped around his did the roar in his ears subside enough for him to hear the choppers. They were closer now, the whap of their rotors clearly audible over the river's rage.

He had to get Carly up, had to get her on the ridge and ready for a sling. One-armed, he worked the rope that anchored him, crabbing back and up slowly, steadily. With the other arm, he tugged Carly. His shoulder socket burned. His muscles were on fire.

"You're doing great, sweetheart. A few more yards."

His left boot had just touched brick when he heard the first pop, almost lost in the rain and wind and deafening beat of the blades. Another pop came a few seconds later, followed by a splat just behind him.

Carly's eyes went wide with shock.

"They're shooting at us!" she screamed. "Ryan! They're shooting at us!"

He whipped his head around, saw the chunk taken out of the brick just behind him. Incredulous, he threw a look above him at the nearest chopper. The hatch stood open. Lifelines hooked to both sides of the hatch braced a helmeted police sharpshooter against the violent pitch and roll of the aircraft. He aimed a high-powered rifle at the roof, waiting for the helo to bank and bring him another clear shot.

The truth hit Ryan between the eyes. Twisting, he shouted to the woman clinging to his wrist with both hands. He had less than a second to make a frantic decision. The rope would hold her. It had to hold her.

"They're not shooting at us, Carly! They're shooting at me! They think I'm trying to hold you, trying to hurt you or use you as a shield. You've got to let go, slide down the roof away from me, or you might get hit!"

Her nails dug into his wrist, frantic, clawing. "No!"

"Yes! Let go! The rope will hold you. I've wrapped it around the chimney."

"No! Dammit, Ryan, no!" The rain pelted into her upturned face, slicked her hair back from her face in a dark river of red. "I won't make you an easy target for them. Pull me up."

Another chunk of masonry exploded. As deadly as a bullet, a long, ragged sliver of brick dug into Ryan's back. He felt the hot, biting sting, the rush of blood, saw more bits of brick flying at Carly. She turned her head, took the hits on her cheek, winced.

Oh, God! They were going to put out her eye! Send a deadly sliver of mortar through her skull! They'd

kill her in their efforts to save her. He jerked his arm,
trying to shake her loose.

"Carly! Let go!"

"No!"

CHAPTER TWENTY

"**H**oly shit!"

The copilot's exclamation exploded through Jo's earphones. She made a minor correction to keep the winds rolling in from the north from driving her too close to the police helos circling the flooded farmhouse and snapped a glance at the copilot.

"Do we have a problem, Lieutenant?"

"Not us! Them! Those people on the roof!"

Jo's heart jumped into her throat. She wrenched her eyes from the instruments and zeroed in on the farmhouse.

Carly and McMann were still there, she saw with relief, clinging like spiders to the shingles. Why the hell hadn't the police choppers gone in with a sling to lift them off?

"What their problem?" she demanded. "Other than several tons of water lapping at their heels?"

"They've got sharpshooters taking potshots at them, for starters."

"What!"

"In the police choppers. Check the hatch."

Jo nudged the cyclic between her legs to the left. The Huey responded instantly, changing the pitch in one of its blades, tipping into a bank. Like a well-trained quarter horse, it turned on a dime and handed back nine cents in change.

Disbelieving, Jo caught a glimpse of a SWAT sharpshooter in black body armor and helmet with a high-powered rifle to his shoulder before the other helo banked into a turn of its own. She jabbed her mike button and came up on the frequency Rescue Control Center had given her to coordinate with the police choppers.

"This is army rescue one-seven-two-one. What the hell's going on? Why are you firing on those people?"

The pilot responded after a delay that had Jo's teeth grinding. "Our orders are to take McMann alive, if possible, but shoot to kill if he makes any attempt to harm Major Samuels."

"He's not trying to harm her!" Jo shouted over the static. "He's hanging on to her, for God's sake! Keeping her from going into the river."

"Negative, two-one. He swung an ax at her. We saw it. She tried to get away from him, and he dragged her back. We've got to take him out or we'll never get her off that roof safely."

Jo knew what she was going to do before he finished his transmission. "I'm going in."

"Negative, two-one! I repeat, negative. This is our operation. Stay out of it."

"Too late, I'm already in."

"Stay the hell out, two-one. We've got . . . hell!"

His transmission broke off as he banked violently to avoid a tall sycamore sticking out of the water like a solitary sentry. At the same moment, Jo felt her own cyclic kick under her right hand. With a coordinated movement of arms and legs, she got her bird back in trim, swearing at herself all the while for jerking the stick like some damned rookie. The copilot shot her a startled look.

"Captain?"

"I've got her under control."

"Are we really going in?"

"That's one of our own on the roof, Lieutenant. We're not leaving her staked out like a goat while these guys use the man with her for target practice. Chief, are you strapped in?"

"Affirmative," the crew chief confirmed. "Try not to get in their crosshairs, will you?"

"Roger that."

The Huey moved with her, banking, descending, buzzing straight for the roof. She came in so low the skids brushed the topmost branches of the pecans fringing the house. So low she could see the desperate expression on McMann's face. The frantic one on Carly's. That silvery glint had to be the ax, embedded in the shingles halfway down the roof . . . and ignored by both of the people trying to signal the swooping helo.

The copilot pushed against his shoulder straps, his eyes pinned on the target. "She's waving us away . . . no! She's waving us in. She wants us to come in!"

"Then I guess we'd better accommodate the lady."

Jo brought the Huey around in a tight bank, wishing fervently that the H-1 carried a jungle penetrator with a seat attached. If it had, she could hover high above the roof to shield Carly and McMann from the effects of the rotor wash, keeping the bird in trim while the crew chief winched them up.

Briefly, she considered dropping a rope for McMann to rig Swiss seats for him and Carly. Then Jo could just swoop away with them dangling like puppets from a string. But the damned winds made it too risky to put all that weight on one side. She'd have to go light on the skids and hover above the peak of the roof while they scrambled aboard.

Setting her jaw, she lined the Huey perpendicular to the ridge and into the wind out of the north. The controls felt sluggish in her hands. Their unresponsiveness chipped away at her concentration. The command from the police pilot that exploded in her earphones didn't exactly help, either.

"Abort, two-one! You're not authorized to go in. Abort!"

She ignored the command, fighting the controls, fighting the backwash as she approached the roof.

"Hang on to that roof, folks," she muttered under her breath. "Big Windy's coming in."

The skids danced crosswise an inch above the ridge, touched down, bounced up. Jo put everything she had into maintaining an out-of-ground-effects hover, countering the violent upwash from the roof, playing with the increasingly unresponsive controls. The pitched angle of the roof made the rotor wash flow in crazy ways.

Sweat rolled down between her breasts. She felt like a rookie again. She could almost sense the sharp eyes of a flight instructor, watching every move, sweating blood while her bird whipped back and forth in the sky for hour after hour until that magical, extraordinary instant when everything started to click and she found the hover button.

She couldn't find the damned button today to save her soul. She got the skids an inch or two off the roof, fought to keep the nose up. It wasn't pretty, but it was the best she could do.

"Chief! Get them aboard! Fast!"

"Roger."

Jo didn't dare take her eyes off the ground references she used for the hover, but the swirling rotor wash on the river gave an optical illusion of movement where none existed. She kept her hands on the stick, gripping it with the same pressure she might a tube of toothpaste. She was swimming inside her flight suit by the time the crew chief came back on the intercom.

"I got 'em strapped in!"

"Roger!" She rapped out a pre-takeoff check. "I've got sixty-four hundred rpm, no caution panel lights, six-hundred pounds of fuel."

The copilot echoed the check while the crew chief did a quick visual through the open hatch.

"You're clear left and above."

"Roger. Here we go."

Jo knew that her biggest challenge coming off the roof would be to gain enough speed for effective translational lift—to move from a hover to forward flight. She'd need at least fifteen knots before the two whirling overhead blades became a disk and the aircraft started flying like a plane instead of a hover craft. To do that, she'd have to slide down the roof to gain airspeed, dropping like a jet off the end of an aircraft carrier, trading altitude for airspeed, using all of her left pedal to keep the bird in trim. A tricky maneuver, but doable under ideal conditions. These were hardly ideal.

Three seconds later, they got a whole lot worse.

The bird went down, the water rushed at them, the nose picked up. Suddenly, she found herself using all her strength to maintain control. At the same instant, the master caution light flashed red on the instrument panel.

"We've got a master caution!"

One glance at the segmented control panel warning light sent her stomach plunging.

"It's the hydraulics!"

The stick was jerking and bouncing around. Jo used every muscle in her body to hold it while the copilot strained against his straps to reach the overhead panel behind him.

"Hydraulic switch is off," he shouted.

"Roger."

His gloved fingers fumbled with the switches. "Circuit breakers are out."

"Roger."

"Breakers are in. Switching them back on."

Jo gritted her teeth. "We still have no hydraulics. Chief! What have you got back there?"

"I'm checking, I'm checking! Jesus H. Christ! We've got a hole in the side of the bird. We're leaking fluid like a sieve. One of those bastard's bullets must have nicked a line."

That explained the sudden kick Jo had felt when she lined up for her approach to the farmhouse. Someone, she vowed grimly, was going to get real sorry about that, real soon.

"And they call themselves sharpshooters," she muttered. "Lieutenant, you'd better come on and help me with the collective."

White as a sheet, the copilot reached for his stick. "I've never landed without hydraulics before, except in simulators!"

"Then you know exactly what we need to do," she told him with brisk reassurance. "We'll come in at about thirty knots, slide onto the skids, throttle back, and put the collective down. Piece of cake . . . if we can find someplace to land."

"Right," the copilot answered weakly.

From that point on, it took both of them to muscle the controls. Jo fought the winds and searched the flooded landscape. Maybe, just maybe, they could make it back to Maxwell. While she watched the instruments and coordinated with her crew, she was mentally handing herself off from one possible forced landing site to another—from that tiny patch of dry field to that flat-roofed, flooded school; from that distant stretch of road rising out of the water to a two-lane bridge. The police choppers flanked her. At least they could pull her passengers and crew out of the drink if the Huey went down. Thank God the rains let up enough to give her some visibility.

Finally, Maxwell's red and white water tower loomed dead ahead. She'd already radioed ahead, advising the tower that they were coming in with police escort and hydraulics off.

"Stay with me on the collective," she instructed her copilot.

"With you on the collective," he confirmed.

"We're on approach."

The concrete rushed at them with a speed that made her forget how to breathe. Jo brought the Huey's nose down to level the skids. Curtains of sparks shot up as they slid down the runway. Sweating, Jo and the lieutenant pushed the collective down and eased back on the cyclic to brake the sliding aircraft. The H-1 slid another few yards, then, mercifully, shuddered to a stop. A twist of the throttle had the rotors winching down.

Jo sat for a moment, willing her rubbery arms and legs to move. When she could trust them to support her, she unlatched her seat restraints and climbed out of the cockpit. Her helmet and gloves came off by reflex. Tossing back her head, Jo sucked in clean, drizzly air.

The grin that stretched across her face when McMann and Major Samuels jumped down from the side hatch was far more natural than the one she'd tried on her copilot.

An answering grin lit McMann's blue eyes.

"Helluva ride, Captain."

"It *was* kind of fun, wasn't it?"

Carly hadn't quite recovered her sense of humor yet. All she could do was wrap both arms around the helo pilot and hug her fiercely.

"Thanks, Jo."

"Anytime, Major."

That got a shaky smile. "You're a good woman to have around when the shooting starts."

"Speaking of which . . ."

Scowling, Jo ran a hand along the Huey's skin, much as a horse trainer would along a sick or nervous mare, searching for the source of the fluid that now slicked the entire tail section. She found it just aft of the cross strut. Small. Neat. Round.

A shocked Carly peered over her shoulder. "They shot at you, too?"

She had to shout to be heard above the noise of incoming choppers.

"The assholes were probably aiming at Ryan," Jo yelled back. "I just got in their way."

Blasts of rotor wash and engine noise precluded any response to that. The Huey's crew and bedraggled passengers turned to watch as the police choppers hovered above the runway, then touched down hard. Their skids had barely kissed concrete before the side hatches burst open. SWAT team members scrambled out, black body armor glistening in the drizzle, guns leveled. They fanned out, raced toward the Huey.

"McMann! Hands in the air, now! Move away from those people!"

Carly felt Ryan edge sideways. She grabbed his arm and yanked him back. "Don't move!"

"I have to! I don't want them firing into you."

She turned on him, almost snarling in her determination. "You did your thing on that roof and saved both our lives. Jo did hers in the air. This is *my* show now, McMann and you're not making a move or saying a word that I don't tell you to!"

His protest got lost in a screech of tires. A midnight blue Lincoln Continental tore around base ops, swerved onto the apron, and raced toward them. It screamed to a stop only yards away, sending the entire SWAT team into a crouch. To a man, they swung their weapons toward the new threat.

Carly felt a bubble of hysterical laughter at the back of her throat. Obviously, these trigger-happy idiots wouldn't recognize the Congressional seal on the Lincoln's license plate if it bit them in the butt. They recognized the slender, elegant woman who jumped out of it, however. She heard a few muttered exclamations as her mother ran across the concrete.

"Carly! Baby!"

Deciding the sharpshooters wouldn't gun Ryan down in front of a member of Congress, Carly met her mother halfway. It was a toss up who cried hardest or recovered first. When they finally pulled apart, Adele's once flawless eye makeup had painted long dark streaks on her cheeks. Carly didn't even want to think about what her own face looked like.

"Are you all right?" Adele asked anxiously, patting her daughter's face, her shoulders, her arms.

"Yes."

"Are you sure? No broken bones? No lacerations, no traumas?"

"Only a near miss with a fast bullet."

"What!"

"Hang around, Mother," Carly said, swinging her gaze to the SWAT team that now had Ryan face down on the concrete. "Things are going to get interesting."

"Really?"

There was nothing like a confrontation to perk Adele up. Raking five perfectly manicured nails through her hair, she followed as Carly stalked over to the group surrounding their suspect, guns to his head, while one of the team jerked his arms behind his back and cuffed him, then patted him down.

"He's not armed," Carly protested.

"We're just making sure of that, ma'am."

Forcing herself to an icy calm, she waited until they dragged McMann to his feet. Her fists clenched at the sight of the bruise already forming above one eye and the bloody patch where the concrete had scraped the skin off his cheek.

"Who's in charge here?" she bit out.

"I am." A dark-suited civilian pushed his way through the heavily armed ring.

Carly recognized him at once. Ed Bolt, warden of the Federal correctional facility here on Maxwell.

"Were you aboard one of those choppers?" she snapped.

"Yes, Major Samuels. I've been up looking for you and McMann since we found Fayrene Preston's body."

"Did you give the order to fire on Mr. McMann?"

"Yes." His gray eyes rested with cold satisfaction on the prisoner's face. "And after I get a few answers out of him, I'm going to take great pleasure in slapping him with charges that will earn him a one-way ticket to Marion."

Carly's stomach rolled. The penitentiary at Marion was where the Feds executed condemned prisoners.

"Before you issue any tickets, Mr. Bolt, you may have to answer to a few charges yourself."

His gaze whipped back to her face. "Such as?"

The fear and fury that had erupted in Carly when she realized the snipers were shooting at them boiled to the surface once again.

"Such as reckless endangerment. Excessive use of force. Willfully discharging a firearm under such circumstances as to endanger human life, or causing another thereto."

The third was a military offense, but Carly was too furious at this point to make such fine distinctions.

"What in hell were you thinking, ordering these men to fire at us like that!"

"They weren't firing at *you*. They were firing at the paroled prisoner suspected of abducting you and holding you hostage. The same prisoner wanted for questioning in the murder of my assistant."

"He didn't kill Fayrene Preston," Carly asserted flatly.

"Was she alive when you and McMann went into the river?"

"She was face down in the mud."

"Was she alive?"

"I didn't see her move, if that's what you mean, but she was alive."

His eyes narrowed. "I think a jury will have to decide that."

"Listen to me, Mr. Bolt. Mr. McMann didn't abduct me or at any time try to hold me hostage. Nor did he kill the assistant warden, and he sure as hell didn't have time to sexually assault her, if in fact she was assaulted. He wasn't out of my sight for more than a minute, two at the most."

"We have an eyewitness that says he saw McMann

bludgeon her. We also have his prints on the murder weapon."

"Gator Burns's statements have to be weighed against the testimony of a rehabilitated prisoner and an officer in the United States Air Force."

The irony almost choked her. She'd begun her Article 32 investigation faced with the same dilemma—whether to take the word of a convicted felon against that of an air force officer. She'd come full circle.

Bolt's eyes narrowed. She was getting to him, Carly saw. Anger stained his face, even the scalp under his salt-and-pepper buzz cut. His gaze traveled from her flushed face and tangled hair to her bare legs and back up again with deliberate, infuriating thoroughness.

"Are you sure you're pleading McMann's cause as an impartial witness?" he asked in a tone that suggested he had a good idea what had happened between her and Ryan in the isolated farmhouse.

The fact that he'd hit the nail squarely on the head only inflamed Carly to the point that she saw red.

"No, Mr. Bolt, I'm not just an impartial witness. I'm Mr. McMann's legal advisor."

Surprise whipped across Ryan's bruised face. Carly flashed him a fiece, silent warning. If he opened his mouth, if he so much as *tried* to open his mouth, she'd cut him off at the knees!

Satisfied that he'd received her message, she gave the warden her full attention. He was as astonished as Ryan by her declaration.

"Then I'd say you've got yourself a little conflict of interest, Major. You're a military JAG investigating the murder of an air force officer. You can't represent McMann. He's a civilian and a witness in your own investigation."

"I've completed the Article 32 investigation to my

satisfaction, Mr. Bolt. I'll have it finalized and submitted today. As to my military status . . ." Her gaze
was as steely as her determination. "I can resign my
commission with the stroke of a pen."

"Carly!"

"What the hell!"

The simultaneous protests erupted from McMann
and Adele Samuels. Carly ignored them both to focus on the warden. He was the key. She had to
convince him, had to make him give Ryan one last
chance.

"You and I have to talk about the allegations
against Mr. McMann. Privately."

His glance flicked to the handcuffed prisoner.
Carly saw contempt and vicious satisfaction flare in
his eyes before he brought them back to her.

"A jury will decide if he murdered Fayrene Preston, Major. There's nothing more for us to talk
about."

She let him take three confident strides toward his
prisoner before she halted him in his tracks.

"Let's try this one more time. Either we talk now,
privately, or I'm going to ensure that the media, the
assistant DA, and at least one member of Congress
receive those portions of my investigation that detail
the complicity by officials at the federal prison in
the sex-for-money scheme known as the Afternoon
Club."

As a bluff, it was pretty weak. The government
agencies, including interested members of Congress,
would have access to those details anyway. The bit
about the media got his attention, however.

"All right, Major. We'll talk."

A half hour later, a small cavalcade of vehicles left
base ops. Special Agent Derrick Greene, chief of De-

tachment 405 of the Office of Special Investigations, was at the wheel of one vehicle. Warden Bolt sat in the passenger seat of another.

Ryan rode in the back of the third, cuffed, bruised, bleeding. They were taking him to the hangars where the wing commander had bedded down the eight hundred prisoners evacuated from the low-lying prison facilities. He'd only remain there a few hours, Bolt had informed Carly at the end of their terse discussion, a day at most, before they arranged transport for him to Marion.

A few hours. A day at most.

Tired and grimly determined, Carly crossed the tarmac to the midnight blue Lincoln. She ached all over, and would have given a month's pay right then for clean clothes, cooked food, and a stiff shot of something other than peach brandy.

Her mother paced beside her, her face a study in calm concentration. Carly felt a weary smile pull at her heart. How like her mother! No questions. No demands for details. No comments about the kiss her daughter had laid on Ryan before the guards escorted him to the vehicle.

Side by side, they walked through the weak, struggling drizzle. Carly lifted her face to the gray sky, her heart twisting when she spotted a patch of blue. It was almost over. The storm. The terror. The . . .

"Major!"

The crew chief hot footed it across the concrete, hefting a daisy-patterned pillowcase in one hand.

"You left your cats in the Huey. They're hissing and spitting up a storm, but otherwise seem okay."

The smile tugging at Carly's heart burst into a flame of something so strong, so fierce, she almost shook with it.

"They're not mine, Chief. They belong to McMann by right of salvage, unless or until he returns them to their original owners." She held out her hand. "I'll see that he gets them."

CHAPTER TWENTY-ONE

With a guard on either side of him, Ryan walked into the hangar where the evacuees from the prison were housed. His shirt hung in tatters from its contact with the rough shingles. His cheek dripped blood onto his bare chest. The cuffs gouging into his wrists behind his back only added to the misery of being back among his fellow malfeasants and transgressors.

Jeers and catcalls greeted his return.

"Hey, boys, lookee here! We got us a warden killer back among us."

"You didn't let that river float you far enough away, McMann!"

"Hey, hockey star! We heard you done Fay-reen with that big stick of yours!"

He endured the taunts in silence as the guards marched him through rows of mattresses laid out with military precision on the hangar floor. He endured, too, the disgust and condemnation on the faces of those prisoners to whom murder was still evil.

"In here."

One of his escorts shoved him into what looked like a small storage area at the far end of the hangar. Partitions and heavy-duty wire caged it off from the rest of the area.

The door clanged shut and was secured with a padlock on an old fashioned hasp. Ryan knew it was useless, but asked anyway.

"What about these cuffs?"

"Warden said to keep you separate from the rest of the men until we ship you out. He didn't say to make you comfortable."

The guard spat a stream of brown tobacco juice on the otherwise spotless, gray-painted floor and yelled across the hangar.

"Hey, Murph! Haul your butt over here!"

The gray-haired guard moved at his normal unhurried pace. Ryan's mouth salivated at the sight of the mug in Murphee's hand. He'd give his soul for a cup of hot coffee right now . . . if he had one to give. He didn't bother to ask for any though. In these men's eyes, he was a brutal, sadistic cop killer. He'd be lucky to make it out of here without severe damage to his internal organs.

"That McMann?" Murphee asked, peering into the dimness of the cage.

"Yeah, we got the bastard. Warden says he wants him kept under visual observation at all times until we ship him out to Marion. He's making the arrangements now. Take the first shift, will you?"

"Yeah, sure."

"Here's the key, but you won't have to use it. He's got no privileges. No telephone, no food, no water, no nothing until we get the word from Bolt. And no talking to anyone. Anyone, understand? That includes any lady lawyers who might come poking around. Got that?"

"I got it."

While the two escorts made their way back to the hangar doors, Murphee took a leisurely sip, eyeing the prisoner through the steam rising from his cup.

"Looks like you're in one helluva mess, boy. I thought you were too smart a coon to let yourself get treed again like this."

Ryan leaned against the partitioned wall, not bothering to answer or even look at the paunchy guard.

"The assistant warden wasn't high on my list of favorite people, either," Murphee confided. "Always nagging at folks to get back to work. But what you did ain't gonna earn you any privileges at Marion."

The prisoner's stony silence brought a touch of red into Murph's cheeks.

"That swim in the river sure didn't loosen you up none, boy. You always were a cocky bastard. Can't say as I won't enjoy seeing you shipped off with shackles on your wrists and ankles. I know a few other folks who'll enjoy it, too. Might even have to call a reporter friend of mine and tip him off when they get ready to haul you outta here so I can watch it again on the nightly news."

Ryan's mouth twisted sardonically. "So you can make a few bucks on the side from your reporter friend, you mean."

The red in Murphee's cheeks deepened. "A man's gotta live. Now you better think about modulatin' that mouth of yours, boy, 'cause where you're going, a crack like that would earn you some real nasty consequences. It might yet, if you're not careful."

Dragging a chair across the hangar, the guard propped it against the wall beside the wire cage and made himself comfortable.

Ryan tried to do the same. Back to the partitioned wall, wrists bruised and aching behind him, he slid down until he could stretch out his legs on the bare concrete floor. An eerie sense of déjà vu swept over him. For a moment, he felt the same shame, the same writhing humiliation he'd experienced the first time he'd been brought in in cuffs. That experience had seared his pride and cost several years of his life. This one, he thought with a swallow that scratched at his dry throat, might well cost him what was left of it.

He closed his eyes, shutting out the gray partitions, the wire cage, the long, echoing hangar. He couldn't shut out the discomfort of the brutally tight cuffs or the ache in his shoulder from hanging on to Carly so long on that roof. Instead, Ryan used the pain, let it carry him back to the roof, to the farmhouse, to those incredible, glorious moments in the kitchen.

If he didn't beat this, if he spent whatever days were left to him in maximum security, he'd have those moments to take with him. Just savoring them now tightened his body. He could picture Carly's head flung back, her perfect breasts quivering at his touch, her eyes dilated from the shock of her pleasure. He could hear her astonished gasps. Feel her slender, supple legs gripping . . .

"Well, well, whadda you got here, Murph? Looks like some kinda river rat to me."

Ryan didn't have to open his eyes to identify the sneering drawl.

"Beat it, Gator," Murph said mildly. "The warden doesn't want him talking to anyone."

"Me and Pauly and Jimbo here don't wanna talk to him, Murph. Nossir, we don't wanna talk. We just wanna finish some business McMann started before he took to bashin' in people's heads. How 'bout lettin' us in?"

"I can't do it, Burns."

"Sure you can." Gator's voice dropped. "How much you want? Fifty? A hundred? You know I'm good for it."

Ryan raised his lids then, curious to know how

much it would take. The sight of Gator's left eye all purple and swollen shut gave him a jolt of intense satisfaction."

"No can do, Burns. I got orders."

Gator shifted his gaze. When he caught Ryan's eye, a smile creased his bruised face.

"Five hundred, Murph, for five minutes."

"Jesus!" The guard shot a quick glance around. "All right, but make it quick." The padlock rattle on the hasp. "Just don't leave any marks where they can be seen."

"Don't worry," Gator purred. "Unlike McMann here, me 'n the boys are experts at this."

The door opened and swiftly clanged shut again, caging Ryan in with the other three. Gator strolled forward, flanked by his lieutenants. He didn't say anything for several moments. Rocking back on his heels, he simply enjoyed the sight.

Then, without warning, his boot whipped back and swung forward, slamming into Ryan's ribs with a force that knocked him onto his side. Clenching his jaw against the splintering pain, he used an elbow to roll himself back into a sitting position.

"I was sure disappointed when I heard the river didn't take you, McMann."

Ryan pulled in a slow, painful breath. "Yeah, I bet you were."

The boot swung again, but this time he was ready for it and took it on the hip. He wasn't as lucky the third time. The toe caught him square in the stomach with all the force of Gator's squat, barrel-chested body behind it.

He was grinding his teeth against the bruising agony when Burns crouched down, dangling his hands between his knees. The stink of his body odor came with him.

"Too bad I can't mark up your face the way you marked mine, pretty boy, but I can still have me a little fun."

"The same . . . kind you had . . . with Preston?"

Gator's lips pulled back in a wide smile. He leaned even closer, his breath a foul wash on Ryan's face. He was flying high, his glee at bringing McMann down shining in his black eyes.

"Just between you and me, boy," he confided in a low, smiling whisper, "she weren't no fun. I had to bash her in the head before I could get me some of that ass. Damned if I didn't hit the bitch too hard. Knocked her right out and spoiled my sport, if you know what I mean. I couldn't even get off on her."

In tight, pain-laced grunts, Ryan told him what he could do with himself. Gator merely laughed.

"Accommodatin' of you to leave your prints on that tie-down rod, by the way. It sure come in handy." He dangled his fists between his knees. "I s'pose I couldda wiped your prints off, the way I wiped Billy-Boy's off after he shot that Smith bitch, but I figured that there iron rod would be just the ticket to send you to the Big House. Afore you go, though, me 'n Pauly 'n Jimbo wanna give you a little somethin' to take with you."

He straightened, signaling his two lieutenants forward. Their faces alight with anticipation, they took up positions on either side of Ryan.

"When we're done with you, pretty boy, you're gonna wish you never came outta that river."

"You're already done with him, Burns! Back off!"

The shouted order spun the three prisoners around. They went stiff with shock as the warden rushed in through the hangar's side door. A small army of uniformed and plainclothes personnel followed on his heels.

An ashen-faced Murphee jumped to his feet, sloshing coffee across his shirt and knocking over his chair in the process. "Warden! I was, uh, just letting these men have a few words with their buddy. McMann and them are, uh, old pals."

"So I heard." Bolt slapped out a hand. "Give me the key, then get the hell out of my sight. I'll deal with you later."

Gulping, Murphee fumbled in his pocket.

The door slammed back against the wire. Bolt strode into the cage, followed by two guards, one of whom shoved Gator up against the partition wall and patted him down before jerking his arms behind him. Sweat sheened the prisoner's shaved head when he was spun around.

"Look, Warden, I was just payin' McMann back for what he done to me before he bashed in Fayrene Preston's head. Maybe I shouldn't oughtta done it, but—"

"Save it, Burns." Bolt jerked his chin at one of the guards. "Get McMann up and those cuffs off."

With the guard's assistance, Ryan controlled his wheezing and got a foot under himself. White, dizzying spots danced in front of his eyes with every breath. He used the few seconds it took for the guard to unlock the cuffs to regain his equilibrium.

The sight of Carly pushing her way into the crowded cage helped considerably. Face scrubbed, hair tamed into a smooth, sleek sweep, she rushed to his side. Ryan gave her a ragged smile.

"You were right, sweetheart. Gator's kind can never resist bragging."

A taut silence filled the cage while an air force special investigator in civilian clothes unscrewed a metal vent cover and retrieved the bug the OSI had inserted into the air duct at Carly's insistence.

Bellowing with rage, Gator lunged. "You sonuva-bitch, you set me up!"

With the coordination of a born athlete, Ryan moved Carly aside, sidestepped the charge, and used the bull-like convict's own momentum to send him crashing headfirst into the partition. Gator hit a stud and dropped like a stone.

"Bastard," Carly snarled at his inert form with an unlawyerlike lack of cool. "I hope you burn in hell."

She was still shaking with the force of her fury a half hour later. She couldn't quite believe that the nightmare was over, that Ryan had been cleared of all charges. She'd congratulate herself for forcing Bolt to agree to the bug later. Right now, she had one more piece of business to take care of before she joined her mother for a hastily called news conference.

Relatively clean and neat in a uniform rushed from her house by her brother Dave, she forced big gulps of air into her lungs to steady herself before entering the small conference room where she'd begun her Article 32 investigation two weeks ago.

The three people in the room looked with varying degrees of wariness and welcome when Carly strode in. Sergeant Hendricks, the court recorder, smiled warmly at her over his array of equipment.

"Hey, Major, glad you're okay."

"Thanks."

G. Putnam Jones echoed his sentiment. "I know I speak for both myself and my client when I say how relieved we are that you're safe. I must say, though, that this abrupt summons to the base came at a highly inconvenient time." He checked his Rolex. "I'm due in court in less than an hour."

"And I'm due at a press conference in twenty min-

utes," Carly threw back. "It's in your client's best interest that he tell me the truth now, before I step in
front of those TV cameras."

Her eyes on the stiff-spined lieutenant colonel
standing by the windows, she slapped a microcassette
recorder on the conference table and hit play. Gator's
guttural growl jumped into the tense silence.

*I s'pose I couldda wiped your prints off, the way I wiped
Billy-Boy's off after he shot the Smith bitch, but I figured
that there iron rod would be just the ticket to send you to
the Big House. Afore you go, though . . .*

She stabbed the off button. "I'm asking you again
for the record, Colonel Smith. Did you drive along
River Road at approximately two o'clock on the
afternoon of April twelfth?"

Michael Smith dragged his stunned gaze from the
recorder. The muscle under his left eye began a jerky
dance. He swallowed once, twice, and dragged his
answer from deep within him.

"Yes."

His lids came down, shutting out Carly, his lawyer,
the conference room. When he opened his eyes again,
the relief and regret were almost indistinguishable.

"I knew Elaine had gone to the stables. I thought
. . . I suspected . . ." He swiped a hand down his face.
"I found her car parked in the lot and her gelding
still in his stall. Then . . . then I heard a shot. I raced
through the woods, thinking she might be in trouble.
She was already dead when I found her."

"So you left her there?"

The question held no hint of condemnation or
blame, but Smith obviously felt both. His head
reared back, and the coldness Carly had sensed in
him before descended like a curtain.

"Yes, I left her. I couldn't help her, and I knew I'd

come under suspicion after all the vicious fights and
accusations."

Carly merely nodded. "You were right. Now, if
you'll excuse me, my mother's called a press conference to announce my safe return from the flood. I
won't discuss the status of your case, but you can expect a swarm of reporters to converge on you if and
when Mr. McMann chooses to make a statement."

Tucking the recorder into her bag, she swept out of
the conference room for the last time. She'd completed the Article 32 to her satisfaction.

Now, another, even more important matter awaited
her.

CHAPTER TWENTY-TWO

"Pull over."

At Ryan's gruff command, Carly slowed the vehicle her mother had put at their disposal. The Lincoln rolled to a stop fifty yards from the hangar situated next to the one Ryan had walked into such a short time ago.

Sweat slicked his palms as he studied the vans that jammed the parking lot outside the hangar. Antennas and satellite dishes bristled from their roofs. Carly had warned him that every television station in the city had responded to her mother's announcement that she'd be holding a press conference at the base.

"I don't want to do this."

Carly nodded, her brown eyes brimming with understanding. "I know."

Everything in him cringed at the knowledge of what awaited inside . . . the blinding lights, the microphones shoved in his face, the frenzy of questions and demands for intimate, lurid detail. He'd gone down this road once, and destroyed three lives in the process.

Jaw clenched, Ryan strained to remember his ex-wife's face the last time he'd seen it. All that came to him was a blurred memory of her eyes hating him across the sea of voracious reporters who mobbed her when she tried to walk out of the courtroom.

Nor could he remember the girl, that pathetic groupie so desperate to add Ryan to her collection. The media and Ryan's own defense team had torn her into little pieces.

Could he risk putting Carly through the same thing? And her mother? Christ!

He knew what this press conference could do to Adele Samuels's re-election chances. The media would latch on to her daughter's involvement with a convicted felon and play both for all they were worth. Adele had insisted that the only way to beat the headlines was to make them, but Ryan had made too many front pages to appreciate her plan of attack.

He wasn't ready for the circling sharks to close in. He didn't want the circus that would erupt the moment he stepped inside that hangar. His fists balled, and that long, deserted road to anonymity he'd dreamed about for so long shimmered like a thin, silvery ribbon in his mind.

That long, empty road.

If he traveled that road, he'd travel it alone. He couldn't take Carly. He knew that. The threat she'd thrown at Bolt to resign her commission and take up Ryan's defense had shocked the hell out of him. Her mother, too, judging by the congresswoman's astonished face. Ryan couldn't let her do it. He'd told her over and over in the past, hectic hours that he *wouldn't* let her do it.

And Carly had told him over and over that she didn't allow anyone to make those kinds of decisions for her.

So here he was, relatively cleaned up, wearing another set of borrowed clothing, his stomach crawling

at the thought of the media who panted eagerly for
the two of them to pull up at the hangar.

Correction, the four of them. To Ryan's disgust,
Carly had insisted on carting along the damned
kittens. They were sleeping now, their bellies full
from another infusion of canned milk, curled into
each other in the cardboard box she'd appropriated from somewhere, but their earlier distempered
squealing hadn't exactly soothed Ryan's lacerated
nerves.

Nor did the question Carly put to him now.

"Well? Are you going to climb out of the car and
walk away now, while you still can? Or are you going to face it with me?"

"There's another option. *You* can walk away. Or at
least stand with your mother. Let me take them on
alone."

"Not this time, Ryan," she said softly.

"Don't you understand?" he growled in a last,
desperate attempt to make her see reason. "I don't
want your association with me to destroy you or
your family."

"You might as well give up. I inherited more than
my red hair from my mother. In case you haven't
noticed, we can both get pretty stubborn when we
want to."

"Yeah, I noticed."

She cocked her head, the movement both provoca-
tive and challenging. "Ready?"

"No, dammit."

Stretching an arm along the back of her seat, he
cupped her neck. His thumb found the soft hollow
between her chin and her neck.

"There are a few things I want to tell you before we
walk in there."

"Like what?"

"Like, one . . . you're a helluva a legal advisor, Major Samuels."

She smirked. "I think so. Two?"

"Two . . ." He leaned over, brushing her mouth with his. "You're also one hell of a woman."

"You certainly won't get a rebuttal from me on that point. Three?"

"Three . . ."

Ryan gave in to the need that spilled through his veins. He had to say it, had to let her know before the jackals ripped the hours they'd shared into pieces.

"I want you, Carly. I have since the first moment I saw you, all stiff and beautiful and so damned cool you burned me with it. At the farmhouse, I was sure that I could get you out of my head if I just had you once. But now . . ."

"Now?"

"Now," he admitted, "I ache all over with the wanting. It's in my blood. You're in my blood."

"That's funny," she got out on a shaky breath. "I ache all over the same way. So what do you say, McMann? You want to get this press conference over with and go jump in the sack?"

He blew out a long breath, wondering if he'd ever reach the point where this woman wouldn't knock him right between the eyes.

"Sounds like a good plan, Counselor." He grinned at her and the warm smile that touched her eyes made nothing else matter.

Heads high, faces solemn, they ran a gauntlet of cameras and mikes. Luckily, the harried public affairs officer who'd responded to Congresswoman Samuels's request for a news conference on Maxwell had roped off a path so they could get through the mob.

A smiling, exquisitely turned out member of Congress met them at a small platform crowded with folding chairs. Ryan caught a glimpse of a grim-faced Ed Bolt and a row of uniformed air force officers in the back row. In the front was the helicopter pilot who'd plucked them off the roof, looking slightly overwhelmed. Beside her sat a big, broad-shouldered man whose sculptured features and reddish brown hair identified him instantly as Carly's brother. Football player, Ryan guessed. Another lawyer, no doubt. Next to him was a wheelchair, occupied by an elderly gentleman with a shock of white hair and a keen, unblinking stare.

The Judge.

Ryan felt his palms start to sweat all over again. He was still dealing with the fact that the entire Samuels clan had turned out to support one of their own when Adele swept to the bank of mikes.

"Ladies and gentlemen, three remarkable people have joined me for this news conference today. You'll meet one, Captain Joanna West, a little later. The other two are standing beside me. Most of you know my daughter, Major Carly Samuels. And for those of you who don't know him, this is Mr. Ryan McMann."

She turned the full force of her brilliant smile on him.

"Mr. McMann saved my daughter's life when the river broke its banks. He's a hero, and always will be to me and my family. I'll let him and Carly tell you their story, then we'll take your questions."

Having firmly and irrevocably put the power of her charismatic personality behind Ryan, the congresswoman gave them both a kiss and stepped aside.

Carly walked up to the mikes, cool, poised, every bit as remarkable as her mother. She turned, waiting with a smile in her eyes.

Ryan took a deep breath and joined her.

ONYX

John McKinna

CRASH DIVE

How long can you hold your breath?

Commercial deep-sea diver Ben Gannon has been assigned to retrieve the bodies from a helicopter crash in the Gulf of Mexico. Instead he discovers the bullet-ridden bodies of the "crash" victims, among them a senator who championed American oil independence. The helicopter was returning from a highly advanced oil rig, where Gannon suddenly finds himself assigned to work. But when the rig is seized by Middle Eastern terrorists, he decides to take matters into his own hands....

☐0-451-40885-3/$6.99